BURNING FOR YOU

BOOK 5: BURNING FOR THE BRAVEST SERIES

KAYE KENNEDY

For my Fairy Godmothers
Thank you for your unwavering support. No matter how crazy my ideas
may get, you always have faith in me. Love you both a million.

ALSO BY KAYE KENNEDY

Burning for the Bravest Series

If you like alpha males with soft centers who love hard and make love harder, then this series featuring New York City firefighters is for you!

Burning for More – Dylan & Autumn

Burning for This – Jesse & Lana

Burning for Her – Ryan & Zoe

Burning for Fate – Jace & Britt

Burning for You – Kyle & Allie

Burning for You: The Wedding – Kyle & Allie

Burning for Love – Declan & Gwen

Burning for Trouble - Coming Spring 2021

Burning for Christmas - Keith & Brielle

Standalone set in the same world

NOTE FROM THE AUTHOR

I can't thank you enough for choosing to read Kyle and Allie's love story. By far, this has been the story my readers, my editor, and even I have been most anticipating in this whole series, thus far. I'm confident that this story will deliver on your expectations, and then some.

This book has wrecked me! I've laughed just as much as I've cried and I hated writing *The End* because I didn't want it to end! You can definitely expect more appearances by Kyle and Allie in future books.

This has been the story I've most enjoyed writing and also the one that has put me through the ringer most. I'm talking snotty crocodile tears that keep me up at night. The struggles hit home for me in a lot of ways, but it's also this beautiful story of transforming tragedy into strength, making this novel a powerful punch to the emotional gut.

And don't even get me started on how much I love Kyle. I wish he was real and I wish I was Allie...just saying (sorry hubby). Neither of them are perfect, but they are perfect for each other. Trust me when I say we all need a Kyle in our lives!

Honestly, I'm going to have a hard time topping this one, but I am absolutely up for the challenge!

Note from the Author

If you're new to me, here's a fun fact: I was a firefighter in a previous chapter of my life, until an injury sustained in a house fire put an end to that. I was actually the third generation of firefighters in my family. I grew up with a father who is now an ex-chief, and I told myself that I would *never* date a firefighter...but then I fell in love with my lieutenant.

After seven years together, we parted ways, but I took away a plethora of knowledge about the inner workings of the FDNY (that's the New York City Fire Department). When I decided to start publishing, I knew I wanted to write from experience and that's how the Burning for the Bravest series came to be.

I knew I could accurately depict the job, having done it myself, as well as the operations of the FDNY. Plus, the stereotype of firemen being sexy comes from somewhere, right? In this series, I stick as close to reality as possible, but I have used some creative freedom for the sake of the stories.

In this book, I've drawn from real-life experiences with two key fire call scenes (Chapters 27 and 43). Keep that in mind, especially when you're reading that last one.

This series is best read in order, as your favorite characters will continue to make appearances, so if you haven't read book one: *Burning for More*, I highly suggest you start there.

Any parallels found here to actual people or places are purely coincidental, as this is a work of fiction. You may notice I refer to some places that actually exist, but what I say about them is purely my opinion and I don't stay completely true to reality.

TRIGGER WARNING: If you don't like spoilers, then you can stop reading now and dive straight into the book. Last chance. You sure you want to keep reading?

Yes?

You're positive?

Really, really sure?

Okay, I warned you...

Note from the Author

SPOILERS: This book has a character who has to deal with fertility issues. It also confronts loss and grief.

I hope you enjoy reading this as much as I enjoyed writing it!

Hugs & Happily Ever Afters,

Kaye Kennedy

PREFACE – ALLIE

As I turned the key in the lock at my apartment, the wine practically called my name. I'd had a day. One of my kindergartener's had had an accident in his pants, leaving a puddle under the activity table. We'd taken a second recess so that the janitorial staff could clean it, and getting my students' already short attention spans back after that had been nearly impossible. While I loved working with the younger kids, they were particularly skilled at testing my patience.

After work, I'd gone to my Pilates class where I'd gotten my zen back, but on the Subway ride home, that had been obliterated. I'd been scrolling through social media and got smacked in the face by a photo my former sister-in-law had posted. My ex-husband and his much younger new wife smiled obnoxiously, both of their hands on her pregnant belly. *Fucking perfect.*

I opened the fridge to get the bottle of chardonnay only to be disappointed. I'd forgotten I'd finished it the night before. "Dammit," I huffed. Standing there with my hands on my hips, I tried to decide whether my desire to curl up on the couch was strong enough to forego wine. Did I mention my ex-husband's wife was pregnant?

I snatched my keys off the counter and checked myself in the mirror by the door. I'd left my chocolate-brown hair in a ponytail after class, so I tugged on the hair tie and shook out my long locks. There were dark circles beneath my honey-colored eyes, but I couldn't be bothered to refresh my makeup, so I left straight for the liquor store wearing my yoga pants, track suit zip up, and sneakers. Thankfully, the store was only a couple of blocks away, so I didn't have to go far. After sixteen years in Michigan, I was still very much adjusting to being back in New York. It had only been a month, but something about it felt right.

The bustle of Manhattan made it easy to get lost in a crowd, which had been exactly what I'd needed after leaving behind my life in Ann Arbor. New Yorkers don't give a shit about the strangers passing by on the streets. They're not gossiping behind your back and smiling to your front. Sure, the streets smell like exhaust, garbage, and urine layered with the sweetness of roasted nuts and the saltiness of soft pretzels and hot dogs, but there was something oddly comforting about it.

While perusing the wine aisles at the store, I thought maybe I'd try something different, but in the end, I grabbed my go-to chardonnay. A deep voice called my name, shooting a chill up my spine. "Allie?"

No, no, no. This can't be happening.

Out of the three million people who crammed onto the island on a daily basis, I somehow managed to enter the same liquor store as the one person I'd hoped to never see again. Life could be cruel.

I glanced up and turned toward him. My mouth hung open, but I struggled to come up with words. Kyle Hogan. My childhood best friend who I'd selfishly abandoned sixteen-years before. The wine bottle fell from my hand and hit my foot, but the pain hardly registered.

In many ways, he looked the same. He was still a big,

muscular guy with those captivating crystal blue irises. His hair was cropped short in a military style and he had lines around his eyes that showed every one of his thirty-four-years.

I fought the urge to run into his arms and tell him how much I'd missed him and how sorry I was because certainly he hated me. "Kyle," I managed to choke out. "Hi."

He blinked several times as though he was trying to decipher if I was an apparition. I was having the same thought. As I stared into his eyes, I got a glimpse of what was beneath his rugged exterior, and I saw the boy who'd loved me in our youth. He was my biggest *what if?* in life. The boy who might have been my forever…if only…

PART I

THE PAST

1

KYLE

Age 4

*I*s there anything better than a swing set? As a kid, it was the closest thing to flying. Head back, feet in the air, wind on your face, stomach in your throat. Flying. The playground was only a few blocks from our house and Mom walked us up there almost every day during the summer. My little brothers, Dylan and Jesse, were in the stroller, but I was old enough to walk by myself as long as I held onto Mom when we crossed the streets. When we arrived at the playground I was allowed to run, and every single time, I bypassed the slide, monkey bars, and seesaw as I charged straight for the swings. There were four in total and two of them we're excessively squeaky, so if you wanted the good ones, you had to be quick when one opened up. And I saw an opening.

My butt landed in the swing seconds before some other kid. I was faster. It was a tough place that playground. Not for the weak. There was a girl beside me on the other good one and she looked to be about my age. Her chocolate-brown hair was braided against her scalp and it was clipped to the side

3

with a red bow. She had on black leggings with red polka dots and a Minnie Mouse t-shirt. *This was gonna be too easy*, I thought to myself.

I pumped my legs and got swiftly off the ground, then said to the girl, "Wanna race?"

"Race?"

"Yeah. See who goes highest."

She shrugged. "Okay."

I worked my knees faster, inching further and further from the ground. Back and forth. Up, down, and up again. I got so high in the air that the chains jerked. No way a sissy girl would get as high as me. A squeal made me turn my head and to my surprise that girl was right beside me, neck and neck, closer and closer to the top bar. And she was laughing.

"Allie, that's high enough," a woman's voice called out.

"But, Mom," the girl beside me protested.

"No buts."

The girl groaned.

"Same goes for you, Kyle," my mom said from the bench where she was sitting holding my new baby brother, Jesse.

It was my turn to grumble.

As we lost our momentum, the girl asked, "So who won?"

Truth? It was a tie, but I wasn't gonna tie with a girl. "Me. You came down first."

"Not fair! I had to."

"Don't be a sore loser," I repeated the words my dad had said to me whenever he'd beat me at Hungry Hungry Hippos, which was my most favorite game.

"I'm not a loser." She pouted.

Arguing with a girl was boring me. I looked around to see if any of my friends were at the playground, but came up empty. My brother Dylan was sitting in the sand playing with some other kids. He was only two and couldn't go on the swings with me because they were for big boys only. He didn't seem to mind though. Dylan liked playing in the sand with his rake.

A boy, who appeared to be a little bit older than I was, walked past Dylan, bent down and picked up a handful of sand, then threw it in my little brother's face, making him cry. I fought to slow down my swing, so I could go defend my brother, but before I could get out of the seat, the girl had jumped off of hers—while in mid-air—and got in the bully's face.

"Say you're sorry," she demanded. Her hands were on her hips and she stood on her tippy toes to get closer to the kid.

He laughed at her. "No."

She poked the boy in the chest with her finger. "Yes. You're a mean bully and you can't throw sand."

I charged over, then bent down beside my brother and wiped his face with my NASCAR t-shirt that my dad had gotten me on a trip he'd taken a few months earlier. "Don't cry, Dyl. I'll fix it." I got most of the sand off and his tears subsided. "Better?" I asked.

He nodded, his pouty lip still quivering.

A smug smile crossed the bully's lips as he said, "What are you gonna do about it? You're a stupid girl."

I hopped to my feet, ready to put the boy in his place, but she beat me to it. Literally. Her fist connected with the boy's belly, knocking him onto his butt.

The parents all converged on us, demanding to know what had happened. The bully pointed at the girl. "She punched me," he whimpered.

"Allison Dupree is that true?" the girl's mother asked in horror.

The girl proudly crossed her arms over her chest and smiled. "Yup. He's a bully. He threw sand in the little boy's face and he wouldn't say sorry, then he called me a stupid girl."

The boy's mom asked, "Did you throw sand?"

He shook his head. "It was on accident."

"No," I shouted. "I saw you pick it up and throw it at my little brother."

He tried to protest again, but his mother grabbed him by the arm and dragged him away. "You have to stop doing this, Robbie," she said as they left the playground.

The girl's mom got down on her knees and looked her daughter in the eyes. "You can't punch people, Allie, even if they're being bullies. You get an adult and let us take care of it. Understood, young lady?"

She huffed. "Yes, Mama." Then she sat on the ground next to Dylan. "Can I play with you?"

My little brother handed her his rake—his most prized possession that he never let me play with—and I sat down on his other side.

The girl dragged the prongs through the sand. "I'm Allie."

"I'm Kyle. This is Dylan."

She looked up from the sand and said to me, "Wanna be my friend?"

I shrugged. "Okay."

Little did I know she wouldn't just be my friend for the day, but she'd be my *best* friend for the next fourteen years.

2

ALLIE

1st Grade

My legs barely reached the ground as I sat on the cool metal bench in the dugout beside my best friend, Kyle. We'd been in the same Kindergarten class, but for first grade we'd ended up in different classes and I missed him. We still had lunch together and played at recess, though that time always went by too quickly. When he'd said he was going to play little league baseball that spring, I'd decided to join the team, too. I was the only girl.

On the first day of practice, the boys hadn't been very nice to me. They'd told me I couldn't play baseball because it was for boys only and girls had to play softball, but I'd quickly shut them up during batting practice when I'd hit a home run over all of their heads. Kyle and I had been playing baseball together since we were five. Well, as much as two people could play by themselves. I also had two older brothers who'd let me play with them sometimes, so I was pretty decent at it.

It was our first real game of the season and I was excited to actually play for real. Our team, the Mamaroneck Monarchs

7

(try saying that one five times fast), was first at bat, so Joey Fisher started us off. He was one of the older boys on the team and he was tall so he usually hit the ball above everyone else's heads. After two strikes, his bat finally connected with the ball and it went far enough to get him onto first base.

Kyle was up next and I was after him. I left the dugout so I could see him better and also because I had to take a few practice swings like our coach had told us to. I tugged on the waistband of my shorts. They came down to the middle of my shins and I had a hard time keeping them up on my waist. Coach came over and tied my drawstring tighter so that I hopefully wouldn't run out of them while I rounded the bases. The boys on the other team, the Larchmont Lions, laughed and I heard them making comments about the little girl. As one of the youngest players on the Monarchs, I was the smallest, which didn't help much with my street cred, so to speak.

I sighed.

Coach tapped the brim of my hat and whispered, "Hey, don't listen to them. You're our secret weapon."

I nodded and watched as Kyle got a hit that brought him to first base. I cheered as loudly as I could.

"You're up, Allie. Go show them how girls play baseball." My coach grinned broadly and I returned his smile.

"Good hit, Kyle," I yelled as I passed first base on my way to the batter's box.

"Good hit, Kyle," one of the boys on the other team mocked me. "Cheerleaders don't belong at the plate."

"Yeah, girls can't play baseball," another kid echoed.

My oldest brother, Brandon, called out from the stands, "You've got this, Allie."

I turned and gave him a thumbs up. My parents had been fighting—again—so my brother had walked me to the park for my game because I wasn't allowed to walk there by myself yet. Brandon was in fifth grade and he was one of the most popular guys at our school. No one ever dared to mess with me when

Brandon was around, but the other team must not have realized that because they kept taunting me. "Yeah, *Allie*, you've got this. Set the strike out record."

I gripped the bat tighter, in an effort to fight my desire to take a swing at the fence in the Lions' dugout. After a couple of breaths, I took my position at the plate. The first pitch came in high and outside.

"Ball," the umpire called.

The next one appeared to be inside, but at the last second it looked like it might be in the strike zone so I took a swing and missed.

"Strike," the other team hollered over the umpire.

"Strike her out again," one of them shouted at the pitcher. "Show her how the boys play."

I lowered my bat and pivoted around to yell at them, but Kyle called out and stopped me. "Show them how girls hit, Allie."

That made me smile. Kyle always knew what to say to get me down from the ledge. Admittedly, I had a bit of a temper. I blame growing up with two older brothers for that endearing quality.

"Watch and learn boys," I said as I brought my bat up again and took my stance. I stared their pitcher down, daring him to throw the ball into my sweet spot.

And that's exactly what he did. I felt what was going to happen before it even happened. My bat came over the plate at the exact perfect timing to hit the ball about four-inches from the end of the barrel, sending it high into the sky. I dropped the bat and ran for first base. Kyle rounded second, so I kept going. The other team shouted, but the boy in left field was still scrambling for the ball that had landed far behind him. Of course, they'd brought the outfielders closer for the girl. *Surprise, surprise.* I gripped the waist of my slipping shorts as I headed for third, while Kyle ran home. The crowd cheered. On third, I couldn't see the ball, but Kyle waited at home plate waving me on. "Come on, come on," he shouted.

I stepped on the plate just as the left fielder got the ball to their short stop. I looked straight into Kyle's crystal blue eyes as he gave me a high five, then Joey, who'd also scored on my home run, gave me one, too.

Coach ran out and gave me a double high-five. "See, that's why you're our secret weapon."

I looked over at the Lions' dugout and grinned obnoxiously.

Kyle put his arm around my shoulder. "You hit like a girl, Allie," he said loudly enough for them to hear.

"Yes, I do."

The Lions were silent the rest of the game.

KYLE

2nd Grade

I'd found out at hockey practice that I was getting the MVP award at our fundraiser dinner the following Friday. At eight years old, it was totally a big deal. Of course I wanted my best friend there for the ceremony. Too excited to wait until I saw her in class the next day, I called to invite her, but no one answered, so I had to leave a message on her machine.

"Hi Allie, it's Kyle. Guess what? I won the MVP award on my hockey team this year and there's going to be a celebration at the fundraiser on Friday. It'd be really awesome if you came with me. Mom said you can sit at our table. The bad part is that we have to get dressed up so you'll need to wear a dress. Do you have a dress? Anyways, I think it'll still be fun. I'll see you in class tomorrow. Bye."

Two hours later, the phone rang and I raced to answer it. "Hello, Kyle speaking."

"Kyle, it's Mrs. Dupree. Is Allie at your house?"

That's weird. "No, she's not."

"May I talk to your mom?" she asked frantically.

"Sure." I pulled the phone away from my ear. "Mom! Phone."

My mother came into the kitchen and I handed her the receiver. "It's Mrs. Dupree."

"Leslie, hi," Mom said.

I opened the fridge pretending to look for something so I could eavesdrop, but then I realized I was hungry, so I grabbed an orange and started to peel it.

"I see. Let me talk to Kyle and I'll call you back. Do keep me posted if you find her, though."

I bit into the orange slice and juice ran down my hand.

"Kyle, have you seen Allie this afternoon?" Mom asked.

"Nope. I called to invite her to the hockey dinner, but I had to leave a message."

Mom took a seat at the table beside me. "Have you talked to her at all today?"

I shook my head.

"Are you sure?"

This conversation was strange. "Yup. Why?"

"Allie and her mommy got into an argument and Allie ran away. Mrs. Dupree thought maybe she came here."

I'd been about to take another bite of my orange, but I paused with it inches from my mouth. "Oh. No, she hasn't been here."

Mom sighed. "Can you think of a place she may have gone?"

I knew exactly where she'd be, but it was our secret. "Don't know."

"Well, if you can think of a place, you tell me, all right?"

I nodded. "Sure." I finished my orange. "Hey, Mom, can I go to the park for a little before dinner?" The park wasn't far from our house, so my parents had started letting me go there by myself sometimes.

Mom gave me a half smile. "That's fine. But take your watch with you and be back here by five o'clock."

"K thanks, Mom." I ran up to my bedroom and grabbed the watch my parents had gotten me, then I went back downstairs and tried to look casual as I said goodbye to my mom before putting on my jacket and letting myself out the kitchen door. Once I was on the street and out of view, I ran to the park.

Sure enough, Allie was there, barely swinging back and forth on the old metal swings. It was cold out, so the park was empty. After crossing the sand, bypassing the other playground equipment, I sat in the swing beside her. She sniffled and refused to look at me.

"Your mom called worried about you."

Silence.

"She said you got into a fight."

More silence.

"Wanna talk about it?"

She wiped her nose with her coat sleeve. "No."

"Okay." I pumped my knees, letting myself get higher.

After a few minutes, she finally said, "My mom won't let me go to your party."

I let myself slow down, then I dragged my feet in the sand until I was stopped. "Why not?"

She sighed. "I don't think she wants me to be friends with a boy."

I laughed. "But we've been friends for years."

"I know. Guess that's not so okay now that we're older."

"How come?"

"She doesn't like it when Daddy talks to other girls either." She shrugged. "And I think she's worried you're going to kiss me."

"Gross." I stuck out my tongue. The thought of kissing Allie —any girl really—was not in the least bit appealing.

"That's what I said."

"Why would she think that?"

"She caught Brandon kissing a girl at his birthday party last week."

I kicked the sand. "But your brother is in middle school. We're only in second grade."

She sighed. "I know."

"That stinks."

"Yup."

"Is that why you ran away?" I asked.

She nodded. "I'm mad at her. Also, she was fighting with Daddy again." Allie's parents had been fighting a lot lately. It always got her upset.

I rubbed my lips together. "It's okay if you don't come to the ceremony."

She finally looked up. Her bronze eyes were puffy and blood shot from crying. "You don't want me to go?"

I ran my fingers over the cold chain links. "Of course I want you to, but it's not worth fighting with your mom over. We can have our own party during recess. Just you and me. It'll be way better and we won't have to get dressed up."

She laughed. "That sounds fun."

"Good. No more crying."

She reached across the gap and punched me playfully in the arm. "I wasn't crying."

I laughed. "Sure you weren't."

"I mean it. I'm not a cry baby."

"No, you're not. You're the toughest girl I know. That's why we're friends."

She grunted. "I'm tougher than most boys you know, too." That was probably true.

I rolled my eyes. "Yeah, yeah."

"I am!"

"Sure you are." I hopped off the swing. "Come on. I'll walk you home. Your mom's worried."

She sighed and reluctantly stood, tucking her hands into her pockets. "Okay."

That Friday, we had the best recess celebration. We shared a cupcake during lunch and Allie drew me her own friendship MVP certificate, which was way better than any hockey award.

4

ALLIE

3rd Grade

*T*he sun's warmth felt good on my beige skin as I sat with my friends at a table on the pool deck wearing my rainbow tie dye one-piece. For my friend Melissa's ninth birthday she had every girl in our class over to her house for a pool party. Melissa's father is the guy who came up with mini M&M's, so their family had a lot of money. Like rock-cave-with-a-waterfall-in-the-pool and movie-theater-in-the-basement kind of money.

Everyone always loved getting invited to Melissa's house. When I'd told Kyle I couldn't hang out with him that Saturday because I was going to her party, he'd wanted to come with me, but it was a girls only party. Can't say he understood that. Actually, he'd gotten kinda mad and upset about the whole thing, although he'd never come straight out and admit it, but I could tell because he'd gotten real quiet after.

While I applied another layer of sunscreen, Melissa gushed about Ian Baxter. "He's like the cutest boy in our whole class, so I'm totally going to date him." In Melissa's world, Ian being the cutest obviously meant he belonged to her.

I'll admit that Ian was cute. When I'd played little league baseball, Ian had been on my team, but I hadn't been into boys back then. Being nine was way different than being seven, though. Boys weren't quite as icky.

Melissa wiped her wet blond hair off her face. "He totally wanted to come to my party, but my parents wouldn't let him. He said he's going to bring me a present at school on Monday though."

Veronica swooned. "You're so lucky, Melissa. Ian is so nice."

Lila nodded as she added another coat of glitter nail polish to her forefinger. "He is, but I kinda like a different boy in our class."

"Tell me," Melissa demanded as she reached for the neon pink polish. "Which boy?"

Lila blushed. "Kyle."

"Oh, he is super cute," Veronica replied.

Was there another Kyle in our class? Because surely, she couldn't mean...

I scrunched up my face. "Kyle *Hogan*? Are you serious?"

Lila continued, "He has really nice eyes."

I had to give him that. His eyes were so crystal blue they were almost like ice cubes. Sometimes, I found myself getting distracted by them.

Melissa added. "Yeah, he's cute, too. Aren't you and Kyle like dating or something, Allie?"

I coughed on my own saliva. "What? No! We're just friends."

Melissa blew on her freshly painted nails. "You spend recess with him a lot."

Veronica nodded. "Yeah, and those other boys, too. Shawn and Reece."

"That doesn't mean I'm dating them. We're just friends." I'd always preferred hanging out with boys over girls. Over the years, there had been boys who hadn't liked that I wanted to play with them at recess and Kyle had always made it clear that I was invited and if they had a problem with it, they could go play with someone else. I liked that. Besides, it was way more entertaining to play box ball with the boys than to do hand clapping games like Miss Mary Mack or Rockin' Robin with the girls for forty-minutes straight.

"Good. You can talk to Kyle about Lila then," Melissa urged.

"Uh, sure." I stood up. "I'm getting hot. I'm gonna go for a swim." I jumped into the deep end before they could respond, not caring that the water was cold. My feet bounced off the bottom, catapulting me to the surface.

Why'd I think going to an all-girls party would be fun? Every time I found myself stuck with a bunch of girls for an extended period of time, I was reminded why most of my friends were boys. All girls wanted to do was gossip and talk about boys and do their nails or makeup. That really wasn't my thing. After treading water for a minute, I swam into the shallows and got out. Once wrapped in my towel, I went to find Melissa's mom.

"Excuse me, Mrs. Russo?"

She turned away from the other mom's she'd been talking with. "Yes?"

"I'm not feeling so well. Could I use your phone to call my mom?"

"Of course, sweetie." She walked me inside to the kitchen. "Do you need anything?"

I shook my head. "I think I just had too much cake."

She handed me the portable phone. "You let me know if there's anything I can do while you wait for your mom."

"I will. Thanks." I punched in the numbers to my house while Melissa's mom went back outside.

"Hello?"

I was surprised to hear my dad's voice. He'd been working a lot of extra hours and was gone a lot.

"Daddy, the party ended a little early. Can I walk to Kyle's house and hang out there for a bit?" Cold water dripped down my back from my hair and I inched my towel up to catch it.

"It did?"

"Please?" I knew he probably heard through my lie, but hey, I tried.

"Sure, Allie. Call and let us know when you get to Kyle's house." His voice was hoarse, but that was nothing new. He was probably fighting with mom again.

"Thanks, Daddy."

"I'll have your mom pick you up in time for dinner."

"Will you be home for dinner?" I asked, even though I knew what his answer would be.

"Not tonight. I've got to go into the office."

"Okay." I tried to hide my disappointment. "Bye."

I went back out to the pool and told Mrs. Russo I was leaving, then I slipped my cover-up on, gathered my things, and snuck out the gate without bothering with goodbyes. It only took me about five minutes to get to Kyle's. When I arrived at the white brick house with black shutters, I let myself in through the kitchen door like I always did. "Hello?" I called out, but heard no response. It was a nice June day, so I went through to the back of the house and opened the sliding door. Kyle was having a water gun fight with his brothers. Way more fun than painting nails and talking about how cute my best friend supposedly was.

I dropped my stuff on the patio. "Got one for me?" I asked as I took off my cover-up.

Kyle pointed to the shed at the back of the yard, grinning mischievously. "You'll have to get through us to get it." His dirty blond hair was stuck to his forehead.

I formulated a plan. "Okay." I darted into the yard, scooped up Kyle's two-year-old brother, Ryan, and held onto him as I ran toward the shed.

"No fair," Dylan hollered. "We can't shoot at the baby."

Mission accomplished. I located a water gun and tucked it under my arm. "Ready, Ry?" I scooted the giggling toddler around to the side of the shed where the hose was so I could fill up my water gun. I put Ryan down and he wobbled away. Once my gun was ready, I put the cap back in place and ran out into the yard, squirting water at the boys.

We were all good and soaked and panting when Kyle's dad came outside with juice pouches. "Who's thirsty?" He set them on the table. "Allie, your mom called. I told her you were here."

Shoot. I'd forgotten to call home when I'd gotten there. "Thanks, Mr. H."

He grinned and went back inside.

We all dropped our weapons and walked over to the patio. Kyle handed me a juice, poked the straw into one for Ryan, and then grabbed one for himself before taking a seat beside me at the table.

While Jesse and Dylan were busy competing to see who could finish their juice first, Kyle turned to me. "So, how was Melissa's party?"

I shrugged. "I'm here, aren't I?"

He swiped a wet strand of his sandy blond hair off of his forehead. "What'd you girls do?"

"You didn't miss anything, if that's what you're asking. Trust me."

"No?"

I shook my head. "No. This is way more fun."

He laughed. "Well, duh. I'm a lot of fun to play with, Allie."

I laughed, too. "Guess so." I nibbled on my straw. "Would you believe that Melissa thought you and I were dating?"

He nearly spit out his juice. "What? That's stupid."

"I know. I told her we're just friends."

"Good."

"But I found out that Lila likes you."

His brows shot up. "Lila Waters?"

"Yup."

He hummed.

"She thinks you have nice eyes."

"That's because I do have nice eyes."

I elbowed him in the arm.

"Hey," he feigned offense.

"Don't be such a dork."

He smiled. "Wanna play Twister?"

I loved that game. "Sure." I followed him to the shed to get the mat.

Saturdays at the Hogan's were always a blast and I couldn't believe I'd thought going to Melissa's party would be more fun. Last time I'd make that mistake.

5

KYLE

5th Grade

$\mathcal{S}$itting at the family computer in the living room, I typed the final words on my current events homework and hit print. Just as I was going to log out, my Instant Messenger dinged.

ALLIECAT3: You busy?
HOCKEYBOY11: Just finished my homework. What's up?
ALLIECAT3: Want to come over and hang out?
HOCKEYBOY11: Let me ask

I went into the kitchen where my dad was working on fixing the garbage disposal. "Dad, I finished my homework. Can I go over to Allie's house?"

He didn't bother to pull his head out from under the sink. "Sure, son. Just be back for dinner."

We had a family rule that we always had dinner together on Sundays, even if Dad was at work, Mom still made the rest of us do it. "I know."

"Have fun."

I went back to the computer.

HOCKEYBOY11: On my way.

ALLIECAT3: K. I'll be in the back

The bike ride to Allie's took less than five minutes. I rode down her driveway and leaned my bike against the six-foot fence before opening the gate and letting myself into the yard. Allie was laying in the hammock that hung between two trees over a bed of recently bloomed flowers.

"Hey," I said as I walked over.

She sat up and turned sideways so I could sit with her. "Hi." She offered me a half smile over her book.

I collapsed beside her and pointed to her hands. "*Shiloh*, again?" I teased.

She shrugged. "I like it."

She put her bookmark into the book and closed it, then place it down beside her. "How was your weekend?"

"Homework today and I had a game yesterday." I'd gotten really good at hockey, so my parents had found a few leagues that way I could play almost year-round.

"Did you win?"

I nodded. "Of course."

She leaned her head back and closed her eyes. "Good."

It had been a tough year for her and I could tell that something was bothering her. "What's up, Allie?"

She sighed. "Tired."

Getting my best friend to open up was no easy task, but she'd asked me to come over which told me she wanted to talk, I'd just have to pull it out of her. "Are you not sleeping well?"

"Not really."

"Want to talk about it?"

She shrugged.

"Nightmares?"

She nodded.

"Same ones?"

Another nod.

"I'm sorry, Al, but your dad is an idiot."

She sighed. "Yeah." Her dad had left them that fall and they hadn't heard from him since. She'd been having nightmares where she's trying to get to him, but he stays just out of reach. Allie opened her eyes. "What is it about *it* that makes people crazy?"

I arched my brows. "That's probably a question better suited for Brandon." I had nothing to contribute to a conversation about sex.

She pointed up at her brother's window where we could clearly see him kissing his girlfriend.

"Oh," was all I could manage to say.

"Tyler says Dad left because he wanted to do *it* with some other lady. Now Brandon has a girlfriend and it's like I don't exist anymore."

"Brandon isn't like your dad. He's been dating that girl what like two weeks?"

She nodded.

"I'm sure that'll wear off soon and he'll go back to normal."

She tugged on her long, chocolate-colored hair. "You think so?"

"Yeah."

She sighed. "I don't get what's so great about it."

I shook my head. "Ask me this question when we're older."

She waited a second and then said, "Okay, we're older."

I laughed.

Allie crossed her arms over her chest. "Have you ever kissed a girl, Kyle?"

"You know I haven't."

"I don't *know* that. Maybe you did and never told me."

"You're my best friend. I tell you everything."

Looking down at her lap, she picked out the dirt beneath her fingernails as she said, "Maybe we should try it."

I couldn't be hearing her right because it sounded like she was saying she wanted to kiss me. "Try what?" I asked.

She wasn't looking at me, but she was biting her lip. "Kissing."

My stomach flipped. "Like you and me? Together?"

She nodded. "You said it yourself. We're best friends. It doesn't have to mean anything. Then maybe we'll understand why it makes people do crazy things."

I hummed.

"As long as you promise not be a crazy boy afterward."

A laugh escaped me. "I promise. But are you really sure you want to kiss *me*?"

She finally looked up. "The way I see it, you're better than a lot of the gross boys in our class."

I grinned. "Gee, thanks."

She tapped my arm with her fist. "You know what I mean. Why not try it since it won't mean anything and we'll still be friends after." She froze. "You will still be my friend, right?"

I chuckled. "I'll always be your friend."

"Good." She bit her lip again. "So, what do you think?"

I suddenly found myself sweating. "I, uh, guess we could try it."

She blinked a few times. "Now?"

My breathing grew shallow and I swallowed. "Okay."

I had no clue what I was doing. I knew a couple of guys who'd kissed girls before, but I'd never even gotten close enough to a girl to consider trying it. That's not to say that I didn't want to. I'd had a few crushes on some girls and I would've liked to have kissed them. But kissing Allie...

She was like my sister. Sure, she was pretty, and I knew a lot of boys in school liked her, but to me she was one of the guys. I'd never thought about her in any other way.

She spoke softly, "Maybe we should, um, close our eyes?"

"Right."

Slowly, she let her lids drop. I did the same. But then I realized I couldn't see her and that would definitely result in me missing when I leaned in, so I opened my eyes again. I took a deep breath. "Ready?" I whispered.

She nodded slightly.

I leaned closer until our noses were almost touching and then I shut my eyes as I closed the gap and let my lips touch hers. I simply held them there for a few seconds and then pulled back. We both opened our eyes.

I stared at her, admittedly a little scared.

"I don't think we did it right," she uttered.

Well, yeah, I knew that, but it was weird. I ran my hand over my mushroom haircut. "I guess not." I swallowed. "Should we try again?"

"Umm, maybe. If you want to." Her big, bronze eyes stared up at me, clearly asking me to take charge.

"Okay."

She closed her eyes and I leaned down, then closed mine, too, as my mouth touched hers again. This time I let my lips part a little and she did the same. I sort of sucked on hers for a few seconds and then we pulled away from each other and opened our eyes.

I couldn't read her blank expression. "Well?" I asked.

She let her fingers touch her lips for a second and then dropped her hand. "I'm not sure I'm any closer to understanding why people think that's so great."

I laughed. "Me neither."

She grinned. "My mom made brownies this morning. Want one?"

"Of course, I do." I'd yet to turn down Mrs. Dupree's baking. I got up from the hammock and offered Allie my hand, which she took, and I helped her to her feet.

"Do you want to watch Jumanji?" She knew it was one of my favorite movies.

"Definitely."

Neither of us brought up the kiss again.

6

ALLIE

6th Grade

*M*ovie nights at the Hogan's were always a lot of fun. We'd fill the floor of the den with pillows and blankets and all five of us would cuddle up, eat popcorn, and watch movies. Mrs. H would put on some kiddie cartoon for Ryan, who being five-years-old, usually lasted ten minutes. Then she'd leave us be. Once Ryan was asleep, Kyle would pop in a better movie that the rest of us would actually enjoy, while still being age appropriate for Jesse. That night, we were watching Mr. Magoo, and once Jesse fell asleep, we planned on watching *Men in Black*. Halfway through the first movie, my stomach was feeling really crampy, so I got up to go to the bathroom.

When I pulled down my pants and saw the blood stain on my underwear, I gasped. *I couldn't be getting my period*. I was twelve, and sure a few girls at school had gotten theirs, but I wasn't ready. I didn't want to deal with that. My guy friends would treat me differently once they found out I had my period, and that was the last thing I wanted to happen. Cradling my face in my hands, I cried.

At some point, Kyle knocked on the door. "Allie? You okay? You've been in there a while."

I sniffled. "Go away."

"What's wrong? Are you crying?"

"Leave me alone, Kyle."

Then I heard Mrs. H's voice. "What's going on?"

Kyle replied, "Something's wrong with Allie."

"What do you mean?"

"I think she's crying and she won't come out of the bathroom."

"You go back to your brothers. I'll take care of this."

I heard Kyle stomp away and then there was a soft knock on the door. "Allie? Are you all right, dear?"

My lip quivered. "Not really."

"Can I come in?"

I reached over and unlocked the door.

It cracked open and Kyle's mom slipped inside. "What's wrong?"

My eyes filled up with tears again. "I—I think I'm bleeding."

She gave me a compassionate grin as she sat on the edge of the tub. "You got your period?"

I sniffled and nodded.

"First time?"

I nodded again.

"Congratulations."

My head snapped up and I looked at her like she had three heads. "What?"

"That's a big deal. You're becoming a woman, Allie."

I bit my lip.

"I know it's scary, but you're going to be just fine." She opened the cabinet beneath the sink and pulled out a pad, then handed it to me. "Here. Use this."

"I...umm..." I didn't quite know how to tell her that I'd made a bloody mess of my underwear.

"Do you want me to show you how to use it?"

"Umm, yes, but I can't because...umm..."

"Oh, dear. Did you bleed on your underwear?"

More tears clouded my vision as I nodded.

She stood and ran a hand tenderly over my hair. "Don't worry. We'll wash them. It'll be fine." She reached for the door knob. "I'll be right back."

After a few minutes she returned with a new package of boys' underwear. She ripped open the wrapping and handed me a pair that had Teenage Mutant Ninja Turtles on them. "These are Jesse's size, but I think they'll fit you." She turned away from me. "Go ahead and try them on."

I kicked off my pants, removed my dirty underwear, then stood and slipped on the pair she'd given me, which were a little snug, but mostly fine. "They fit," I said as I lowered them to my knees, then pulled my pants back over my ankles and sat down.

She turned again and picked my bloody underwear up off the floor and dropped them in the sink. Then she removed another pair out of the package and unwrapped the pad. She showed me how to stick it to the underwear, then handed it to me. "Go ahead and put it on while I rinse these out for you." She turned to the sink and began to wash the blood out.

I was mortified. Doing as she'd demonstrated, I put the pad in place, then pulled up my pants, closed the lid on the toilet and sat back down. It felt weird. Like I was sitting on a million cotton balls.

She rang out my underwear and said, "I'll throw these in the wash for you."

"Thanks, Mrs. H."

She gave me a reassuring smile. "You'll be okay, Allie. This is a good thing even though I know it probably doesn't feel that way."

"Definitely doesn't. Does it always hurt?"

"Sometimes. Are you in pain now?"

I nodded as my stomach tightened. "Yeah."

She opened the medicine cabinet and took out the Tylenol. After filling one of the small paper bathroom cups with water, she handed it to me along with two of the capsules. "This will help."

I swallowed the pills and drank all of the water.

"Would you like me to take you home?"

I shrugged. I had been looking forward to movie night. Plus, my mom had gone out for the evening and wasn't planning on picking me up until late. Brandon was at a party with his girlfriend, which meant I'd be home with my brother Tyler, a high school freshman, who had made it perfectly clear that he wanted to have friends over without his kid sister bothering him.

"You're welcome to stay, but I understand if you would rather go home."

The thought of being surrounded by my brother's cute, older friends while I was feeling so icky was not high on my list of most desired evenings. "That's okay. I'll stay for the movie." I stood.

Mrs. H pulled me into her arms for a hug and I held on tight. There was something about a mom hug that always fixed things. She released me and said, "You'll want to change the pad every three to four hours. You know where they are now so help yourself, all right?"

"K. Thanks."

"Of course. Mr. H and I are in the living room. You come get me if you need anything."

I nodded. "I will."

She opened the door and I re-entered the den, avoiding Kyle's gaze as I settled back into my spot.

"You okay?" he whispered.

I nodded.

"Are you sick?" he asked, clearly not letting it go.

"No."

"But you were crying."

"Drop it, Kyle. Please."

He sighed and turned his attention back to the movie.

The last thing I needed was for my best friend, who I was pretty sure thought I was more boy than girl, to find out I was *becoming a woman.* I liked the way things were between us and while I knew it was inevitable that our relationship would change because eventually, we'd both be older and dating people and things would be different then, I wanted to hold onto what we had for as long as possible.

Ryan started to stir in his sleep so I scooted away from Kyle and cuddled up next to his little brother. Well, if I'm being honest, I felt like he was my little brother, too, since I'd known him from birth. Ryan and I shared a special bond. I let him lay his head on my chest and I stroked his hair, easing him back into dreamland.

7

KYLE

7th Grade

*M*elissa Russo had an epic basement. I'd never been to her house before, but for her thirteenth birthday, her parents had allowed her to have a co-ed party. Since it was raining, the planned pool party had been turned into a basement party. The best part was that her older sister was the chaperon so there were no parents to bother us, which was great because Lila Waters was there and she and I had some unfinished business.

Lila was into figure skating, so I often saw her at the ice rink with her coach before I had hockey. For the past few weeks, she'd been hanging around to watch us practice and I'd always catch her staring at me. Two weeks before Melissa's party, I'd approached Lila at the rink. We got to talking about skating and then she'd kissed me right outside the locker room. A few of my teammates had seen, so of course we'd quickly become the subject of the Mamaroneck Middle School's gossip mill. Lila had been avoiding me ever since. Except I didn't want her to ignore me. It had been my first real kiss and I'd liked it. Really liked it. Kinda wanted to do more of it. So I was hoping she and I could talk at the party.

Shawn and I finished up the air hockey game we were playing and I noticed Lila was talking to a few of her friends nearby, so even though I'd won the game, I told Shawn he could play next. Yeah, I was nervous to talk to Lila, but I couldn't let anyone see that, so I mustered up the courage and sauntered over to her circle like it wasn't the hardest thing I'd done lately.

"Hey," I said to the girls and smiled, trying to play it cool.

Lila's hazel eyes widened.

Melissa, the unofficial gossip president of the seventh grade, said, "Hi, Kyle. Thanks for coming to my party."

I tucked my fingers into the pockets of my jeans to keep from fidgeting. "Yeah, thanks for inviting me."

She twirled a strand of blond hair around her finger and there was an unmistakable sparkle in her eyes that suggested she was up to something. When she opened her mouth, that became clear. "Lila was just asking about you."

Lila's eyes darted to Melissa. "I was not."

Melissa giggled. "Come on girls, let's give these two love birds time to...chat." She dragged her posse away, leaving Lila and I alone.

Refusing to look at me, Lila tugged on her mousy-brown hair and I shifted my weight on my feet. I spoke first. "Are you having fun?" Not my best line by any means, but it was the only thing I could think to say in the moment.

She nodded. "You?"

"Yeah. Melissa has a cool house."

Lila crossed her arms. "She does. The movie theater is pretty neat."

"I haven't seen it yet. Want to show me?"

Her eyes darted around and she hesitated before saying, "Um, sure." She turned and I followed her to a room on the other side of the basement. Lila slid open the barn-style door revealing the empty theater room. The walls were painted in a dark color and there was a large projector screen on one wall. Two over-sized sectional couches formed a giant U-shape with a gap in the middle for an aisle.

"This is it," she announced from the doorway. Then she went to slide the door closed.

"Wait." I put my hand out and stopped her. "Can we maybe go in there and talk for a minute?"

She bit her lip.

"Please?" I urged.

She walked into the room and took a seat on the couch. I sat next to her, but left enough space between us so that she wouldn't feel uncomfortable. Then I came right out and said, "You've been avoiding me."

She stared down at her hands. "Sorry."

"Was the kiss that bad?" I mean, I was no expert, but it had seemed good to me. Sure, it probably could've been better, but it hadn't been terrible.

She shook her head. "No. You're a good kisser, Kyle."

I grinned. "Yeah?" The prospect of getting to kiss her again made excitement well up inside me. "Then why have you been avoiding me?"

"My mom's best friend is a teacher at our school and she told my mom that people were talking about us kissing." She sighed. "I'm not allowed to date until high school and Mom said if she hears I'm not sticking to that she's going to cancel my skating lessons."

I knew Lila was just as passionate about skating as I was about hockey, so I felt for her. That was definitely a dilemma. I tried to put myself in her shoes. I'd choose hockey over a girl. "I'm sorry, Lila. I didn't want to get you into trouble."

"You don't have to apologize. I wanted to kiss you," she gave me a lopsided grin. "I've been avoiding you because I like you."

My stomach did a happy flop. "I like you, too."

She folded her arms over her chest. "Which is exactly why we can't hang out. I can't get into trouble. And if we spend time together, then we're going to end up kissing again. I'm training for the Olympics. I can't lose my lessons."

The disappointment sucked, but I understood. "I get it." I scooted closer to her. "But do you think I could have one more kiss? To hold us over until high school."

She giggled. "I think we could do that."

Not wanting to risk her changing her mind, I leaned in and kissed her. It didn't last long, but it was enough to tell me that I was well past the girls-are-icky phase. When I pulled away, we both smiled.

Allie had once asked me if I knew what the hype was all about. I hadn't at the time, but I'd finally got it. Kissing was totally worth the hype. And I wanted to do more of it. We got up from the couch to go back out to the party, but Melissa and her gaggle of girls appeared in the doorway.

"There you are," she said dramatically. "We've been looking for you, Lila, but now I see you've been busy."

Lila's eyes widened and she went to protest, "No, Mel—"

"Lila was showing me the theater. That's it. You can stop the presses on tomorrow's gossip mag, Melissa," I cut in. "Don't go getting your *friend* into trouble for nothing."

Melissa laughed a little too hard and flipped her wavy hair over her shoulder. "Whatever. We're here to hang out. She led her followers into the space and told everyone to sit down. "We're going to play a game. I'll be right back."

Lila went to sit with her friends while I attempted to escape, but when I got to the door, I froze. Standing in the middle of the room was a stunning girl in a short dress with long, tan legs. I only caught a glimpse of the side of her face before she turned. But her body told me all I needed to know. I thought she was hot, and she definitely had to be friends with Melissa's older sister because girls my age didn't look like that. Her straight brown hair fell to the mid-point of her back and she was surrounded by nearly every boy at the party, all of whom were salivating over her curves.

As I went to go join the circle and get a better look at the mystery girl, Melissa came up beside me and followed my gaze. Then she shouted across the room, "Yay! Allie, you made it."

What? No.

The girl spun around and sure enough it was my best friend. My jaw nearly hit the floor. Noticing me, she waved and made her way out of the circle of admirers and over to me.

"Hey, Kyle." She gave me a quick hug.

Too shocked to reply I simply gawked like an idiot. Not my finest moment.

"Sorry I'm late, Mel. My cousin's bridal shower took longer than I'd thought."

Melissa replied, "Girl, you don't have to apologize for showing up to my party late when you look like that. You should totally wear makeup more often." She grabbed Allie's arm. "Come, we're about to play a game." She dragged Allie into the room and I followed like a hungry puppy. I wasn't the only one. Several other boys flooded in, too.

Melissa pushed the coffee tables out of the way. "Everyone sit in a circle on the floor."

Ian and Shawn weaseled their way into the circle on either side of Allie while I sat across from her. In the nine years that I'd known her, I'd never seen Allie wear makeup, but whatever the black stuff on her eyelids was, it made her pretty bronze eyes seem even more beautiful. And the shiny gloss on her lips made it hard not to stare. Sure, I'd always thought Allie had been pretty, but I'd never thought of her as anything more than a friend.

I don't know when it had happened, but Allie had boobs. They hadn't been there when I'd seen her in a bathing suit the previous summer. My mind was already scheduling trips to the pool for when we got home from sleep away camp. Allie's typical outfit consisted of jeans and a basic t-shirt or sweatshirt. The black dress she was sporting was something I'd never in a million years picture my best friend wearing. But wear it she did. It fell almost to the middle of her thigh, tightened around the waist, and had off the shoulder straps that showed off a heck of a lot more of her chest than a t-shirt did.

Melissa stood in the center of the circle. "We're playing spin the bottle." She placed an empty glass soda bottle in the middle and then found a spot in the circle. There were ten of us and at the mention of the game, the boys clapped and hooted, while the girls giggled. I did nothing. The shock was real.

"Who's first?" Melissa tempted.

Shawn reached for the bottle and spun. I squeezed my eyes shut a moment and prayed that it landed on anyone but Allie. When I opened my eyes, it slowed to a stop in front of Veronica. I sighed in relief. While they kissed, I glanced around them and my eyes met Allie's. She gave me an awkward half-smile, which I matched with one of my own. Spin the Bottle wasn't something we'd played before. At least not that she'd ever told me anyway, and seeing as we basically went to everything together, I felt fairly confident in that assessment.

Ian's bottle stopped on Lila and I probably should've been mad about it since she had kissed me not too long before that, but strangely it didn't bother me. Again, I was more caught up in the relief that the bottle hadn't landed on Allie. Maybe Lila was the reason I was thinking about kissing Allie. She'd gotten me all worked up about kissing and it had only confused me.

Reece spun next and his landed on Melissa. I sighed in relief once more, but the feeling was short-lived because it was my turn. My heart pounded against my ribs as I reached for the bottle. Without question, I found myself hoping it would land on Allie, but then I felt bad about that. She was my friend. Kissing her would be wrong.

Fate intervened. The bottle slowed to a stop and my gaze followed to where it was pointing. A pair of nervous, surprised, bronze-colored eyes stared back at me.

Ian laughed, "Damn, Hogan."

I cleared my throat.

"You have to do it," Melissa announced.

I equal parts wanted to and didn't want to. "Uh," I uttered. Neither of us moved.

"Don't be babies about it. It's just a kiss," Veronica added.

"Right." I ran my hand over the top of my head, but I didn't advance toward her.

Allie sighed. "Let's just get it over with." Her words felt like a slap, but I didn't have much time to think about it because she crawled forward into the circle.

I swallowed hard as I moved toward her. Right as I met her in the middle, someone hollered from the door, "Melissa, I told you no kissing games."

Allie and I both scurried backward.

Melissa protested, "Come on, Jamie. It's harmless."

"No. I promised Mom and Dad I wouldn't let this kind of thing happen. Everyone up, let's go."

The group grumbled and exited the theater. I couldn't get out of there fast enough and I found myself a corner to stand in. I'd almost kissed *Allie*. Like kissed her-kissed her, not like that time when we were in fifth grade and just messing around. This time, I wanted to kiss her. *What the —*

"Hey."

I looked up and blushed as though she had somehow heard what I'd been thinking. "Hi."

She thumbed over her shoulder at the theater. "That was weird."

I laughed. "Yeah."

She leaned against the wall beside me. "So, what'd I miss?"

I just realized that you're a girl.

I shrugged. "Not much. You arrived when things got...interesting." I pointed to her dress. "You look nice."

She tucked her hair behind her ear. "I feel ridiculous. Mom

insisted I wear this to the shower. I wanted to go home and change before coming here, but I was already so late."

"I'm glad you didn't." The words slipped out without thought.

She crossed her arms. "You are?"

I lifted a shoulder. "Looks good on you."

She sucked in her bottom lip, once again drawing my attention where it shouldn't be. "Thanks."

All I could do was smile.

She dug into her small purse and retrieved a disposable camera. She'd taken to bringing one with her everywhere. "We should get a picture with Melissa."

I nodded. "Sure."

When she turned, my gaze wandered to her hips as they swayed with each step. *I'm so screwed.*

8

ALLIE

8th Grade

I twirled a curl around my finger as I assessed myself in the mirror for the zillionth time. This night was a big deal. Everything had to be perfect for my first ever school dance. Dress? Check. Shoes? Check. Makeup? Check. Jewelry! I crossed to my dresser and opened the jewelry box I'd had for as long as I could remember. The maple wood gave it a distinguished smell that always reminded me of my grandparents' house, which had been filled with maple furniture. Since they'd retired and moved to Florida, I hardly got to see them anymore. Well, that and the whole my dad leaving our family thing.

I fished out my silver Tiffany heart bracelet. All the girls at school had them and I'd been so excited when I'd come downstairs a couple of months earlier to see the distinctive blue bag on the kitchen counter. My brothers had gotten it for me for my fourteenth birthday and it was my most valued possession. After a couple of tries, I got the clasp fastened around my wrist.

41

"Allie? Kyle's here," Tyler called out from downstairs.

"Be down in a minute." I checked the mirror one last time and I almost didn't recognize myself. Mom had done my makeup and she'd even used one of those eyelash curler contraptions, which, for the record, was terrifying. Seeing that thing coming at my eye was like volunteering for some kind of medieval torture. But, I had to admit, my lashes looked like the movie stars'. My hair, which I wore in a pony-tail ninety-five percent of the time, was loosely curled and it reached halfway down my back. The rhinestone belt sparkled on my one-shoulder, navy-blue cocktail dress. It had lace on the top and a few layers of tulle that flared slightly at the waist. The girl staring back at me in the mirror was not the Allie Dupree I knew. She was older, sophisticated—beautiful, even.

After taking a deep breath, I opened my bedroom door and descended the stairs.

"Dude, you should really think about football next year," Tyler's voice came from the living room. "Being on the team is a sure way to get in with the right crew as a freshman."

I rounded the corner

"Yeah, but it interferes with hockey," Kyle replied.

I came up behind him. "Kyle, there are other sports besides hockey, you know."

"No, no, no." Brandon jumped up from the couch. "Allie, you are not going anywhere looking like that."

Kyle spun around and Tyler stepped around Kyle so he could see me, too.

"Whoa." Kyle's eyes grew big.

"Hell, no. Too short," Tyler added.

I rolled my eyes. "It's not that short, I just have long legs." I spun around to show them that my butt was fully covered. "You guys are being ridiculous."

Brandon put his hands on his hips. "No, we're not. We know teenage boys better than you do, lil' sis, and you are far too young to be going anywhere wearing that and," he pointed to my face, "looking like that."

"One hundred percent." Tyler mimicked Brandon's pose. "Not happening."

I huffed. "Too bad you guys aren't the boss of me. Besides, Mom got me this dress and she helped me get ready, so this is her doing. If she doesn't have a problem with it, neither should you."

I turned toward my best friend who was staring at me entirely too weird. "Kyle likes it," I said, trying to communicate with him telepathically to agree with me.

Tyler let out a sarcastic laugh. "Tell her, Kyle."

"Uhh," he uttered, pathetically.

I narrowed my eyes at him. "Do not tell me you agree with these overprotective maniacs."

Kyle's gaze darted between my brothers and me. "You look..." He chewed on his lower lip. "Different."

I frowned at his assessment. While Kyle and I were going to the dance together, we weren't *going together*. Actually, I was hoping that Ian Baxter would notice me, so I didn't want to look *different*, I wanted to look pretty. Ian knew me as the girl from little league, but I wanted to change that.

I must've scowled because Tyler came over and put his arm around me. "There will be plenty of time for you to be a heart-breaker, but I really don't want to have to punch some four-teen-year-old hormonal dweeb for putting a hand on my baby sister. You're not old enough for that yet."

I shrugged him off. "I appreciate your concern, Ty, but I can handle myself. And we're going to be late if we don't leave now, so you're just gonna have to deal."

Brandon, who was a senior in high school, threw his hands up. "Fine you can go."

"Gee, thanks." I stuck my tongue out at him. "But I wasn't asking for your permission."

"You can go because Ty is going with you."

43

"He is?"

"I am?"

Brandon grinned smugly. "Yes, you are."

"I think you mean *you're* going with her," Tyler countered.

"Can't. Molly and I have plans." She was his girlfriend.

"I've got plans, too," Tyler grumbled.

"Neither of you is coming with me. Kyle, let's go." I grabbed my best friend's wrist and pulled him toward the door out to where his mom was waiting for us in her minivan. My mom had some meeting to go to so she had to rush off, but Mrs. H was practically my other mom. She was also the new high school principal, so I figured if anyone could talk some sense into my brothers, it would be her.

Upon approaching the van in the driveway, I released Kyle and went straight to her window. "Mrs. H, please tell my brothers that they are not coming to chaperon me at the dance." I glanced up to see them both barreling down our front steps.

Mrs. H laughed. "You look lovely, dear."

"Thank you," I huffed. I stepped aside so she could get out of the van.

"Brandon, Tyler," she acknowledged the buffoons.

Brandon replied, "Principal Hogan, would you mind giving Tyler a ride to the dance as well?"

She smirked and addressed Tyler. "Mr. Dupree, are you going to the dance as the date of an eighth grader?"

He pointed at me. "Yeah, Allie's."

I screamed through my teeth. "No. You. Are. Not."

Mrs. H said, "Allie and Kyle are going together so I'm afraid you'll need another date if you plan on getting into the dance."

I loved that woman.

Brandon came back with, "He's taking one of Allie's friends."

I balled my hands into fists at my sides. Before I could

respond, Mrs. H replied, "Oh? Well then we'll pick her up on the way, that way we can stop to get photos of you two together for the yearbook."

Tyler turned to Brandon. "No way, dude. I will not be seen on a date with a kid. You go. No one would believe you're really dating the chick."

Brandon sighed. "Can't. I'm eighteen. That would be illegal."

"Then it's settled." I pulled open the sliding door of the van. "See you guys later." I hopped in and scooted over to make room for Kyle who stood there looking like a lost puppy. "Kyle." I patted the seat beside me. "Get in."

Brandon grabbed Kyle's shoulder. "Watch her back. I'm counting on you."

Kyle nodded. "I've always got her back."

Brandon sighed and stepped away. Since my father's departure, Brandon has taken his big brother role very seriously. My mother practically had to force him to apply to colleges out-of-state. In a few months he'd be leaving for college in Texas and the closer it came to him going, the harder he held onto the reins.

I waved to my pissed off brothers as we drove away.

The gym had been transformed for the event. A giant balloon arch in our school colors—navy and gold—adorned the entrance, and each table had more balloons as centerpieces. Kyle offered me his arm as we entered, which I reluctantly took. I was still a little mad at him for the *different* comment. Okay, mad might be extreme because I guess he was right, I didn't look like myself, but still. The tables bordered a make-shift dance floor and there were entirely too many streamers hanging from the basketball hoops. The DJ was playing a Destiny's Child song and a bunch of girls were dancing while the boys huddled together off to the side. Melissa noticed me and waved.

Releasing Kyle's arm, I said, "I'm going to dance." I didn't wait for him to respond. My heels clicked on the wooden floor and I took care with each step so that I wouldn't slip. Lila stepped to the side and let me into the circle. Melissa had on this hot pink, glittery dress and I made it my mission to stay as far away as possible because glitter was the devil.

Lila peered over my shoulder and said, "Kyle looks really good in a suit."

With the whole big brother debacle, I hadn't had a chance to truly look at Kyle, so I spun around and spotted him standing with Reese and Shawn. Admittedly, he looked nice in the black suit. He was even wearing a tie, which I imagined he'd borrowed from his dad. Kyle always had the whole boy next door thing going for him and I understood why so many girls thought he was cute—with his piercing blue eyes and his contagious smile, but to me he was my goofy best friend.

I scanned the gym in search of Ian, finding him at a table with some of the other guys on the baseball team. He'd taken off his suit jacket and his tie hung loosely around his neck. His dark eyes and spiked up brown hair gave him a Freddie Prinze Jr. vibe, so it was no wonder a lot of girls in our class thought Ian was cute.

Melissa snuck up behind me and said, "So you're into Ian, huh?"

I flinched, startled by her sudden appearance and I pulled my gaze away from Ian. Trying to play it off like it was nothing, I shrugged. "He's cute."

Melissa sighed. "Yeah, but Kyle Hogan is looking hot tonight."

I nearly choked on my saliva. Kyle and hot were by no means synonymous.

"He's kinda got a JTT thing going on."

"You think so?" Without a doubt Jonathan Taylor Thomas

was the subject of every tween girl's fantasies, but Kyle and JTT? I didn't see it.

"For sure. They both have that killer smile and those blue eyes and dirty blonde hair."

I tilted my head as though somehow that'd make me see the resemblance. "I guess so."

"We should like totally get them to dance with us."

Dance with Ian? Yes, please! But the thought of asking him made me quiver. "You mean like ask them?"

She tossed her head back and laughed as though my question were preposterous. "No, Allie. Girls like us don't ask. Ever. We *get* asked."

"Girls like us?" I'd never considered myself to be in the same league as Melissa. She was the head cheerleader type, whereas I was on the volleyball team and spent my free afternoons hanging with the guys at intramural sports.

"Face it, Allie, you have real potential. You should like totally try out for cheerleading with me next year. It's important for us to establish ourselves at the top right from the beginning of high school."

A very unladylike laugh escaped my lips. "I don't think that's my thing, Mel."

She hooked her arm in mine. *So much for avoiding the glitter bomb.* "Trust me, sweetie. It's your thing. Now, let's get those boys."

We tapped our heels over to where Ian and his crew were, my pulse quickening with each step. Melissa said to the table, "You know boys, this is a dance, not a sit around and do nothing party."

Ian looked over his shoulder and upon making eye contact with me, he stood. "Allie? Wow you look..."

"Different?" I filled in for him. Not sure why.

He shook his head. "Pretty."

I blushed. "Thanks."

Melissa released my arm and gave me a shove in Ian's direction. "Doesn't she though? You two should dance."

Ian grinned and I returned it with a smile of my own. He held his hand out to me. "Wanna?"

"Sure." I put my fingers in his palm and tried not to freak out about a boy—who wasn't Kyle—holding my hand for the first time.

A fast-paced Jennifer Lopez song was playing and we'd managed to get all of two steps onto the dance floor before Kyle bombarded us. "Hey guys. Having fun?"

I glared at him, but he pretended not to notice as he danced along with us, ruining any romantic moment that Ian and I might've had.

Melissa joined our circle. "Hi, Kyle." She smiled flirta- tiously.

He gave her a chin dip. "Hey."

The song changed to, "I Turn to You," a slow ballad by Christina Aguilera. Ian stepped forward, his eyes locked on mine, but Kyle cut in between us just as I was sure Ian was going to grab me to dance. "Let's dance, Al." Kyle's hands found my hips and he dragged me away from Ian and Melissa before I could protest.

Over his shoulder, I saw Melissa and Ian dancing. I sighed and, resigning myself to reality, I put my hands on Kyle's shoulders while Christina sang about two people being strong for each other.

I sighed. "Kyle, what was that about?"

"What was what about?" He tried to play dumb, but I saw right through his rouse.

"I was trying to dance with Ian."

"Were you? Oh, I didn't realize."

I tilted my head and gave him an expression that said, *yeah right.* "What's the deal?"

He shrugged. "Just looking out for you."

We swayed side-to-side. "Would this have anything to do

with my brothers?"

"Can't a guy just want to dance with his best friend?"

"Nope."

He sighed. "Or maybe I was trying to avoid having to dance with Melissa's dress brushing against me."

I pursed my lips. That seemed logical, but still... "Fine, but I want to dance with Ian next."

"You *want* to dance with Ian?" His brows furrowed. "What do you have against Ian? I thought you two were friends."

"Yeah." He spun me around, unexpectedly, making me giggle. "Guess it's weird hearing you talk about Ian like you've got a crush on him."

"I don't have a crush on him." My vehement denial made it painfully obvious that I was lying.

"Sure..."

"Okay, fine. Maybe a little."

"Why?" He furrowed his brow.

I shrugged. "He's cute."

"That's it?" His eyes pierced mine.

"I guess we also have stuff in common."

"Like baseball?" he suggested.

I nodded. "For one."

"I don't think it'll work." He spun me again as Christina belted out the chorus.

I stopped swaying. "Why not?"

"Because he's a dumb jock."

"Wow, Kyle. Do you always speak so kindly about your friends behind their backs?"

"I just think you can do better than Ian Baxter."

I let go of his shoulders and stepped away. "Like who?"

He slipped his fingertips into his pockets. "I don't know." His refusal to meet my gaze told a different story.

"Yes, you do."

"Let's just drop it."

Fueled by frustration, I had a newfound sense of confidence. "Fine." I stomped straight up to Ian and Melissa. "Mind if I cut in? Mel, Kyle said he wants to dance with you."

She happily released Ian before embracing Kyle, covering him in pink glitter. *Good.*

Ian smiled as he reached for my hips, pulling me against him. We got in two eight counts before the song changed to something upbeat, but it had been the best few seconds of my night.

9

KYLE

9th Grade - September

"*I* just realized something," Allie said as we walked to our third period biology class. We'd scheduled as many classes together as we could that year and would only be apart for three periods.

"Care to share?"

"We're high school freshman."

I chuckled. "You're just realizing this?" School had started exactly one week earlier.

"No, jerk. I mean four years from today we'll be in college."

I smirked. "And one year from today, we'll be sophomores."

She elbowed me. "Not the same."

We took our seats—Allie in front of me, so we could pass notes back and forth—and the bell rang, but our teacher, Mr. Riley, wasn't there yet, which was strange because he was a stickler for punctuality.

Melissa, who sat in front of Allie, turned around. "Are you excited for our first practice this afternoon?"

Allie shrugged. "I guess."

"You're really doing this?" I leaned forward and asked her, still in disbelief that she was officially a cheerleader.

She turned sideways in her seat. "Well, I made the team, so, yeah."

Melissa chimed in, "It's a squad."

Allie turned her head so only I could see her roll her eyes, "I made the *squad*."

When she'd told me she was going to try out, I was sure she'd been kidding, but then she actually had. After school the day before, they'd had uniform fittings. She'd met me at the ice rink afterward sporting the navy and gold micro-length pleated skirt and tight cropped top that showed off a sliver of skin on her midriff. No joke, two of the guys on my team had skated straight into each other because they'd been staring at her instead of paying attention. I couldn't blame them. My initial reaction to seeing her had been far from platonic. It was getting more difficult by the day to deny that I was developing feelings for Allie beyond friendship. She was beautiful, no doubt, but it wasn't only that. We'd spent a decade building our relationship and I couldn't imagine my life without her.

Ten minutes late, Mr. Riley arrived all disheveled and his skin was sallow. He dropped his briefcase, then perched himself on the edge of his desk in front of the class. "In a minute, Principal Hogan is going to come over the loudspeaker with a very important announcement."

What the hell? The whole class looked at me. I shrugged. It was news to me, too.

My mother's voice filled the room. "Students, this is Principal Hogan. It is with a very heavy heart that I must tell you not long before nine o'clock this morning, a plane crashed into one of the twin towers. A second plane crashed into the other tower shortly after." Her words shook, which was very unlike my mother, and my blood drained to my feet.

"Some of your parents will be picking you up early. If this is the case, a teacher will come and get you from your class for early dismissal. For the rest of the day, classes will be canceled, but school will be open. You'll remain with your current teacher and if your classroom does not have a television, you will be moved into one that does where we will be airing the news. This is a somber time for our nation and please know that you can speak openly with your teachers about how these events are making you feel."

A girl a row over from me was crying and I heard her mutter that her dad was a cop in Manhattan.

Mom cleared her throat. "I realize that several of you have parents who work in the city. Please know that our staff will be personally reaching out to every single one of your families. This may take some time as cellular service is limited, but we will keep you updated. It's okay to be scared. It's okay to cry. We will get through this together. God bless America."

I hadn't realized I was biting my lip until the metallic taste of blood hit my tongue. Allie turned and looked at me, but I couldn't meet her gaze for fear I'd lose control of my emotions. My father was a fireman in the Bronx and I knew in my gut that he'd be responding to the attacks. Allie reached across the desk and grabbed onto my hand, squeezing it tight. "He'll be fine," she whispered, reading my mind like she tended to do.

I couldn't even manage a nod.

Mr. Riley cleared his throat. "We're going to be sharing a classroom in the English department where there's a television, so pack up your things and we'll go down together."

No one said a word as we silently gathered our stuff. In the hallway, we passed other shuffling students, all of whom wore somber expressions, as well. We arrived at our destination and since there weren't enough desks, many of us took seats on the floor. Allie sat beside me on the tiles, clutching my hand as the news streamed live footage of the burning twin towers in downtown Manhattan. No one said a word. Several people cried. Many students held each other.

A knock at the door drew our attention just before it crept open. My mother was there. "Kyle?"

I stood up and Allie rose beside me.

"We've got to go."

My worst fear was confirmed: my father was responding. My mom would never leave the school in a crisis otherwise. I slung my backpack over my shoulder. Allie did the same. "I'm coming with you."

We both exited the classroom and Mom pulled us into a hug. "We've got to go pick up your brothers. Allie, I'll let your mom know you're with us. Did Tyler drive to school today?"

Allie nodded.

"All right, I'll have him dismissed. He can come to our house, too."

We followed Mom to the main office where she tasked someone with going to get my brother. Her cell phone rang and she ushered us into her office and closed the door as she pulled the antennae up and answered it.

"Brian," her voice was rich with emotion as she addressed my dad.

She took a steadying breath. "Of course...Yes...Be careful...I love you, too...Yes, here's Kyle." She handed me the phone.

"Dad?

"Hi, son." Sirens blared in the background.

"You're going."

"Yes, I am."

I blinked a few times.

"I have to."

"I know," I reassured him. He'd instilled in all of us the sense of duty and honor that accompanied his job in the New York City Fire Department (FDNY).

"It might be a while before I can call again. I don't know how long I'll be there."

I inhaled a shaky breath. "Okay."

"Take care of your mother and your brothers, son."

I squeezed my jaw tight to hold in the emotion. *This could very well be the last conversation I ever have with my dad.* I swallowed. "I will. I promise."

"I'm proud of you, Kyle." The truck's air horn blew.

"Thanks, Dad. Stay safe."

"I will. Give your mom a hug for me, okay?" For the first time in my life, I heard a hitch in his voice.

"Of course."

"I love you."

"Love you, too, Dad."

The silence after he hung up was painful. I handed my mom her phone and we headed outside then piled into the minivan. The middle school was a block away, so we didn't have to go far to get Dylan. Once he was in the car, I explained to him that our dad was going to the World Trade Center (WTC). He seemed to understand the gravity of that and we rode to the elementary school to pick up Jesse and Ryan in silence.

Ryan sat next to Allie and she kept her arm around him the whole ride home. While Jesse got that this was serious, Ryan was mostly confused. When Mom pulled into our driveway, Tyler was already there. Allie's mom worked at a nursing home in Connecticut so it was good that the he came to our house instead of going to his home alone.

In a daze, we all filed into the living room and I turned on the news. Tyler sat on the edge of one of the chairs and he leaned forward on his forearms, which balanced atop his legs. Dylan and Jesse sat together on one part of the sectional while Ryan and I sat on the other part with Allie between us. Ryan put his head on her shoulder and she stroked his blond hair with one hand while her other hand rested on my thigh. Mom went into the kitchen and called my grandparents in Ireland to let them know that our country was under attack and their son was there.

Seeing the towers burning was like something out of an apocalyptic movie. It didn't seem real. Sometime between my mom's announcement at school and when we'd gotten home, a third plane had hit the Pentagon. Words like *terrorism* and *attack* were being thrown around as the camera panned over the financial district. The twin towers were pillars of smoke and flame.

And then the unthinkable happened.

The reporter gasped in horror when one of the towers imploded and disappeared from the skyline in a matter of seconds. My hands went to my mouth and it was as though everything around me had ceased to be. I was hyper-aware of my accelerating heart rate and all I could think was, *please, God, don't let my dad be there yet.*

Allie's hand moved to my shoulder making me flinch. "He'll be okay, Kyle."

Tyler got up. "Come on boys, let's go make a snack." He led Ryan and Jesse into the kitchen, which was good because they didn't need to see what happened next.

Dylan stayed. "Is Dad...?"

I shook my head and scooted over. Patting the empty spot beside me, I said, "No. Don't go there. We need to believe he's fine."

"He *is* fine," Allie emphasized.

Dylan sat down next to me. "Okay." A few tears trailed down his face, so I draped an arm over his shoulder.

The news switched to a camera on the street and it looked like a blizzard, which wasn't possible on such a perfect blue-sky day in September. People were coated in what appeared to be white powder as they sprinted down the streets, ducked into buildings, and vanished. Others who were injured and bleeding wandered about in a daze.

The camera switched again, this time it zoomed in on a crushed fire truck. Dylan cried out, "Dad!"

I bit my lip as I squeezed my eyes shut forcing the tears back. "It's not Dad's, bud." I held him tightly against me.

Mom came into the room. "Tyler said one of the towers exploded."

Her gaze fixed on the television and her mouth dropped open at the scene.

The reporter, who sounded like she was in utter shock, announced, "We've just gotten word that a fourth plane has crashed in a field in Pennsylvania. It is believed that this plane was heading toward Washington, D.C."

All my blood drained to my feet and I shivered with a chill. I kept my arm around Dylan and Allie kept hers around me.

Mom perched on the armrest next to Dylan. "Everything is going to be okay, boys."

I was certain she'd said it as much for herself as for our benefit.

We continued to watch in shock and I secretly hoped to catch a glimpse of my dad, but no such luck.

And then the second tower fell.

I got up and hugged my mom. Without me needing to ask, Allie scooted over to hold Dylan.

This had to be what it was like when the world came to an end. Helpless, we stared at the screen. Waiting. For what? I'm not sure, but we held out for any glimmer of good news.

Tyler got Ryan settled in one of the bedrooms to watch cartoons, then he and Jesse sat with us as we stayed glued to the television for hours. Our phone wouldn't stop ringing and Tyler and Allie did a great job of intercepting concerned friends so that mom wouldn't have to do it. Later, a third building at the WTC that had caught fire collapsed, and with it, so did our hope.

As the sun set, a few neighbors dropped by with food, but none of us could bring ourselves to eat. Sometime that evening, Mrs. Dupree arrived and she watched the news with us for a bit. She even got my mom to eat a little and drink some coffee.

I overheard her offer to stay the night, but my mom declined. We still hadn't heard from Dad, but the reporters claimed that cell service was basically non-existent in the area, so I crossed my fingers and prayed that was the reason why.

Mrs. Dupree helped get the younger boys ready for bed and then she rejoined us in the living room.

"Ann, are you sure you don't want us to stay?" she asked my mom.

Mom nodded. "Thank you for all of your help."

Mrs. Dupree waved her off. "I'm off tomorrow, so we'll come back in the morning, okay?"

"I'd appreciate that, Leslie."

"Of course. You call me anytime if you need anything at all." She turned to her children. "Let's go you lot."

Tyler stood, but Allie remained planted to my side. "Mom, I'm gonna stay."

Mrs. Dupree nodded. "Sure, sweetie. I'll bring you a change of clothes and whatnot in the morning." She kissed her daughter goodbye and they left.

It was after midnight by the time my mother shut off the television. "We need to go to bed."

"Ma, can Allie stay in my room?" Our parents hadn't let us share a bedroom since we'd hit puberty.

She didn't hesitate. "That's fine."

I gave my mom a hug that seemed to last for days. As she pulled away, I said. "Or I can stay with you tonight if you want." My mom was one of the strongest people I knew, but a part of me recognized that staying alone in the bed that she and my father shared wouldn't be an easy thing.

She cupped my cheek. "I love you for offering, but I'll be okay."

"You sure?" I asked for good measure.

She nodded. "Try and get some sleep, you two," she said as she went upstairs.

I gave Allie a pair of my boxers and a t-shirt to sleep in so she didn't have to wear the clothes she'd worn to school. After getting ready for the night, we slid under the covers of my full-sized bed.

Allie cuddled up against me and put her head on my chest. Holding her and having her near like that managed to ease a little bit of my tension. I truly couldn't imagine my life without her and that day had been the perfect example of why. She intuited what I'd needed from her without a word. Every single time. And she had a way of comforting me when no one or nothing else could. We stayed like that for a while, neither of us speaking, no sound but our breathing and the ceiling fan clicking above us. I doubted sleep would come easily because my mind kept reliving the horror of the day.

After some time, when I'd assumed Allie had fallen asleep, she surprised me by saying. "It's going to be okay, Kyle."

I sighed and her head bobbed on my chest. "Yeah."

"I promise you it is," she whispered in the darkness. "I have a feeling."

The idea of my father being hurt or...worse, crept in. I swallowed. "I hope you're right."

"I am. And I'm going to be here with you every second until he comes home."

And I knew without a doubt that she would be. For the first time, I allowed the tears to drip down my cheeks without fighting. I'd been holding them in all day, trying to be strong for my family like my dad had asked, but everyone had a breaking point.

Allie didn't say anything, she just held me tighter until I managed to get control of myself. Sometime later, Allie whispered, "I love you Kyle, you know that, right?"

That made me smile. "Yeah, I do."

"And..." she teased.

A small laugh escaped my lips. "And I love you, too." No words were truer. Except, I was pretty sure that the love I felt for her was different than what she'd meant. But I didn't dwell on that. My heart was hurting enough.

The next morning, we once again huddled around the television, praying to catch a glimpse of Dad. Mrs. Dupree handled the friends and neighbors who'd decided to stop by to check in on us. Mom wasn't up for company. Hell, neither was I. Since we'd yet to hear from Dad, my Mom had chosen to keep us home from school and she'd called out of work as well. Tyler went, but Allie, true to her word, refused to leave me.

Around noon, the phone rang and instead of coaxing the concerned friend off the line, Mrs. Dupree brought the cordless handset in to my mom. "Ann, you should take this one." She looked pale and my stomach immediately sank.

Mom clutched it to her ear. "Hello?" The desperation in her voice told me that Mom was hurting much more than she'd been letting on. "Yes, hi, Jimmy."

Dad worked with a guy named Jimmy at his firehouse. My hands clenched into fists on my lap and I strained to try and hear the conversation. As though she read my mind, Allie muted the TV.

My mom fell back against the wall and the phone dropped from her hands. Mrs. Dupree grasped Mom's shoulders. "Ann, what is it?"

I went for the phone. "Jimmy? This is Kyle."

He sounded like he hadn't slept in years. "Kyle, I'm sorry to have to tell you this, but your father is missing."

Missing wasn't good, but it wasn't dead. I squeezed the bridge of my nose. "When?" was all I managed to get out.

"We haven't heard from him since before the second tower fell."

My hope shattered. I glanced at my mom who was crying on Mrs. Dupree's shoulder. It broke my heart to see her like that, so I looked away. Allie was holding Ryan, trying to soothe him. Jesse and Dylan stared at me expectantly.

I took a deep breath. "Thank you, Jimmy."

"A few of the wives from the firehouse are going to stop by to help you guys. I'm heading back to the site soon, but one of us will give you a call tonight with an update. You call the firehouse anytime if you need anything, son."

Son. I remembered my last conversation with my dad. "We will. Thank you."

"Be strong, Kyle. You can handle this."

I nodded even though he couldn't see me. "Be safe out there, Jimmy."

He sighed. "We won't stop until we find him."

"I know." That I believed. Dad had always said the firehouse was family.

"Talk to you later."

"Goodbye, Jimmy."

I clicked the hang up button and stared down at the phone.

Mrs. Dupree had gotten my mom into the kitchen and I wanted to go check on her, but Dylan stopped me. "Well?" His voice shook.

I went over and sat on the coffee table, directly in front of them. "Dad's missing."

Allie clutched Ryan tighter and I noticed her eyes water up. Jesse stared at his lap and Dylan gawked at me in disbelief.

I continued. "They're going to find him. You hear the reports, it's a mess down there. Most of the radios aren't working and cell phones have become useless pieces of plastic."

"Your dad is going to be okay, boys," Allie stated with the confidence I wished I had.

Later that day, as Jimmy had said, a few of the wives of other firemen came by with tons of food. They sat with Mom, helped with my brothers, and after a while, we all started to regain some hope. They had people they loved out there, too, which meant that they understood, while others could only sympathize.

Marci, Jimmy's wife, stayed the night. She and mom had always been good friends. Her husband was a few hours into his forty-eight hour stretch at Ground Zero, so her staying was just as good for her as it was for Mom. Her kids were off at college and I bet she hadn't wanted to be alone either.

Just like the night before, Allie stayed in bed with me. Even though her mom had brought her pajamas, she chose to wear my boxers and t-shirt again. I hated myself for thinking it, but I really liked seeing her in my clothes. With everything going on, sex should be the furthest thing from my mind, but I was a fourteen-year-old boy with hormones that raged beyond my control. Of course I adored seeing Allie all dressed up because she was sexy as hell, but nothing would beat the image of her in my boxers, with no makeup on and her hair piled atop her head in a messy bun. That was *my* Allie: the girl I'd loved for years.

She cuddled up beside me and I immediately raised my knee slightly so she wouldn't notice the hard-on in my gym shorts. "Thanks for staying with me."

"There's nowhere else I'd be."

My chest warmed beneath her head.

"Your heart is racing," she noted.

I took a deep breath and uttered the words I'd been feeling since I'd heard my mom come over the loudspeaker, but hadn't vocalized. "I'm scared." My voice was so low, I wondered if she'd hear me.

"I know. Have faith a little longer. I don't know how I know, but I just know that your dad is okay."

Beyond reason, I believed her.

The phone ringing jolted me awake. Sunlight was barely inching through my curtains. I leapt out of bed and practically flew downstairs. As frazzled as I was, I got to the phone just before Dylan and Mom appeared in the kitchen.

"Hello?"

"Hey, son."

I squeezed my eyes shut but it was no use. The tears fell. "Dad?" I asked in disbelief.

Mom clutched Dylan to her side as they both cried, too.

"Yeah, it's me."

"You're okay?"

"I'm fine. I'll be home tonight."

I ran the back of my forearm over my eyes. "You're really okay?"

"I promise you."

"They told us you were missing."

He sighed. "I was trapped in an alcove. Some guys found me this morning."

Bile rose to my throat at the image of my Dad being buried in the rubble. "Are you hurt?"

"Nope. Damn miracle. How's everyone there?"

"Hanging in. It'll be better now we know you're safe."

"Good. Can I talk to your mom?"

"Yes, of course, she's right here."

"Kyle?"

"Yeah."

"I love you, son."

"I love you, too, Dad."

I handed the phone to my mom and she both laughed and cried into it. Everyone had crowded into the doorway and I happily announced, "Dad's safe. He's coming home."

We all cheered and hugged. Allie threw her arms around me and I held onto her like she was my lifeline.

"What'd I tell you?" She muttered into my ear.

"You were right." I squeezed her tighter. "Thank you for being my faith."

"I'm not." She rubbed my back. "You had it all along, I just reminded you."

"No. You had it for me. And I had you."

I finally released her and she smiled up at me as she wiped the tears of relief off my face using the sleeve of my sweatshirt she was wearing. She must've found it in my room and tugged it on before coming downstairs. A sudden urge compelled me to bend down and kiss her forehead. I knew then that as long as I had her, my life would be full. Right then and there, despite wanting more than friendship, I vowed to myself that I'd never cross that line because if things didn't work out and I lost her, I'd never get over it.

10

ALLIE

9th Grade - February

*M*elissa re-tied the gold satin ribbon around the base of my braid. It had slipped off during our half-time dance. This was the biggest night of the season for our school's basketball team. We were going up against the high school one town over, so it was a major rivalry. Our boys were leading by nine, but they had been flip flopping the lead all game. I glanced over at our team's bench and caught Ian staring at me. He smiled. I blushed and smiled back.

Melissa rolled her eyes. "When are the two of you going to go out?"

"Huh?"

"You and Ian. You've had this flirtation thing going on for like a year already."

I shrugged. "He hasn't asked me out." Even if he had, Mom had made it clear that I couldn't date until I was a sophomore and my brothers were all too happy to enforce that.

"He's practically undressing you with his eyes, Allie."

I snort-laughed. "Yeah, right."

"I'm serious. He's into you."

God, I hope so.

"We could totally go on a double date this weekend." Melissa had been casually dating Kyle for the past few weeks. It was too weird for me to think about. I gave them two months. Tops. She waved to him in the stands.

I shook my head. "Can't."

"Why not?"

Because my brothers would murder Ian if they found out. "I've got plans."

"Plans more important than going on a date with Ian?"

Melissa could be relentless. Thankfully, I didn't have to answer because the captain told us to get into formation since the game was starting back up. Ian had made varsity as a freshman, but he didn't get as much play time as the older guys, so when he did make it onto the court, I paid extra attention.

He dribbled the ball around one of the defenders and tossed it into the air, sliding it along the backboard and into the basket. We went straight into the cheer we did for individual players. "A cheer for Ian Baxter let's hear it," we shouted in unison. "Ian, Ian he's our man. He rocked the court, he scored the shot, he's the one we trust a lot to lead us to V-I-C-T-O-R-Y. Victory! Go Ian!"

When we finished, I scanned the court for him. He ran past us and winked at me. I nearly died. Our team won by three. It was hands-down the most exciting game I'd cheered for. When it was over, the boys ran past us to go to the locker room and I had a moment of bravery.

I shouted, "Great game, Ian."

He stopped and grinned. "Thanks, Allie." Sweat pinned his dark hair to his forehead and he swiped the strands away. "See you tomorrow."

I bit my lip and nodded. When I turned back around, Melissa was wrapped in Kyle's arms and it made me wince.

. . .

At lunch the next day, I sat with our usual crew in the cafeteria. Kyle, Shawn, and Reese were talking about hockey, Melissa was showing off her new iPod to Lila, which I must admit was much cooler than my Walkman CD player, and I was staring into space fantasizing about Ian. Melissa had planted a seed in my head at the game and ever since all I could think about was dating Ian. *Sigh.*

"Hey," a familiar voice behind me made my heart flutter.

"Great game last night, Ian." Melissa grinned at me.

"Thanks."

I scooted over so he could pull a chair in beside me. "Want to sit with us?"

"Sure." He smiled and grabbed an empty chair from a nearby table.

Melissa wasted no time. "So, Ian, what do you think of Allie's new haircut?"

I squinted and was about to ask her what she was talking about because I hadn't gotten a new haircut, but she gave me a look that told me to go with it.

Kyle arched a brow. "What—ow!" He glared at Melissa who must've kicked him under the table or something.

Ian replied, "Beautiful as always, Allie."

I blushed. "Thanks."

"She is, isn't she?" She gave me a grin that said she was plotting. "Allie, give me your camera. I'll get a picture of you and Ian."

I dug the disposable camera out of my bag and handed it over. Ian put his arm on the back of my chair and we smiled as Melissa snapped the photo. She handed the camera back and swung her finger back and forth pointing at Ian and me. "You two look cute together. Don't they, Lila?"

"So cute."

I wanted to crawl under the table.

Kyle asked, "Mel, what are you doing?"

She shrugged all innocently. "What? I'm simply making an observation. Ian and Allie should totally date don't you think?"

"Melissa," I gritted through my teeth.

Ian tensed up.

Kyle laughed. "Don't be ridiculous."

"What do you mean?" Melissa returned.

I narrowed my eyes and turned to my best friend. "Yeah, what's so ridiculous about that?"

Kyle looked straight over my head at Ian. "Allie's not allowed to date until Sophomore year."

"What the hell, Kyle?" I wanted to punch him.

"What? It's true," he replied as though he hadn't just mortified me entirely.

"I know, dude." Ian put his hands up.

I swiveled my head to Ian. "You do?"

He squirmed in his chair. "Uh, yeah. Kyle told me at the beginning of the school year. I wanted to ask you out and went to him to see if he thought you'd be interested and he told me."

I kicked my chair backward as I rose to my feet so I could tower over Kyle. "I can't believe you! How could you do that?"

He stood as well, making me look up at him. "I was stating the facts, Allie. Don't get all butt-hurt."

I balled my hands into fists at my sides. "It wasn't your place." I spun around and asked Ian, "Would you still like to go out with me?"

He hesitated and looked around me at Kyle.

"He's not the boss of me. We don't need his permission."

"Uh, yeah. I mean of course I do, but I thought—"

"As long as my mom and my brothers don't find out, it's fine." I sat back down so I was closer to his level.

"You sure?"

I nodded. "Tell you what, you think about it, just know that if you ask me, I'll say yes. And no one is going to say shit about it." I turned to glare at Kyle. "Right?"

The bell rang, but I stayed put and continued to stare at Kyle who looked pissed off. That, of course, only made me angrier because I was the one who deserved to be pissed at him, not the other way around.

Kyle broke first. "I'll walk you to class."

"No, thanks. I don't really want to be around you right now."

I pushed my chair back.

Ian cleared his throat. "I'll walk you, Allie." He grabbed my books off the table.

"Thanks." I followed him out of the cafeteria.

Once in the hall, after I'd taken a few calming breaths and distanced myself from Kyle, I said, "I'm sorry, Ian. I shouldn't have put you on the spot like that."

He nudged me in the arm. "No sweat. You're cute when you're angry."

I smiled and the tension melted away.

"And if you really meant what you said, I'd like to take you out."

"Really?"

He chuckled. "Yes, really. I like you. And I think you already know that."

I bit my lip and nodded. "I'd love to go out with you."

"Cool." We arrived at my Social Studies class and Ian handed me my books. "Friday night?"

"Friday works."

Ian surprised me by leaning down and kissing me softly on the cheek. "See you later, Allie."

"See ya." I was screaming with excitement on the inside.

11

KYLE

9th Grade - February

*A*llie hadn't spoken to me for two days, not since she'd gotten mad at me about the whole Ian thing on Tuesday. We'd never really fought before. Maybe a little when we were younger, but it was always over stupid stuff and never lasted more than an hour. This was different. I'd tried talking to her at school, but she'd been doing a hell of a job avoiding me. Even in class, she'd slide into her seat right when the bell rang so I couldn't talk to her and she'd disappear as soon as class had ended. She wouldn't even take the notes I'd tried to pass her.

After dinner, my dad asked me to help him in the garage, so I followed him out there. Except he didn't actually have something for us to do.

His blue-gray eyes narrowed. "What's going on with you?" he asked.

I shook my head. "Nothing."

"You've been moping around here for two days, so talk to me. Is it Melissa?"

I laughed. "No." I wasn't entirely sure why I was even dating Melissa. Truthfully, the girl made me crazy, but it was fun making out with her.

"Then what?"

I leaned against the work bench and crossed my arms. "I got into a fight with Allie."

He nodded. "I should've guessed that first."

"That obvious?"

He perched on the hood of his car. "That you're in love with her? Yeah."

"I'm not—"

"Don't bother lying."

I ground my teeth. Despite my best efforts to move on and forget about my feelings for Allie, it was a struggle.

"What happened?"

"She found out I told this guy she likes that she's not allowed to date until sophomore year."

He slipped his hands into the pockets of his jeans. "And why do you think you did that?"

I kicked my foot against the concrete floor. "Trying to protect her I guess."

"And maybe because you don't want her dating other boys?"

I took a breath and nodded slowly.

"Does she know how you feel?"

"Hell no. I can't risk our friendship."

My dad crossed over to the bench and leaned next to me. "But maybe she feels the same way."

I scoffed. "Doubtful."

"How do you know unless you talk to her about it?"

I ran my hand over the stubble on my jaw. "We're friends. And that's how I want it to be." The thought of losing her terrified me. "Besides, I think she's going to date Ian." I looked around the garage where I'd spent quite a bit of time with my dad growing up. He'd taught me how to change the oil and tires on a car in that garage.

"Have you apologized to her?" Dad asked.

"No. I was going to on Wednesday, but she wouldn't talk to me."

He rested his hand on my shoulder. "She'll come around, son. Don't give up."

"Yeah," I sighed.

Suddenly, I felt like I needed to go for a walk to clear my head, so I excused myself, grabbed my coat, and wandered toward the park. If I couldn't see Allie, at least I'd feel close to her at our spot. As I turned the corner and the swings came into view, I noticed a familiar frame swinging gently on the playground and my stomach turned. I almost chickened out and went home, but I forced my feet forward and took the swing next to her. She didn't run away, so I took that as a good sign, but she also didn't say a word.

"I'm sorry, Allie."

Nothing.

"I really hate fighting with you."

"Me, too." She sighed. "But I'm mad at you."

"I know." I moved my swing back and forth slightly. "And I truly am sorry."

"You embarrassed me and basically told Ian that I'm a baby. Yeah, I know I'm not allowed to date. You know I'm not allowed to date. But no one else needed to know that. If anything, it would have been my place to tell Ian that when he asked me out."

I kicked the sand. "You're right."

"So why'd you tell him?"

The truth fell out of my mouth without thought, "Guess I got jealous."

She stopped swinging and looked at me. "Kyle, you're my best friend. If I start dating, I promise to still make time for you. That's not going to change. I mean, you're dating and we still hang out, so it won't be any different when I have a boyfriend."

"Yeah. You're right. It was dumb." I went with it because telling Allie I liked her as more than a friend would've been foolish.

"So you'll stop interfering and you won't get upset with me for dating?"

I wanted to wrap my arms around her and squeeze her tight and never let her go because she was mine and only mine.

Except she wasn't.

"I promise," I replied.

"Good." She sighed. "Because I really need my best friend right now."

"What's up?" I asked.

"I'm going on a date with Ian tomorrow night and I'm kinda freaking out."

I forced the jealous monster back into its box deep inside me. "Why are you freaking out?"

"It's my first date. Ever. What if I'm bad at it?"

I laughed. "How could you be bad at it? It's like hanging out with a friend except it's called a date."

Her eyes widened. "But what if he kisses me?"

I smirked. "Then you kiss him back."

She bit her lip. "But I've never kissed anyone before. I don't know how."

I feigned offense. "Excuse me? I seem to recall a very romantic moment in the hammock in your backyard in fifth grade."

She laughed. "That so doesn't count. I mean a real kiss. How did you? You know...figure out how to do it?"

"You're serious? You're really worried about it?"

She nodded. "I don't want to suck at it."

I sighed. "You won't. Follow his lead. Lean your head the opposite direction as his, so you don't bump noses, and move slowly so you don't crash your teeth together, then let him kiss you."

"And what exactly does that entail?"

I laughed under my breath. "I can't believe we're seriously having this conversation."

She playful punched my arm. "Don't be mean. I need help here and you've kissed a few girls, so that makes you an expert as far as I'm concerned."

"Shouldn't you maybe ask Melissa about this?"

"And listen to her talk about what it's like to kiss you? No way! That would be disastrous. She'd probably have me making out with a pillow like in those bad teen movies."

I chuckled. "Yeah, you're probably right." I took a breath. "Okay. When he opens his mouth, part your lips and take one of his between yours. Then kinda move around a little and suck gently."

She scrunched up her face. "That sounds ridiculous when you put it that way."

I kept going because why not? I'd already crossed that line. "He'll probably probe his tongue out and then you do the same, but not too much or it'll be sloppy and weird." I knew that from experience thanks to my homecoming date.

"How do I know when to stop?"

I shrugged. "You can kinda feel when it's done. You'll both slow down and pull back."

She pursed her lips. "And what do I do with my hands?"

The idea of her hands on another guy—and his on her— made me cringe. I forced the lid back onto that box. "Umm, well, you can put them on his neck, or his chest, or in his hair, or move them around."

"So I've got to think about what my mouth is doing and what my hands are doing? That sounds complicated."

"Don't think, just go with it."

She got off her swing and stood in front of me. "Like this?" She put her hands flat on my chest and my breath hitched as she slowly eased them up to my shoulders. Her eyes were focused on where her hands were, but my gaze was fixed on her and how beautiful she looked under the moonlight. She glided her fingers up my neck and I shivered from the coldness of them, but also from the contact of her bare skin on mine so intimately. Her hands cupped behind my head, then slid up into my hair and she tugged softly.

When she stilled, I swallowed. "P—perfect."

She dropped her hands and grinned. "Thanks. This was helpful." She got back on her swing.

Discreetly, I tried to adjust the crotch of my jeans to hide my excitement. "Glad I could help."

She changed the subject and I did my best to picture naked old ladies to keep my erection at bay.

12

ALLIE

Summer After 9th Grade

$\mathcal{F}$reshman year was finally over. Kyle had invited me to family dinner at his house because he was leaving the next day for hockey camp. Over that past year, he'd bulked up quite a bit. Between the muscles and him hitting six-feet in height, he no longer looked like a kid. As I'd predicted, he and Melissa had broken up and he'd dated at least five girls since then. Pretty much every girl in school had noticed Kyle's rise on the hotness scale. And since I was his best friend, they all came to me and asked about him. All of the time. I'd told him I was going to start charging him to be his secretary.

"Mrs. H, this shepherd's pie is delicious," I said between bites. Mrs. H was an excellent cook. I suppose it should've been weird because she was my principal, but I was a solid B student and I kept out of trouble, so I was fine with it. Besides, she was basically my second mom.

"I'm glad you like it, Allie."

Family dinners at the Hogan's were always reserved for just family, but I was practically one of them, so I got invited a lot. Kyle's girlfriends had never liked that because they'd never been invited. Oh well. His choice in women was questionable at best. I'd always thought he could do better, but he went for the pretty ones that lacked...substance. And he never got serious with them.

"You all packed to go, Kyle?" Mr. H asked.

Kyle nodded. "Yup." He'd be in Canada for the next six weeks for a hockey intensive. It was a great opportunity. The program was invite only and Kyle had been chosen to be one of the fifty high school students who got to attend. While he'd always been good at hockey, it was becoming clear that he was exceptional. I wouldn't have been surprised if he'd ended up in the NHL one day.

"Dad, can I go to hockey camp, too?" Dylan asked. All of the Hogan boys had gotten into hockey. The whole family was going to drive Kyle up to Toronto and make a vacation out of it.

"Not this year, but maybe one day if you keep working hard," Mr. H replied as he scraped the last bite onto his fork.

I admired Kyle's dad. He was what a father should be. Unlike mine who'd turned his back on us as though we'd never existed. I tried not to dwell on it, but sometimes when I was around the Hogans it made me a little sad. My mom did her best, but it hadn't been easy for her working full-time and raising three kids alone.

After dinner, Dylan and I did the dishes while Jesse and Ryan cleaned up, giving Kyle some time with his parents. Six weeks alone in Canada was a big deal and I knew how much I was going to miss Kyle; it couldn't be easy for his parents either. He'd been to sleep away camp before in New Hampshire, but that was only for a month and it was a five-hour drive.

As I was putting the last plate into the dishwasher, Kyle came up behind me and squeezed my sides—where he knew I was ticklish—making me jump and scream. I slapped him in the chest with my wet hands while he laughed like crazy. "It's not funny!"

"Oh, I disagree. It's hilarious."

"Because you're not the one being tickled." I reached up and smushed his spiked up dirty blond hair that I knew he made an effort to gel like that.

"Hey," he scolded as he hopped away. Using his fingers, he tried to put it back into place. "You're so annoying."

"Now you know how I feel," I retorted as I turned off the faucet and dried my hands.

"Want to go to our spot?"

"Sure." I said bye to his family and we walked the few blocks to the playground. The sandy lot was bordered by woods on three sides. A comforting calmness washed over me as the familiar sight of the seesaw, slide, monkey bars, and of course, the swings came into view. It was simple, but it was ours.

Being June, it was still light out at eight o'clock when we got to the swings. The park was almost always empty at night, which was why it worked well when we wanted to go somewhere private.

I sat on my swing. "So, you excited to head out tomorrow?"

"Yeah." He kicked his legs and got his swing going. "But I'll miss you."

"Aw, how cute," I teased.

"Yeah, yeah."

I got my swing up high like his. "I'll miss you, too."

"What are you gonna do this summer?"

"Not sure." I sighed. "I think I'm going to break up with Ian."

He slowed his swing down and looked at me. "Seriously?"

I slowed down as well. "Yeah."

"Why? I thought it was going well."

Ian and I had been dating for four months, but I simply wasn't feeling it anymore. "He's kinda boring."

Kyle laughed.

"I'm serious. All he talks about is sports, which was cool at first, I mean I like sports, but I think that's the only subject he's capable of discussing and it's getting old."

"Huh."

"What?"

"Just surprised."

"Really?" I narrowed my eyes at him. "You've never been thrilled that Ian and I were dating."

"True, but still. I thought you were happy."

"You know, Kyle, I'm still not sure why you've never been a fan of me and Ian. The two of you are friends."

He kicked at the sand. "Guess I think you can do better than Ian Baxter."

"Like who?"

He shrugged and didn't say a word, but I could practically feel him thinking.

"You're not getting off that easy, mister. Tell me."

He ran his hand over his jaw. "Not sure. I have a feeling I'll never think any guy is good enough for you, Al."

"That's weirdly sweet."

He grinned. "It's true though. You deserve the best."

I smiled back. "Well, when you find him, please send him my way because clearly I didn't do a great job of choosing my first boyfriend."

A flash of sadness crossed his eyes, but before I could ask about it, he changed the subject and I respected that. "Let's have a jump competition."

"For real?"

He couldn't be serious. It'd been years since we'd done that.

"Yeah, why not?"

"Umm because you're much taller than me now so you have an unfair advantage."

He pumped his legs to get his swing up higher. "Yeah, but you're lighter so you'll fly further."

I brought my swing up to speed as I considered it. "Is that actually true?"

"No idea, but it sounded good."

We laughed.

"Okay," I acquiesced. "You jump first."

He swung back and forth a few more times before launching into the air and sticking the landing. Super far away.

"I'll never beat that," I shouted.

"Don't be a chicken, Allie. Jump!"

So, I did. As I'd assumed, I fell several feet short of him. "Best out of three?"

"Hell, yeah."

We got back on the swings and played like we were kids again.

13

KYLE

10th Grade - November

*A*fter the last football game of the season, Allie dragged me to a house party that Chelsea, one of the senior girls on the cheerleading squad, was throwing. I use the word dragged loosely because I didn't need much convincing. It was our first *real* high school party. We'd been to a few, but not any of the big ones with students from all of the grades. Naturally, Allie and I went together. Neither of us was dating at that moment, although, even if we had been dating, we probably would've still gone together. I always had way more fun with her anyway. It was really no surprise that when it came to Allie, all of my ex-girlfriends had serious jealousy issues. But as far as I was concerned, she'd been my best friend for over a decade, so they could just deal with it or leave because she wasn't going anywhere.

Chelsea's dad was the CFO of a major bank, so their house put Melissa's to shame. It looked like a freaking castle. Set back from the road, there was an iron gate at the end of the stone driveway, which led to the giant stone structure complete with a turret. It was opulence at its best.

Tyler had driven us there, but when we'd arrived, he sought out his friends and we went off on our own. There were kegs in the kitchen and an actual ping pong table was set up in the living room where some guys were playing beer pong.

"Want a beer?" I asked Allie as I reached for a red plastic cup.

"Um, sure."

I knew she'd never really drank before, beyond having a few sips here and there. I poured one from the keg like a pro and handed it to her.

"Something you wanna tell me?" she asked.

I smirked. "I may have attended a few parties at hockey camp over the summer." The drinking age in Toronto was nineteen so it had been easy for a lot of the older guys to get convincing fake IDs.

She gasped and pretended to be hurt. It was cute. "You got drunk without me?"

I finished filling up my cup. "Not drunk, no. But I've had one or two beers." Getting drunk for the first time was one of those milestones and I hadn't felt right doing it without Allie.

She took a tentative sip.

I couldn't fight the grin.

"What?" she asked.

"Nothing. You're cute."

She rolled her eyes at me. "Whatever." She hated it when I called her cute. According to her, cute was for children. Truth was, I thought she was gorgeous—sexy as hell in that cheer uniform she was wearing—but telling her that wouldn't come across as friendly.

We weaved through the crowd and found our group in the den along with several of the football players and cheerleaders, including Chelsea. Normally, you wouldn't be able to pay me enough to hang out with Chelsea, but I figured it wouldn't be so bad at a big party. She was one of those stereotypical mean girls just because she was pretty, popular, and had a sizable trust fund.

Melissa, who'd clearly had a couple of drinks already, swung her arm around Allie. "You're here," she slurred excitedly.

Allie laughed. "Yes, I am. And you're here, too."

"Have you met Josh?" She pointed at one of the senior football players. He wore a grin that suggested he thought he'd get lucky that night. I made a mental note to make sure I didn't leave the girls alone.

"Can I try your beer?" Allie reached for Melissa's cup.

"Sure." She handed it to Allie without a fight and Allie passed it off to me. I went straight to the kitchen and returned a minute later with a cup of water. I handed it to Melissa and she took a sip, clearly not noticing our switch.

"Let's play truth or dare," Chelsea shouted over the crowd.

I grumbled to Shawn. "Is she serious?"

Shawn elbowed me. "Dude, you're gonna wanna play. Trust me." He'd been to a few of Chelsea's parties and the look he gave me told me that this would be no ordinary game of truth or dare.

A football player I didn't really know went first. He pointed to one of the cheerleaders. "Lisa, truth or dare?"

"Truth."

"Are you a virgin?"

Allie shot me a look.

I shrugged.

Lisa replied, "You know I'm not."

"Oh, that's right. We fucked in the locker room last week."

The guys hollered and the girls all rolled their eyes or shook their heads, displaying how unfazed they were by his boasting.

The game continued. Secrets were spilled, people were making out, and girls were letting guys feel them up. One girl had even been dared to give a guy a blow job. She took him upstairs without protest. It was insane.

I finished my beer and was gonna get out of there, but then I heard Chelsea single out Allie. "Truth or Dare."

Allie's face was flushed from her beer, and I half expected her to try and pass, but she said, "Dare."

I put my cup down and prepared myself to carry her out of there kicking and screaming before I'd allow her to degrade herself with one of those drunk idiots.

Chelsea said, "I dare you to kiss Kyle Hogan for fifteen seconds. With tongue."

Well, shit. I had a flashback to our almost-kiss during spin the bottle in middle school, but this was no child's game. It wouldn't be a middle school kiss.

"Seriously, Chelsea? That's like asking me to make out with my brother."

Ouch. I suppose it was a fair statement, but I didn't want her to think of me as her brother.

"Tyler is here somewhere, isn't he?" Chelsea continued, "I can go get him and you can kiss your actual brother instead."

"Don't be a bitch, Chelsea," I commented.

She narrowed her eyes at me. "Then kiss her."

Allie looked at me and bit her lip.

Chelsea added, "Or don't. Then you know what you have to do to pass." She was referring to the rule that if a girl passed on a dare, she had to flash everyone.

Allie put her cup down on the table. "Fine, I'll do it."

My heart raced as she crossed over to me.

"You cool with this?" she asked.

Hell, yes. I shrugged. "Sure."

Allie looked over at Shawn. "Will you time us?"

He nodded and hit the stopwatch button on his watch.

Allie played it off like it was no big deal to her, but I knew her better than anyone. Her chest rose and fell quickly and tiny beads of sweat formed just above her neckline. If that weren't enough of a giveaway, her honey-colored eyes stared up at me with apprehension. I leaned down and whispered, "We don't have to do this. We can just leave. It's a stupid game."

She placed her palm on my chest, giving me chills. "Just kiss me," she whispered right before closing her eyes.

I rubbed my sweaty palms on my jeans for a second before cradling her face in my hands and taking a deep breath. My lips connected with hers and I tasted the cherry Chapstick that she loved. Her lips were soft and, after a moment of reluctance, she opened up for me, letting me kiss her—really kiss her—and she kissed me back as her fingers laced tightly behind my neck. Surprising me, her tongue sought out mine and I greedily let myself lean into the kiss.

Never in my life had a kiss ever felt like that. When Shawn said time was up, the last thing I wanted to do was stop and given how her lips were moving, I don't think she wanted to either, but I knew she'd become a target for Chelsea if we kept going, so I backed off and let her go.

For half a second, she stared at me, with dark, lustful eyes, but then she turned abruptly and said to Chelsea, "There. Happy now?"

Chelsea smirked. "That was hot."

Allie crossed her arms and kept her gaze on Chelsea. "Truth or dare."

"Dare."

Allie's grin told me that she was about to get even. Allie was sweet as could be ninety-nine percent of the time, but if someone pushed the wrong buttons, she could stoop to the levels that Chelsea played at. "I dare you to kiss Evan for fifteen seconds. With tongue."

Several people gasped and others uttered something along the lines of, "Oh, shit." Evan had been Chelsea's boyfriend for a year until a month ago when he'd cheated on her with a freshman.

Chelsea narrowed her eyes at Allie. "You bitch."

Allie crossed her arms over her chest. "Or if your brother is home, I could go find him instead."

I was damn proud of her. Normally, I'd never condone mean behavior, but trust me, Chelsea deserved it. She'd been a bitch to Allie all year because Allie had briefly dated one of Chelsea's ex-boyfriends that fall. Allie had nearly quit cheering because of the girl's evil streak.

Chelsea glared at Allie like she was going to pounce on her.

Allie held her ground. "You could always turn it down."

While Chelsea was kissing Evan, Allie, the clear victor, grabbed Melissa out of the chair she'd been sleeping in and dragged her from the room. I followed them out.

"We need to get her home," Allie said as she held onto a swaying Melissa.

"I'll go find Tyler."

We brought Melissa to her place and then Tyler dropped us off at Allie's before he headed back to the party. It was his senior year and he was living it up. Mrs. Dupree was working that night so I was finally alone with Allie, and I wasn't sure what to say. She sunk into the couch and I sat in the armchair. Certainly, we had to talk about that kiss, but I didn't really know how to. For the first time in our friendship, I thought that Allie might actually reciprocate my feelings for her. And it scared the crap out of me.

Allie sighed. "Interesting night."

"That's one way to put it."

"Things aren't going to be all weird between us now, are they?"

"What do you mean?"

"Because we *kissed*." The way she said it told me that she'd felt what I had. It wasn't the kind of kiss we'd forget anytime soon.

I rubbed my hand over my jaw. "Yeah, we did, didn't we?"

She kicked off her sneakers and pulled her knees up to her chest like she always did when she was nervous, but then she must've realized she was showing off the spanky pants beneath her cheer skirt because she put her feet back down. "I didn't mean to kiss you like that. I guess that beer went to my head a little and I got carried away."

"Yeah. Me, too." I agreed for the sake of our friendship.

She pinched her lower lip between her fingers.

I took a breath for some courage. "Is it bad that I liked it?"

Allie didn't respond right away, but I waited. She released her lip. "I kinda did, too."

My brows arched. "So what does this mean?"

She folded her arms across her chest. "Does it have to mean anything?"

I thought about that. Did it? Lots of people kissed without it meaning anything. Hell, I had. "I guess not." Except I kinda wanted it to. "Unless you want it to mean something." I practically held my breath waiting for her answer.

"You're my best friend."

I nodded. "Yeah."

"You've *always* been my best friend."

I nodded again.

"We can't be more than that. Can we?"

I never could've predicted things going this way. "Do you want us to be?"

"Do *you* want us to be?"

"I asked you first."

She giggled and I joined her. Then she joked, "Should I go get a piece of paper and write: *Do you like me? Circle yes or no* on it?"

I got up and sat down beside her on the couch. "We're being childish, aren't we?"

"Little bit."

I sighed and rubbed my hands over my face. "You know I love you."

"Yeah, I love you, too."

My heart pounded so hard I could hear it. *Tell her, tell her, tell her.*

Before I had the guts to tell her how I felt, she said, "But if we dated, it could ruin that."

My courage shrank back within. "Potentially."

She drummed her fingers on her knee. "It's probably stupid of us to make this decision off of one kiss on a dare."

"What are you saying?"

"This may still be the beer talking, but maybe we should try it again. This time without an audience."

I held her gaze, shocked by her suggestion, but also intrigued. "You wanna?"

"Do you want to?"

I swallowed. "Not this again."

She smirked. "Well, I suggested it, so..."

I scooted closer so that our legs were touching. Of course, I wanted to kiss her. I'd only thought about it at least once a day for like two years. The rational side of my brain was telling me to back quickly out of the danger zone, but my heart and my dick were urging me to go for it full speed ahead. Tentatively, I reached up and brushed the back of my hand along the side of her cheek while I stared at her lips. She must've licked them because they glistened and I desperately wanted to taste her again.

She leaned into my hand. "One rule. This is tonight only. An experiment. Then we're going to go our separate ways to think about it and we'll talk tomorrow. If one of us decides no, we go back to how things always were like none of this happened. Okay?"

I probably would've promised her anything right then, but what she'd said seemed rational. At least one of us was thinking straight. All of my blood was rushing to a body part that was one-hundred-percent clouding my judgment. "Deal." I lowered my mouth to hers and kissed her with everything I had.

An hour later, the sound of a car door slamming in the driveway startled us both to our senses. I was on top of her on the couch with my shirt off, she was in her bra, we looked like birds had landed in our hair, and our lips were swollen beyond the point of plausible deniability. After grabbing our clothes, we bolted up the stairs, getting to the top just as we heard Tyler open the front door, then we tiptoed the rest of the way to her room. She softly closed her door then spun around to face me and we laughed.

"That was close." She held her cheer top up, hiding herself from me. It was futile considering I'd seen, touched, and kissed what she was hiding, but things had been different in the heat of the moment.

I turned around to give her privacy and I put my t-shirt on while I heard her dresser open. She came up beside me wearing the hockey tee I'd gotten her from camp that summer, then she sat down on her bed. I followed suit.

She popped her lips. "So, that happened."

I laughed. "Yup."

"Are you drunk?"

"Definitely not."

"Tipsy?"

"Nope. Are you?"

"Nope."

I nodded.

She laid back. "Well, then."

I laid beside her and we just listened to each other breathe for a while.

"Kyle?"

"Yeah?"

"Would you want to stay over?"

I flipped onto my side and propped up on my elbow so I could look at her. "Yeah?"

"Yeah."

"Okay."

"Good." She grabbed my shirt and pulled me toward her.

14

ALLIE

10th Grade - November

*M*y alarm clock went off and I quickly smashed around my nightstand to silence it. My back was cuddled against Kyle's chest, his arm was draped over me and I was wearing his shirt, which meant he was bare chested. There was something about waking up in his arms that felt good. Right. Safe. I wiggled against him and felt his hard-on through his boxers. The events of the previous night came flooding back. Not only had I had an epic make out session with my best friend, but his fingers had given me my first non-self-induced orgasm and it had been way better than any I'd ever given myself. I'd actually questioned whether I'd been doing it wrong.

Plus, I could officially claim to have touched a penis. All I'll say is the thought of one of those pushing inside me was terrifying. I'd never gone beyond basic groping with a guy before, but no way I'd tell Kyle that. He didn't need to know how inexperienced I was. Although, given how he'd coached me through the hand job, he'd probably figured it out, but he'd seemed to enjoy it.

How we'd managed to get that far was beyond me. I mean, I was there, so of course I knew *how* we got there, but I was pretty sure that neither of us had planned on any of that happening. But it had. And I kinda liked it. And by kinda, I mean a lot. I wanted to do it again.

Kyle stirred and kissed my shoulder. "Good morning."

"Morning," I whispered back.

He pulled his arm in, squeezing me tighter against him. "Mmm, this feels good."

"Yeah, it does."

He kissed my shoulder again. "Last night was something else."

"Like in a good way?"

"In the best way."

I smiled, even though he couldn't see it. "Yes, it was." I glanced at the time on my night stand: seven-forty-eight. "But as nice as this is, you've got to get up and go in Brandon's room before my mom gets home and realizes you slept in here."

He grumbled.

"Besides, we broke the one rule."

"We did?"

"We were supposed to go our separate ways last night so we could think about this independently."

He hummed. "Well, we also were just supposed to kiss, but..."

I playfully slapped his forearm. "I'm serious though. We need to think about this."

He sighed. "Fine. Why don't I go home now and we can meet up later to talk?"

"Good idea."

His hand moved down to the hem of my shirt and he inched his hand under it, up my stomach. "But technically, since we're still here, we could maybe do it again." He pulled my ear lobe into his mouth and my nipples hardened as he grazed the underside of my breast.

I groaned and pinned his hand in place through the shirt. "As tempting as that is, my mom will be home in like ten minutes."

He whined as his hand retreated to safety. "Fine." He gave me a kiss on the cheek before rolling over and getting up. Immediately, I missed his warmth. Shimmying out of his shirt, I kept myself hidden beneath the blanket because it was one thing to let a guy see you naked in the heat of the moment at night in the dark and another thing entirely in the daylight the next morning. Besides, since my head wasn't distracted by my raging teenage hormones anymore, I understood that the guy in my room was Kyle—my best friend, Kyle. And that was too weird to think about. Once dressed, he gave me a quick kiss goodbye and he left with the promise of later.

I went back to sleep for an hour, since it was Sunday and I savored sleeping in on the weekends, then I got up and made coffee before curling up on the couch with a notebook and a pen.

Pros and Cons of Dating Kyle

Pro

He's hot.

We have chemistry. Lots of chemistry.

He's an incredible kisser. And doer of other things.

I know him better than anyone and he knows me better than anyone.

I already love him, so I could probably fall in love with him.

My family likes him.

My friends like him.

I already know his flaws.

I enjoy hanging out with him.

It felt right.

Con

He's my best friend and I wouldn't know how to survive without him if we screw this up.

When I got to the playground after dinner, Kyle was already on the swings waiting for me. I held my denim jacket tightly against myself even though the cold wasn't the real reason I was shivering. He stood when I approached and he pulled me in for a hug, but when he leaned down for a kiss, I turned away.

"Uh oh," he said as he released me. "What's up?"

I sank into my swing. "We're here to talk, not to do other stuff."

He sighed and I knew then that I was going to hurt him.

I took a deep breath and just got on with it. "Last night was special and, as unexpected as it was, I'm glad that it happened."

"But?"

This was hard. "But I made a list."

"A list?"

"Of pros and cons."

"Oh."

"And the pro column was filled with all of the reasons why I love you and why I'd want to date you. It was quite convincing, really. On the con list, I could only think of one."

He squeezed his eyes shut as he said, "It could ruin our friendship."

I nodded. "And I don't think I could live with that."

He kicked at the sand. "That's the only con on my list, too."

"You made a list?"

He shook his head. "Not one that I wrote down, but when I was thinking about this—us—that was the only downside I could come up with."

I gripped the chain link by my ear and leaned my head against it. "But it's a massive con."

"Yeah, it is." He swallowed. "It would kill me to lose you."

I felt the sadness in his eyes. "Same here."

"So as much as we may want to do this..."

"We shouldn't," I finished for him.

"Right."

I gave him a half smile.

"Well, this sucks."

A sad little laugh escaped my lips. "That it does."

We barely swung on the swings for a while as we wallowed in our despair. Eventually, Kyle stood up. "Come on, it's getting late. I'll walk you home."

I hooked my arm in his and leaned against his bicep for a bit while we walked. That was something I'd been doing for a while, but this time it felt different because I knew what it was like to have those strong arms wrapped around me in the heat of intimacy. And I'd never get to feel that again.

15

KYLE

11th Grade - October

*A*llie followed me down the horror aisle at Blockbuster while I searched for the perfect movie for us. It had been our Halloween tradition since the third or fourth grade to watch a scary movie together on Halloween. Granted, back then an *Are You Afraid of the Dark?* marathon was our idea of scary. This year, I had the bar set much higher. I searched the shelves and found one last copy of *The Ring*.

Upon seeing my choice, Allie vehemently shook her head. "No way."

"Come on, Al. Please? I've had this one picked out for tonight since it came out last year."

Allie hated the *really* scary movies. "The freaking commercial gave me nightmares!"

I laughed. "Don't be a baby."

She hated when I called her that, and yes, I knowingly used it to my advantage.

"Fine, but if it's going to give me the nightmares I anticipate it's going to give me, then you're coming over and checking under my bed and in my closet for monsters before I go to sleep for at least a month. I might even make you sleep on the floor in my room for weeks."

I laughed. "Deal."

"And I get to pick a happy movie for us to watch afterward and you can't bitch about it."

"Fine."

She scampered off toward the Disney section.

We'd decided to watch the movies at her house so we wouldn't terrorize my younger brothers. Plus, we had the place to ourselves since Tyler had joined the Army after graduating high school, so he was gone for training and Mrs. Dupree was at her boyfriend's house. She'd started dating this guy who was divorced with young kids, so she stayed there quite a bit. I'd taken to sleeping over in one of Allie's brothers' rooms on most of the nights when her mom was gone so that she wouldn't have to be by herself.

Allie's most recent ex-boyfriend hadn't liked that much when he'd found out. The bastard had actually tried to fight me. I had let him get one punch in before laying him out with a right hook. Once he'd regained consciousness, Allie had scolded him, "You know Kyle's a hockey player, which means he's practically a professional fighter. Are you insane?" Then she broke up with him for being stupid. I'd been glad to see him go. He hadn't been good enough for her. I'd yet to meet a guy who was.

After she and I had shared that night together nearly a year before, it had taken some time for things between us to not be so awkward, but we'd gotten there eventually. If I could've figured out how to stop being in love with her though, that would've been great. No such luck.

While Allie made popcorn, I cued up the movie, and put a giant bowl of candy outside for trick-or-treaters so we wouldn't have to keep getting up to answer the door. After moving the coffee table aside, I took all of the cushions from the couch and arranged them on the floor like we'd done for movie nights when we were kids. I piled blankets on top while I waited for Allie.

She waltzed in balancing a bowl of popcorn and two sodas, which I grabbed to help her. She laughed when she saw what I'd done in the living room. "I guess we'll never be too old for a pillow pile, huh?"

"Never." I set everything down on the table and we crawled across the cushions into a comfortable spot.

I balanced the popcorn on my lap and started the movie. From the opening scene, Allie gripped my arm, pressed against me, and hid her face against my neck. And that was why I loved our Halloween horror tradition. After that night when we had crossed the line, Allie had stopped touching me as much as she'd used to, and I missed feeling her close like that. Which was why I had not been above manipulation to get her to watch a movie as scary as *The Ring*.

By the time we got to the scene with the horse on the ferry, she was practically my new appendage. I was certain I'd have bruises on my bicep from her fingers, but it was worth it. And I also appreciated the irony given the movie. Toward the end, when it seemed like there'd be a happily ever after moment— well as much as a horror movie could have—she finally let go of me. She was chugging water when she realized that maybe it wouldn't end so happily. The image of the well appeared on the guy's TV screen in his studio and Allie dropped her near-empty cup on her lap, not seeming to care about getting wet. She grabbed me again, and buried her face into my shoulder.

"What the fuck, Kyle? I thought it was over."

And that is why I laughed through one of the scariest endings in modern horror.

Once I'd turned off the DVD, I got a good look at Allie. Her skin was red, she was sweating, and she looked like she had the flu. Immediately, I became concerned. I touched her forehead and it was on fire. "Holy shit, Al. Are you all right?"

"No." She hit me in the chest. "That was terrifying." Her eyes watered. "My head hurts and I think I have a fever."

I felt like such a dick. "I'll go find a thermometer and I'll get you some Advil and water." As I tried to stand, she grabbed my shirt and tugged me back down.

"No! You are not leaving me in a room alone with a television ever again."

"It was just a movie. It's not real."

"I don't care. Right now, it feels real."

I wrapped my arms around her and held her tight. "I'm so sorry. If I knew you'd get this scared I never would've made you watch it." I pulled her to her feet. "Come on, let's get you what you need."

Not only did she follow me to the bathroom and the kitchen, but she clutched my arm the entire time. Sure enough, she had a low-grade fever, so after she took the medicine and drank an entire bottle of water, I got her settled on our pillow pile and she laid her head on my chest while I held her and we watched *The Princess Diaries*. Twice. Five minutes into watching it a third time, she finally fell asleep. Once I was certain she was really out, I carried her up to her bedroom and got into the bed with her. I didn't want to leave her in there alone in case she had a nightmare.

After settling in beside her, memories of the last time I'd slept in there with her came to mind. I'd since dated a few girls, even lost my virginity, but nothing had ever felt as good as being with Allie had. Even though I knew we'd decided to stay friends for a very good reason, I often doubted that decision. I was at my happiest when I was holding Allie. Taking advantage of the moment, I cuddled up against her and drifted off to sleep.

16

ALLIE

11th Grade - April

I sat in the stands wedged between Jesse and Ryan as we watched Kyle and his team kick ass on the ice. Kyle's girlfriend, Bambi—yes, that's her real name, and no she's not a stripper...but I wouldn't be surprised if that was in her future—sat in front of me between Dylan and Mrs. H. Bambi didn't know the first thing about hockey, but she wore Kyle's practice jersey with his number on it and she cheered when we cheered, so at least she looked the part.

Undeniably, Kyle was one of the hottest guys at school, so he dated the prettiest girls, which wasn't always a good thing. Bambi, a sophomore, was pretty like a Barbie with her blond hair and blue eyes and model-length legs. While she was sweet, she wasn't exactly the smartest, but Kyle wasn't keeping her around for the stimulating conversation. It was funny watching Mrs. H try and talk to Bambi. She had to be nice because she was our principal, but knowing Mrs. H as well as I did, she kept the forced conversation to a minimum. Mr. H had stopped trying after Bambi had referred to the puck as "the flat ball thing."

The relief on their faces when the third period started after the break was priceless. Using every cheerleader skill in my arsenal, I made sure the entire crowd knew that Kyle Hogan was on the ice. Since it was spring and the players on his team were juniors and seniors, there were scouts present looking to scope out talent for their teams, college and pro, and I was determined to get them to notice my best friend. Even though he was planning on being a firefighter like his dad, Kyle had what it'd take to go to the NHL. He was a natural on the ice. Thanks to our lifelong friendship, I knew hockey well enough to play the game myself if I'd wanted. It was fun going to games with the Hogan brothers because they all played, so we spent the majority of the time shouting directions like we were coaches or yelling at the refs while the crowd around us stared like we were crazy.

Kyle was a defender, so when there was less than two minutes from the end of the match and the other team attempted to score, the goalie rebounded the puck and Kyle came up from a blind spot on the other team's forward and stole it right out from under him. This pissed the guy off, so he intentionally targeted Kyle and body checked him hard into the wall. Bambi screeched and we all jumped to our feet as the gloves came off and the two guys wailed on each other like it was a cage fight.

I cringed each time the guy landed one on Kyle as though I could feel the hit. The ref broke it up and the guys cursed at each other all the way to the penalty box. They'd be out the rest of the game. I could practically feel the anger emanating off of Kyle from across the rink. Kyle's team won, but I knew when we saw Kyle after that he'd probably be harping on the fight.

Sure enough, when he came out into the arena after the game, he was pissed. I drove Bambi home, since she'd gone there with Kyle and he wasn't in the mood to talk to anyone. Thankfully, Ryan went with me and he was able to keep Bambi occupied talking about his favorite new show on Nickelodeon, one that, not surprisingly, Bambi also watched, but I'd never heard of.

"Thank you for saving me," I said to Ryan after dropping Bambi off.

"No problem," he replied from the back seat. "The key is to connect with her on a level that she understands."

I shook my head and laughed. "For a ten-year-old, you're quite wise, Lil' H."

He shrugged. "That one was easy. I can see why my brother likes her, but I bet they don't do much talking."

"Ryan!"

"You know I'm right."

All I could do was laugh. I was certain that kid was going to break a lot of hearts in a few years. He had always been adorable, but he was also the most personable out of all the brothers. Jesse was a close second.

I pulled into the driveway and Ryan and I went inside for family dinner. Kyle was sulking outside on the patio, so I went to join him and cheer him up.

"Bambi has been safely delivered to her corner of the forest with Thumper and Flower," I announced as I forced myself onto the couch beside him.

"Shut up."

"You're welcome, Mr. Grouch."

He sighed. "Thanks."

"Dude, you *won* the game. You do realize that right?"

"I know."

"So why are you so butt-hurt right now?"

He ran his hand over the stubble on his chin. "Because there were some scouts there that I wanted to impress and getting thrown into the box and leaving my team down a player at the end of the game isn't a good look."

I pulled my cherry Chapstick out of my pocket and applied it, then rubbed my lips together. "Are you telling me that you're actually considering going pro now?"

He shrugged.

I nudged his arm. "Kyle! This is a big deal."

"Exactly. That's why I'm mad."

"No, I mean you changing your mind about being scouted. When did that happen?"

He crossed his arms over his chest. "Recently."

"Your vocabulary this evening is stellar."

"Shut up."

I waved off his insult. "Which scouts were there?"

"That I knew of? Boston College and University of Michigan."

I got so excited I actually hopped to my feet. "If this is a joke, I'm going to kill you."

He cracked a smile. "Not a joke."

"You mean to tell me that we could be going to college together?" Michigan was my top choice, but because Kyle had always planned to go into the FDNY, he needed to stay in New York and establish city residency, so this was huge news.

He shushed me, grabbed my wrist, and pulled me back down onto the wicker couch. "Can we not tell the whole neighborhood please?"

"But this is so exciting. Those two schools are like the best for hockey, aren't they?"

He nodded. "They're up there."

"You killed it on the ice today, Kyle. Don't let what happened at the end make you feel like you hadn't performed well. You scored a freaking goal as a defender for heaven's sake."

He grinned. "I did do that."

"Yeah. And you didn't start the fight, the other guy was the instigator and you definitely dominated him. The scouts probably wanted to see that you can fight, too, right?"

"I guess."

"Then you should stop sulking and we should celebrate."

He placed his hand on my thigh. "I appreciate your enthusiasm, but I haven't told my family yet."

"That you changed your mind about firefighting?"

He sighed. "I haven't decided. I'm exploring my options. All I've ever wanted to be was a firefighter, but that was before I realized how good I was at hockey."

I was so freaking proud of him. "You're not good, Kyle, you're exceptional and you owe it to yourself to explore where your talent can take you."

Jesse poked his head out the sliding glass door. "Mom said to tell you guys that dinner will be ready in a couple minutes."

"Thanks, Jes," Kyle replied, then Jesse retreated back inside. "We can keep this secret between us, right?"

I held out my pinkie. "Of course."

Kyle linked his finger with mine.

"But we are not done talking about this because can you imagine if we went to college together?"

He put his arm around my shoulders. "That would be perfect."

"So perfect."

"Thanks, Allie."

"For what?"

"For always knowing how to cheer me up when I get in one of my moods. You're the only person who can do that."

I pinched his cheek. "Anytime, sugar."

He laughed as he pushed me away and stood up. "Let's go eat. I'm starving."

"I couldn't possibly imagine why. I mean, it's not like you skated a few miles today or anything."

"I also ran this morning."

"Underachiever." I followed him inside and took my usual seat beside him at the table.

Kyle smiled and Mrs. H caught my eye and mouthed, *thank you.*

I nodded. Cheering Kyle up always made me happy as well. He could get mean if left to fester in his anger for too long, which was never good for anyone. Plus, I liked being that person for him because he was that person for me, too.

17

KYLE

12th Grade - October

*A*fter the football game, Allie, Dylan, and Jenna, Dylan's new girlfriend who was also a cheerleader, all got into my car and we went to the diner like we'd been doing the past few weekends after the games. It was a routine I could get used to.

We settled into a booth and the waitress came to take our order. Dylan and Jenna got chicken fingers to share, then the waitress turned to Allie.

"I'll have cheese fries and a Coke," she ordered.

"You sure you don't want a shake?" I asked, knowing full well that she did.

She shook her head. "Nope, that's it."

I looked at the waitress. "I'll have a chocolate shake and potato skins."

"I meant to ask you earlier," Jenna addressed Allie, "before next weekend can you work with me on my herkie? I want to get the height like you do."

Allie nodded. "Absolutely." She had always been a great

teacher and I was glad that she'd decided to go to college for education. Allie had more patience than a lot of people. Certainly, more than I had.

"You'll want to do some squat jumps. Two sets of twenty-five at least four times a week," Allie instructed.

While they continued to talk cheer, Dylan and I talked hockey. When the waitress arrived with my shake, I removed the paper from the straw, put it in the glass, then slid it over to Allie with a grin. Without stopping her conversation, she took a sip, which made me chuckle. Our orders had been the same for weeks. I would ask for a shake, Allie would say she doesn't want one, and then she'd drink half of mine. I didn't mind one bit.

When her fries arrived, she put the basket between us so we could share. I glanced over at Dylan and Jenna while they shared their chicken fingers, noticing how cute they were together, and I had an epiphany. Allie was the closest thing I'd had to a serious girlfriend. Sure, I'd dated, but I'd always moved on after a month or two. Allie, though...

I turned to her and she smiled up at me as she reached for my shake. Having her next to me felt like the most natural thing in the world. Allie had been with me for thirteen years. She was the only girl I'd ever loved. We functioned like a couple, minus the sex part, and I was seriously starting to think we'd fucked up by deciding to be nothing more than friends. Hell, it'd been more than a year since that night we'd made that decision and our relationship was stronger than ever. I decided then, over a shared chocolate shake, that I was going to talk to Allie about revisiting the idea.

After leaving the diner, I dropped the girls off at their houses, then Dylan and I went home ourselves. We'd promised Dad we'd help with the yard work after the game. While I plucked weeds out of the mulch, I fantasized about being Allie's boyfriend. And I really liked it.

. . .

My parents were having a date night, so I ordered pizza for us for dinner. I'd texted Allie and invited her over, but she hadn't answered, which was strange because she rarely left me hanging like that. An hour later, my phone beeped.

Allie: Can you meet me at our spot?
Kyle: Of course. Be there soon.

I left Dylan in charge and jogged to the playground. Allie was already there and as I got closer, I noticed that she had been crying. In all the years that Allie and I had been friends, I could count on one hand the number of times I'd seen her cry. Immediately, I dropped to my knees in front of her swing so that we were eye level and I cupped her face in my hands.

"What's wrong?"

She opened her mouth to try and speak, but instead a wail came out that slayed me.

"Oh, Allie. Come here." I scooped her out of the swing and pulled her down onto my lap, letting her cry it out in the safety of my arms. It broke my heart that she was hurting and I desperately wanted to know why so I could fix it. Realizing she needed to purge first, I tried to be patient. In an effort to calm her, I placed kisses on top of her head and whispered soothingly. Eventually, her sobs quieted and she ceased shaking.

"I'm sorry," she muttered.

"Don't be." I grasped her chin and tilted her face up to look at me. Using the sleeve of my sweatshirt, I wiped the tears from her face. "Do you want to talk about it?"

Her lip quivered. "Tyler..." Tears began to fall again.

I feared the worst. Although he was stateside at Fort Bragg in North Carolina, training accidents could happen. "What about Ty, Allie?"

She chewed on her lower lip. "He's being deployed to Iraq on Monday."

I took a relieved breath, but the feeling was fleeting

because my best friend's brother—my friend—was heading for the front lines of the war on terror. "Fuck."

"I mean, we knew this was inevitable, but still..."

I kissed her head. "I know."

"I'm scared," she whispered almost imperceptibly.

"You're allowed to be."

"What if—?"

"No. You can't let yourself think that way. He's been training for over a year. We need to have faith that he'll be safe." I thought back to September 11th and how Allie had unwavering faith that my dad would be okay. This was my turn to return the favor. I brushed a few tear-soaked strands of hair off her face. "Do you trust me?"

"Without question."

I locked my eyes on hers. "Then trust me when I say Ty's going to be fine. We have to believe that."

Sadness and fear darkened her bronze eyes.

"Like when my dad was missing. You had faith for me, remember?"

She nodded.

"Say it."

She took a shaky breath. "He's going to be okay."

"Again."

"He's going to be okay."

"Again."

"He's going to be okay." Her voice was less shaky and the fear in her eyes was beginning to subside, so I made her say it several more times until she seemed to believe the words.

I smiled at her. "Better?"

"A little."

Seeing her upset like that was worse than any punch I'd ever taken. I bent my head forward and rested my forehead on hers. "We'll get through this. Promise."

Surprising me, she placed her lips on mine and kissed me

softly. It was brief and innocent, but it said so much. Then she whispered, "I love you, Kyle."

My chest warmed. "I love you, too."

With her forehead still resting against mine, she sighed. "I don't know how I got so lucky to have you as my best friend, and I know I don't say it enough, but you mean everything to me."

I squeezed my eyes shut because I knew then that we couldn't risk losing that, no matter how much I wanted her to be mine. A best friend was exactly who she needed at that moment. I pulled back and kissed her forehead. "You mean everything to me, too."

We sat in the sand for a while until it got too cold and then I walked her home before heading home myself. The further away I got from her, the more my chest ached and I resolved myself to the fact that there would always be a part of me that was in love with Allie Dupree.

18

ALLIE

12th Grade - January

I was a walking cliche. Austin Clarke was the quarterback. I was a cheerleader. And we were dating. We hustled from the car down the driveway to Shawn's house in an attempt to escape from the January cold. It was Kyle's eighteenth birthday and since having a house party at the principal's home wasn't an option, Shawn had graciously offered his up for the celebration. I wrapped myself tightly in Austin's letterman jacket as we sprinted up the front steps and into the house. My dating Austin had been rather unexpected. Well, to me at least. Matchmaker Melissa had orchestrated it.

Melissa had joined the film club because she had the hots for the faculty advisor, Mr. Ackerman, but she ended up enjoying it. After Thanksgiving, she had been directing a short film and of course I had to star in it. Seriously. She'd made me. Conveniently, she had cast Austin in the role of my love interest. Two weeks later we had started dating.

I'd always found him attractive with his sandy-colored curly hair, much like Justin Timberlake, but once I found out how fun he could be, I'd been hooked. Prior to that, Austin and I had been friendly, but we'd never been *friends*. We hadn't ever had any classes together so there hadn't been an opportunity to get to know him, but we'd hit it off almost immediately once we'd started rehearsals.

I knew I had a good one when I'd told Kyle that Austin had asked me out and all he'd said was, "Hmm." It was the closest thing to an approval any of my dates had ever gotten from him. Austin was smart and he'd accepted a football scholarship to Penn State, which was the only bad part about us dating. We'd been together a month and if it continued to go well, come fall we'd be in a long-distance relationship because I'd already committed to the University of Michigan.

Austin weaved through the house in search of the keg and I followed closely behind. We found it in the kitchen along with Shawn.

He put his hand up for me to slap. "Good. You made it."

"Did you think I wasn't coming?" I asked while Austin poured me a drink.

"Kyle's been whining since he got here because you hadn't arrived yet."

I laughed. "Where is he?"

Shawn pointed toward the living room.

I handed Austin his jacket. "I'm going to find the birthday boy."

"Sure thing, babe."

I found Kyle by the fireplace chatting up some brunette who couldn't be any older than sixteen. When he spotted me, he charged my direction and wrapped his arms around me, lifting me off the ground.

"Allie," he shouted loudly enough for people to stare.

I laughed and slapped his shoulder. "Put me down, you're going to spill my beer."

Kyle had obviously had plenty of that already judging by

his goofy grin. He put me down and the girl he'd been talking to glared at me before storming away.

"Hey, birthday boy."

"Hi." He took the red plastic cup from my hand and gulped my drink.

"Excuse me." I took it back. "That's my beer."

He laughed. "We always share, Al."

Austin snuck up from behind me and snaked his arm around my waist. "Happy birthday, Kyle."

Kyle lifted his chin. "Thanks, man." He looked me over. "Doesn't she look hot tonight?"

I glanced down at my outfit. I was wearing blue denim skinny jeans, a gray cropped hoodie, and my well-worn black and white Adidas sneakers. Pretty much a standard outfit for me.

Austin pulled me closer and kissed the top of my head. "She always looks hot."

"Thanks." I smiled up at him.

Kyle high-fived Austin. "Smooth."

I shook my head.

"Babe, I'm gonna go find the guys. You good?"

"Yup," I replied.

Austin kissed me like he was marking his territory, then he went in search of his friends.

Kyle gagged.

"Oh, grow up."

"Just did, *babe*. Eighteen, remember?" He winked at me. "All I'm saying is, watching you kiss other guys wasn't one of my birthday wishes."

I tucked the hand that wasn't holding my beer into the back pocket of my jeans. "*Other* guys?"

"Yeah. If a man's wishing for a birthday kiss, he should be the one doing the kissing."

I rolled my eyes and got up on my tiptoes, then planted a kiss on his cheek. "One birthday kiss delivered."

He covered his cheek with his hand. "I'm never washing this cheek again."

I slapped the back of my hand against his abs, which I'm pretty sure hurt me more than him. "You're such a dork."

He wiggles his brows. "But I'm a sexy dork." Kyle always got flirtatious when he was drunk, but he was super fun to be around.

Melissa hollered from across the room, "Shots, bitches!"

Shawn, Reese, and Lila were behind her carrying shot glasses filled with a brown liquid. They handed some to Kyle and I, then Melissa raised hers in the air. "To the birthday boy."

We all raised our glasses then shot them back. The whiskey burned the whole way down, making me cough.

"Woo," Kyle shouted. "Now it's a party."

Shawn handed him a red plastic cup.

It was going to be a night to remember.

Or not remember...

A couple of hours later, between make out sessions with my hot boyfriend and dancing like a fool with my best friend, I was feeling *great*. I went outside to get some air, but immediately regretted it when I realized it was nine-degrees, so I went upstairs in search of an empty room instead. The first one I tried was...otherwise occupied, but a surprise waited for me in the next one.

Kyle was splayed out on Shawn's bed staring at the ceiling. I went in and closed the door behind me, then laid beside him.

"Whatcha doin'?" I asked.

He sighed exaggeratedly. "Staring at the stars."

I laughed. "See anything good?"

"Nah. Too cloudy."

I shook my head. "Had a good birthday, huh?"

"I'm eighteen."

"You are."

"I applied for the FDNY test today."

I flipped onto my side and stared at him. "You did?"

He nodded.

"Not wasting any time, are you?" You had to be eighteen to apply. "What happened to the hockey plan?"

He yawned. "Haven't ruled it out."

"No?"

"I got offered full scholarships to a few places."

"What! And you didn't tell me? Where?"

He shrugged. "A bunch of division twos and threes and some division ones."

"Which D1s?" I focused on those because let's be real, Kyle was D1 quality.

"Boston University, Boston College, Pelham University, Arizona State, University of Denver—"

"Holy shit, Kyle. Denver won the championship last year."

"Yup." He smiled devilishly.

"What?"

"I also got into Michigan."

My eyes widened. "University or State?"

"Both."

I squealed. "Are you freaking kidding me?"

His smile lit up his face. "Crazy, huh?"

"That's unbelievable." I laid my head on his chest and hugged him. "I'm so proud of you."

"What do you think, Al, you wanna go to college together?"

I squeezed him tight. "A million times, yes."

He laughed. "Can I tell you a secret?"

"Always."

"I want to be a pro hockey player," he whispered.

My heart smiled. Hockey was Kyle's passion and he'd worked hard at it for a decade. "Then do it."

He sighed. "But what about firefighting?"

"Is that *your* dream? Or is it your dad's?"

He ran his fingers through my hair. "Both. I think I'd love firefighting, but I also think I'd regret not giving hockey a go."

"Then you have your answer."

"But if I do this and I fail, I might never get on the FDNY. I need the city residency credit to rank higher on the list and even with that and taking the test this year, it will still be years before my number comes up. If I try to go pro and don't make it, then I'll be way behind in applying and my number may not get called before I age out."

I tapped my fingers on his chest. "Which would you regret more: missing out on hockey or missing out on the FDNY?"

"Hockey," he responded without hesitation.

"Then congratulations, Kyle Hogan. You're going to be a hockey player."

He laughed. "Holy shit."

"Now, for the most important question. You're picking Michigan, right?"

He kissed the top of my head. "Hell yeah I am."

I squeezed him tight. I couldn't think of anything better than going to college with my best friend.

19

KYLE

12th Grade - February

*D*uring practice, as I skated backward on the ice, I decided that was going to be the day I would man up and tell my family that I was pursuing hockey. I'd had a good talk with Allie about it the night before and she'd convinced me that my dad and my brothers wouldn't be disappointed in me for choosing hockey over the FDNY.

After practice, I drove home with Dylan and when we pulled into the drive, we were surprised to see our dad's car in the driveway.

"That's odd," Dylan said as I parked. Dad was supposed to have left for Ryan's hockey game over an hour ago.

"Very." I got one of those feelings that makes the hairs on the back of your neck stand up and I knew that something was wrong.

While Dylan grabbed his hockey bag from my trunk, I jogged toward Dad's car. As I got closer, I noticed the soles of his boots poking out from in front of the car.

"Dad!" I sprinted.

He was laying on the cold asphalt. Unconscious. Blue.

"Dylan, call 911," I shouted as I shook my father's shoulders. "Dad! Dad!"

He didn't move. I ran through the training in my mind—Dad had made us all get CPR certified. I lowered my ear to his nose and mouth to feel and listen for breaths while I watched to see if his chest was rising.

Nothing.

Dylan ran up. "Holy shit, Dad."

"Call 911. Now," I ordered as I felt Dad's wrist for a pulse. His skin was cold—too cold—but it was February...

No pulse.

Then I felt for the artery in his neck.

Nothing.

"Fuck." Dad had developed heart disease after 9/11. A parting gift from the rubble. I pinched his nose and tilted his head back while I gripped his chin with my other hand and gave him two rescue breaths.

Then I began compressions. One and two and three and...

On the tenth one—*crunch*—I felt my dad's rib crack. I heard his voice in my head say, *that means you're doing it right, son.* My jaw clenched as I fought to keep my composure.

"An ambulance is on the way." Dylan dropped to his knees by Dad's head.

"Twenty-seven and twenty-eight and twenty-nine and thirty." I stopped compressions.

Dylan was already in place to give two breaths.

I resumed compressions.

By the time the ambulance arrived, I was drenched in sweat having done eight rounds of CPR. The medics took over, shoving us out of the way. They got the pads hooked up to his chest while they continued CPR. But they never shocked him. When they stopped mid-compressions, it confirmed what I'd already known. We'd been too late. If we hadn't fucked off with our friends after practice, we would've been home sooner. We could've saved him.

But instead, my dad was dead.

The next few days were a blur. Mom was a wreck, my brothers were devastated, and my father was gone, so I stepped up to make sure everything got done. A bunch of the guys from my dad's firehouse had helped me with the arrangements. We'd had four wakes over two days and each time slot had been packed. Pretty much my entire school had shown up along with hundreds of firefighters and of course our family and friends. It had been a whirlwind of going through motions.

Sitting on the wooden pew in the front of the church at my dad's funeral was the last of the formal ceremonies, and I was grateful for that. I sat beside my mom and kept my arm around her during the whole thing. Dylan sat on Mom's other side, then Jenna. Jesse was next to me, then Allie, then Ryan. Allie held them both through the entire thing. She'd been incredible ever since it had happened. She hadn't left my house and she'd taken care of my brothers while I'd focused on planning. The other firehouse wives had made sure my mother had never been left alone. If I'd ever doubted how much support our family had in the world, my dad's death had shattered that.

Several of the guys from Dad's firehouse had gotten up to share stories about my father and it was comforting to hear how much he was adored as their captain. When the priest called me up to the podium to deliver the eulogy, I stood and buttoned my suit jacket. Dylan took over holding our mom while I stepped up to the altar. From the podium, I grasped the magnitude of how many people were in attendance. The church itself was large and every seat was filled, plus people stood, filling both side aisles. The number of glistening badges I saw adorning the chests of the men and women my dad had worked alongside made my eyes sting. I swallowed back the emotion though because I couldn't cry. My family needed me to be the strong one.

I removed the folded piece of paper from my inside breast pocket and smoothed it out on the podium. Then I cleared my throat. "My father was a hero. Not only because of the countless lives he's saved over the course of his career, but because he was also my hero. He was my brothers' hero. He was my mom's hero. I've always looked up to him and I always will because the legacy he leaves behind is one that we should all be proud of." I clenched my jaw.

"No one loved harder than my dad. Because of the example that he and my mom have set, my brothers and I have had the honor of witnessing true love, and I know I'll never settle for anything less because that's what he taught me." I glanced at Allie, but quickly looked away for the sake of my composure. "When I have kids of my own, I can only hope to be half the father my dad was."

"His passion and his aptitude for his career is evident in the sea of uniforms surrounding us today. Dad had always said that the firehouse is family and I'd like to personally thank every single one of you for helping us through this loss and for being here to honor him. I can guarantee that he's looking down on us right now in awe of this display of love for a man who loved unconditionally without expecting anything in return. My father was a humble man. He was thoughtful. He was kind. He was a man of principle. He was a thousand different things, but above all, he was a family man."

I gestured to where my family was sitting, but I kept my eyes on the paper. "To us, he was a husband and a father." I pointed to the firefighters in attendance. "To you, he was a brother. And today, we all say goodbye, but I know that my dad will live on in every single one of us. He'll be in our memories, our stories, our actions. Every time I put on my hockey skates, I'll remember the first time my father laced skates to my feet. I'll remember how he came to as many of my practices and games as he could. Dylan, Jesse, and Ryan can say the same. My mom will remember him every time she makes shepherd's pie because it was his favorite. And all of you will remember him when you get on a fire truck or you crawl down a hallway because at some point, he'd been there alongside you."

I could hear my mother crying and bit down hard on my lip. "But I want us all to make a promise to my father today. When we remember him in those moments, we'll smile because when he'd been a part of each of those moments, that's what he had done, and I know that's how my dad would want us to remember him."

I looked over at the coffin draped in the American flag as I folded the paper back up. "We love you, Dad. Always will." I made my way back to my seat and my mother gave me the tightest hug as she cried into my chest.

I ran a hand over her hair. "It's okay, Ma. You've still got us."

After the funeral, our house became a revolving door of visitors toting condolences. I made it until nightfall, but then the overwhelming feeling to get away overtook me and I found myself sneaking out the kitchen and walking to the playground. I sat down on the cold swing and stared off into the distance. It was the first time I'd had silence in days and there was something oddly comforting, but also unsettling about it.

While I'd been occupied with making arrangements, I hadn't had the time to think about reality. When I'd been home, I'd made sure my family had been taken care of. Sitting there in silence, it was the first time I didn't have a distraction. It was the first time I realized that my dad was really gone. That I'd never again go home and find him working in the garage, or watching a movie with my mom, or sitting at our dining room table for family dinner.

Distant footsteps crunching on the old snow told me she was coming before I saw her. Frankly, I'd known Allie would come looking for me before I'd even gotten to the park. She was a constant in my life. My forgotten coat was in her hands and when she approached, she wrapped it around my shoulders. Then she draped a blanket over my legs and sat in the swing beside me. Her swing.

For a while, we honored the silence together, but then she whispered, "You know, Kyle, it's okay to cry."

I nodded. "I'm fine."

"No, you're not fine. You're strong."

The threat of tears stung my eyes.

She put her hand on my shoulder. "You don't have to pretend with me. You never have before. Don't start now."

I clenched my jaw and tried to blink away the emotion, but it was no use. My eyes welled up and spilled over as my shoulders shook.

Allie was there, standing in front of me, and she held me in her arms while I cried into her chest. It was the first time I'd cried since losing my dad and all of the emotion I'd been bottling up purged from my system. Allie didn't say anything. She simply held me and let me work through the pain. The heat trapped between my face and her bosom was getting to me, so I pulled back and took a few deep, shaky, breaths.

Allie wiped my face with her coat sleeve—snot and all. Not my best look.

"Sorry," I muttered.

"Don't you dare apologize." Her tone was threatening and I knew better than to argue. She cupped my cheek and I leaned into her palm. Her other hand rested on my shoulder.

I sighed. "Well, fuck."

She gave me a lopsided grin. "That's one way to put it."

I reached for her and pulled her against me again. This time, I was very aware of the fact that I was leaning against her boobs and while it was probably inappropriate, I didn't care because holding her and being held by her felt too good. That moment, listening to her heartbeat, was the most comforted I'd felt in a long time.

She kissed the top of my head and let her lips linger there. "I'm incredibly proud of you."

I pulled back and looked up at her, but held onto her waist.

"Your dad would've been proud, too."

I flinched.

"Don't," she warned.

"What?"

"His death is not on you. Even if you'd had some kind of sixth sense that made you leave practice early that day, there's no guarantee he would've lived." She knew me too well.

I exhaled hard making my nostrils flare.

"He would've been damn proud of the way you handled it when you found him. You did everything he'd taught you to do and I know he was standing over your shoulder beaming with pride."

I blinked a few times to try and clear the image from my mind.

"And if that weren't enough, you've taken care of your family, planned his wake and his funeral, and that eulogy was absolutely perfect, Kyle." She poked me in the chest with the tip of her pointer finger. "And you were right in saying that we should all be proud of the legacy he left behind. Guess what? *You* are a big part of that legacy."

My breath hitched. "You're gonna make me cry again."

"Good. Let it out now because I know as soon as we leave here, you'll go back to being everyone else's shoulder to cry on. But I'm yours. Don't forget that."

The next tears that fell weren't only for my dad, they were also for her. More specifically, my love for her.

20

ALLIE

12th Grade - March

*I*t'd been a little over a month since Kyle's dad had died and I was worried about him. I couldn't blame him for trying to fill his father's shoes for the sake of his family, but he needed to take care of himself, too. That's how I ended up in his bedroom wearing a gold sequined dress and high heels on the Saturday before my birthday.

"I'm only going to turn eighteen once, you know." I tapped my foot beside his desk where he was sitting.

"I know and we'll celebrate, I promise, but I'm not really feeling up for a chaotic party."

I'd been at the party Austin was throwing me for an entire hour before I'd decided to leave and collect Kyle personally. Austin hadn't been happy about it, but there was no way I'd celebrate my birthday without my best friend.

I went to his closet and started putting together an outfit for him to wear. "That's where you're wrong. A party is exactly what you need. It'll be good for you to get out of this house and loosen up." I laid a dark-gray button up shirt down on his bed along with a pair of khaki dress pants. Then I returned to his closet for shoes.

He groaned. "You're really not going to give up on this are you?"

"Nope." I tossed the Dockers his direction.

He sighed. "Fine, but I'm not staying long."

I draped a belt around his neck and pulled him close. "It's my birthday. I make the rules."

His fingers dug into my waist. "If you want to play with a belt and talk about rules while looking like *that*, we're not going to leave this bedroom."

My jaw dropped and I was at a loss for words. Especially because I felt his threat between my thighs.

He started to laugh. "I'm messing with you, Al. Chill."

I let go of the belt and stumbled back. "Right. Of course. I know that."

"Now get out of here so I can change." He stood. "Unless you wanna watch." He pulled his t-shirt over his head and my gaze dropped to his abs.

I spun on my heels. "I'll be in the car."

While I drove to Austin's, I said, "I can't believe you really weren't going to come to my birthday party."

"We're celebrating on your actual birthday. I wouldn't miss that."

"Not the same. I'm going to remember this and I'll be expecting you to throw me one hell of a party next year in Michigan to make it up to me."

When he didn't have a comeback, I knew something was wrong. I glanced at him through the corner of my eye. "What?"

"I, um, I've decided to go to Pelham University."

I pulled the car over and put it in park so I could look at him while we had this conversation. "You what?"

"I'm going to be a firefighter."

I closed my eyes and sighed. I'd half expected that to happen after everything with his dad, but my heart broke knowing he'd be giving up on his hockey dream. "Give it a little more time to think this through. I'm sure Michigan will understand if you need an extension on the commitment deadline given what you've been going through."

He couldn't meet my gaze. "It's already done. I committed to Pelham yesterday."

"Oh, Kyle." Pelham University was the least prestigious of the division one schools he'd gotten into.

"It's the only school that will give me city residency for the FDNY. Since it's only ten minutes from here, I can get an apartment right over the border in the Bronx." He ran a hand over his jaw. "My family is going to need me, so it's my best option. My only option."

I covered my nose and mouth with my hands. "Pelham hasn't qualified for a tournament since the eighties."

He'd never get scouted there and he'd never be pushed to his fullest potential by that coach.

"I know, Allie."

"But you got into schools that have *won* the championship these last few years."

He threw up his hands. "What am I supposed to do? Abandon my family six months after my father dies? My mom can't do it all on her own. Dylan will get his license next year and that'll help, but Jesse is thirteen and Ryan is ten. They need me."

I took a deep breath and put my hand on his thigh. "I know. I get it, I do. But do you really think your dad would want you to give up on your dream?"

He pushed my hand off. "That's fucking low."

"I'm not trying to be callous. Your dad knew you loved hockey. He would've wanted you to pursue it."

"You don't know that and we will never know because I never got to tell him."

I shook my head. "I'm not trying to pick a fight. I just want to make sure you're thinking this through and you're not making a rash decision because of your situation."

He leaned his head back against the seat and covered his eyes with the top of his forearm.

"Kyle, I'll support you in whatever you decide, but please at least talk to your mom about it."

"My mind is made up. I'm going into the FDNY. End of story."

I bit my tongue and did what I had to do as his best friend. "You'll be a great fireman, Kyle."

He stared out the passenger side window. "Can you take me home?"

I put the car in drive and drove back to his house. Selfishly putting him through a party, when it was the last place he wanted to be, would've been screwed up for me to do.

He opened the door and said, "Have fun at your party, Allie." Then he got out and went inside without so much as a glance back at me.

After that conversation, my party mood had been killed, but since I was the guest of honor and my boyfriend had gone through the trouble of throwing me a party, I didn't have much choice but to go. The entire drive there, all I could think about was how much my heart hurt because my best friend was home sulking all because his honor was making him sacrifice his dream in order to do the right thing for his family. I admired the heck out of him for it, but it didn't make the situation any less tragic.

I tried to put on a happy face when I got back to Austin's, but he saw right through it.

"You okay, babe?"

"I'm not feeling very well all of a sudden."

"What's wrong?"

I shrugged. "My stomach hurts." It wasn't a lie because my gut was definitely angry.

He cocked his head. "Does this have anything to do with you leaving to get Kyle and coming back without him?"

"No. He's got to take care of his family tonight. I get that."

"Do you want to go lay down in my room?"

"If you don't mind, that'd be good."

He brought me upstairs and tucked me into his bed before giving me a parting kiss.

Some time later, I was woken up by Austin sliding into the bed behind me. He reeked of beer and he draped his arm over me, cupping my boob as he kissed along my neck, making me squirm and not in a good way.

"Austin?"

"Mm," he grunted between kisses.

"Can we just sleep?"

He pulled his mouth from my neck and rolled away from me.

I'd somehow managed to piss off the two men in my life on the same night. Happy birthday to me.

21

KYLE

12th Grade - May

*T*here was one month left of my senior year. And what
a year it had been. I'd lost my father, I'd sacrificed
my hockey career, and I'd managed to fall even more in love
with the one girl I couldn't have. Fucking fantastic.

I was driving home after dropping Ryan off at a friend's
house when my phone beeped.

Allie: Busy?

Not wanting to text and drive, I called her on speaker and
the second she answered I knew something wasn't right.

"Hi." Her voice was raspy and she sounded like she was
crying.

"What did the fucker do?" I'd been looking for an excuse to
punch her boyfriend anyway. Not that he deserved it, but him
having Allie was enough of a reason for me.

"Uh uh. Pain."

"Your period?" Sometimes Allie got hers so bad she was debilitated for days.

"Uh huh."

"What do you need?"

"You."

"I'll be right there."

I arrived not even five minutes later and used my key to get in. Allie had given me one when I'd started sleeping there on the nights she was alone. When I didn't see her in the living room, I went upstairs. She was curled up in a ball on her bed, so I sat down next to her. Her hair was soaked with sweat, she was pale, and she wouldn't stop whimpering. It killed me to see her like that.

"Allie," I said soothingly as I rubbed her back, which was also damp with sweat. "Have you taken one of your pain pills?"

She'd gotten a prescription for pain killers when she'd badly sprained her wrist playing volleyball earlier that year. She'd only taken one and had saved the rest for emergencies. This definitely seemed like an emergency to me.

"Uh uh."

"Where are they?"

"Dress..."

"Dresser?"

"Uh huh."

I got up and started going through her dresser drawers. I found the bottle tucked in with her bras. On any other occasion, I would've enjoyed teasing her about me riffling through her underwear drawer, but seeing her in that much pain trumped that thought. I opened the bottle and removed a pill, which I put into her mouth for her and she swallowed it.

Not knowing what else to do I sat beside her and rubbed her back as she rocked her body while we waited for the pill to kick in. I'd never seen her that bad and it terrified me. I wished I could take the pain for her. Feeling helpless sucked.

I glanced around her room. I'd been in there many times,

but in a lot of ways it had never changed. It was still the same sunny yellow color it had been when were young, although she'd hung posters as we'd gotten older. They started off as the Spice Girls and Britney Spears, but they'd since been replaced by the Backstreet Boys, NSYNC, and 98 Degrees. My favorite part though was her wall of photos. Allie had always carried a disposable camera with her, so there were tons of photos of us and our friends.

"Kyle?" she said, roughly twenty-minutes after she'd taken the medicine.

"Yeah?"

"Thanks."

"Of course. Feeling better?"

She stretched her legs out. "Getting there."

"Good. That was scary, Allie. This can't be normal."

"It's rarely this bad."

"Still, it shouldn't be like this, right?"

"I don't know." She rolled onto her back. "What time is it?"

I looked at the clock on her nightstand. "Four-fifteen."

"Shit. Could you please get me the pack of pills on top of my dresser?"

"Sure." I got up but didn't see any pills. "You sure they're here?"

"Positive. It's a round plastic disk."

I found what she was talking about and recognition hit. "Is this birth control?" I asked as I handed her the package.

"It is." She scooted so she was sitting up, popped a pill out, and swallowed it.

Shit. "Are you and Austin having sex?" The question blew right through my mental filter.

"You know these pills help with other things, too. Not just to prevent pregnancy."

"Right."

"Besides, I don't see how it's any of your business." She put the pills on her nightstand.

"Sorry. You're right." I wanted to drop it, really, I did... "But are you?"

She laughed. "Why do you want to know?"

"Umm, because we're best friends and you should tell me these things."

"Did you tell me when you lost your virginity or did I find out when I overheard the girl talking about it in the locker room before cheer practice?"

I'd forgotten about that. "Point taken." Except I really wanted to know. It'd give me more of a reason to hate Austin. "So to avoid me having to hear about it in the locker room, are you and Austin...?"

She reached for her water. "Jeez, Kyle. Fine. Yes, we are. Happy now?"

"Oh." That hurt. I knew it wasn't fair of me to think she'd remain a virgin forever, especially when I'd been with other girls, but the possessiveness in me—which seemed to get worse by the day—still thought of Allie as mine.

"I really need to shower."

"Please do. You stink," I joked. It was better than imagining her naked especially since I knew she was fucking Austin.

"Hilarious. You have plans tonight?"

I shook my head. "What do you have in mind?"

"Movie night?"

"You shower and I'll make the popcorn."

While she was in the bathroom, I changed her bed sheets for her and tossed the sweaty ones into the wash. Then I went downstairs and made our pillow pile in the living room as the popcorn popped in the microwave. When she came downstairs, she looked a million times better. She had on shorts and a University of Michigan sweatshirt she'd gotten when she'd visited the campus earlier in the year.

I wanted to be happy for her. No, I was happy for her, but

I was sad for me because in a few months she'd be gone and I truthfully wasn't ready for that. Not that I thought I'd ever be ready for us to be separated, but I definitely wasn't ready then. Losing my dad had put life into perspective for me. He'd known I was in love with Allie and ever since his death, I struggled to keep those feelings I had for her at bay. There was no way I would've gotten through losing him without her and every day that's passed since has made it more difficult for me to fight my feelings.

She snuggled up beside me and covered us with a blanket.

I handed her the remote. "You pick the movie."

"So my being in pain is the secret to getting you to relinquish the remote, huh? I'll have to remember that."

I laughed. "Extreme pain only. And no faking."

She found a decent comedy, but I struggled with concentrating on it. I needed to tell her how I felt. But she had a boyfriend. A serious one. That wouldn't be fair of me and so I resigned to stay silent, even if it killed me.

Then I thought of something. "I have a question."

"Maybe I have an answer," she replied.

"Why did you want me to come over instead of Austin?"

"And let him see me like that? No way. I was a disaster."

I poked her on the nose. "A cute disaster."

She shook her head. "Nice try." She popped a few pieces of popcorn into her mouth and swallowed. "Besides, you always know how to make me feel better. I'm pretty sure Austin wouldn't have been able to interpret my grunts as well."

That made me smile. "I've had fourteen years to learn how to speak Allie."

She nudged me with her shoulder.

I nudged her back.

22

ALLIE

12th Grade - June

*P*rom was our reward for surviving high school. I got ready at Melissa's house along with Lila. Melissa took a curling iron to my hair while Lila glued lashes onto her eye lids.

"So did you go for a bikini wax?" she asked as she wrapped a strand of my hair around the hot wand.

My brows shot up. "Why would I do that?"

"Duh. Because guys like that. I got a Brazilian."

"As in...everything?" Lila questioned as she fanned her one closed eye with her hand.

Melissa nodded.

"Didn't that hurt?" I asked.

"Pain is beauty girls."

I laughed. "You're insane. Besides, you and Josh aren't even dating."

"Don't be so naïve, Allie. It's prom night. Everyone gets laid on prom night."

My mouth dried out. "Right."

"You forget how much it sucks to be single. I don't get laid all the time like you do, so give me this night and don't be so judgy."

Except that I didn't, but I let her believe that so she'd stop bothering me about being a virgin. "Not judging. You do you."

I was the only one in our friend group who hadn't had sex and the last thing I wanted was to have a reputation for being the resident prude, so I may have let them believe that Austin and I were doing it. It's not that I didn't want to have sex. Austin and I had gotten close a few times, but it hadn't felt right. As cliche as it sounds, you only get one first time and I wanted it to be special. I simply hadn't had that magical moment with Austin yet. Prom added pressure, though. He'd have expectations and we'd been dating for six months so it's not like we weren't serious, I just...I didn't know.

"I freaking hate these things," Lila cursed at the lashes that were stuck to her finger.

Melissa handed me the curling iron and went to help Lila. I had no clue what to do with a curling iron, so I just held onto it and waited.

Once we were zipped into our dresses, we went outside into the garden on the side of the house to take pictures. Reece, who was going with Lila, had arrived and so had Melissa's date, Josh, as well as Shawn and his date. They all took couple photos while I waited on Austin. Kyle and Kayley (yeah, I know) hadn't gotten there yet either, so I hung out in back by the pool.

"Wow."

I spun around to find my best friend looking dapper as hell in his tux. His broad shoulders stretched the jacket and his dirty blond hair was perfectly combed. And those crystal blue eyes. Kyle had the best eyes.

"Wow yourself," I returned.

He continued to admire me in my emerald-green satin fishtail gown. It was very different from anything I'd ever worn. Showing off my boobs had never been my style, but for prom, the girls were on full display in my spaghetti strap, cowl neck dress. When I'd put it on in the dressing room, my first reaction when I'd looked in the mirror had been that I could be Jessica Simpson's brunette cousin. The dress hugged curves I hadn't realized I'd had. Once I'd stepped out and Melissa saw the dress, she'd said, "If you don't buy that right now, I'm buying it for you."

Kyle took a few steps forward with hunger in his eyes. "Damn, Allie."

Not knowing what to make of that, I blushed.

"Oh, wow," Austin smiled at me from behind Kyle.

Well, at least the dress got me a consistent reaction. I felt pretty *wow* in it.

Austin stepped around Kyle and gave me a kiss that said he couldn't care less about my lipstick. Luckily, I'd let Melissa talk me into the long-wear kind. "Babe, you look stunning."

"Thanks." I smiled at him.

I turned to Kyle. "Where's your date?"

He pointed to where everyone else was taking pictures. "I came to get you."

Austin wrapped his arm around my waist and pressed himself against me. "We should go take photos now because I don't know how long I'll be able to restrain from relieving you of that dress."

"And that's my cue." Kyle went to join the others.

Austin kissed my neck just below my ear and whispered, "I can't wait for tonight."

I swallowed. "Yeah."

We couldn't have asked for a nicer June evening. Prom was at the Country Club right on the Long Island Sound, so we had a perfect waterfront view. I'd given up on my heels after an hour of straight dancing. Austin was a terrible dancer, but he tried anyway and I appreciated that. After dinner, he had to meet the football players for a group photo, so I waited at the table for him.

Kyle slid into the seat beside me. "Having fun?"

"Actually, yeah. I am."

"You surprised?"

I shrugged. "A little." I'd spent most of the preceding week scared about what may or may not happen between Austin and I after prom, but being there I was able to live in the moment and enjoy the night with my friends. "Where's Kayley?"

"Not sure. I lost her about half an hour ago." Kyle and Kayley weren't dating, he'd simply asked her because…well, she was Kayley. "What about Austin?"

"Doing a football thing."

The music changed to a slow song and Kyle held his hand out. "Want to dance?"

I put my hand in his. "Sure."

He led me onto the dance floor and we swayed middle-school-style with his hands around my waist and mine around his neck while Kelly Clarkson belted out the lyrics to "Because of You."

"We've never danced like this before, have we?" I asked. To my recollection, whenever we had danced it'd always been to upbeat songs.

"Once," he replied. "The eighth-grade dance."

"That's right. You totally blocked Ian and I from dancing."

He smirked. "And then you stuck Melissa on me. I was washing glitter off my skin for weeks after."

I laughed. "And then we ended up dating them so it was kinda like I was predicting the future."

He gripped my hands and spun me around before pulling me against his chest and he *really* danced with me.

I hummed in surprise.

"What?"

"You can dance."

"Guess you don't know everything about me after all."

"What else don't I know?"

Kyle's blue eyes stared into mine and his expression became serious.

My smile fell. *Could there really be something he hasn't told me?*

His lips parted and he took a breath.

I stilled.

"Can I cut in?" Austin interrupted us.

Kyle released me and stepped back. "Yeah, man." He was gone before I could stop him.

Austin placed his hand on my back and pulled me against him. He smelled like whiskey.

"Find a little something extra at that group photo?" I asked.

He buried his face into the side of my neck and kissed me. "Maybe."

"And you didn't share?"

"I've got something I wanna share with you all right." He nibbled on my ear.

I placed my hands on his shoulders and eased him away. "Okay. Save it for later."

"It's always later with you, Allie."

I tilted my head. "Excuse me?"

He let me go. "Nothing. I'll be back."

And I was left standing alone on the dance floor. Clearly, I needed to have conversations with both of the men in my life, so I went in search of Kyle first. Walking the perimeter yielded me nothing, so I headed outside onto the patio, which is where I found Kayley. She and I had never been friends. Not even close. She was a mega bitch, but she was a model, so I guess you could call her attractive. Undoubtedly that was why Kyle had asked her. That being said, the less I had to talk to her the better.

"Hey have you seen Kyle?"

She pouted her lips at me, "Did you lose your boyfriend?"

I put a hand on my hip. "Did you lose your soul?"

Seemingly unamused, she rolled her eyes and turned her back to me.

"So you haven't seen him because you've been dumped at the prom. Got it. Thanks." I gathered up the bottom of my dress and kept going. Sparring with Kayley was not on my to-do list for the evening.

Melissa and Josh were devouring each other's faces over by the railing, so I kept walking along the path. I found Shawn smoking pot with a few other guys.

"Shawn, have you seen Kyle?"

He coughed up smoke. "Took off a few minutes ago," he replied, holding the blunt out for me.

Fuck. I shook my head. "I'll pass, thanks." Guess I'd been right about him having something big to tell me. I went back inside and found my purse tucked under my seat along with my heels. After digging out my phone, I opened a message.

Allie: Did you seriously leave prom?

I waited.
And waited.
And waited more.

Allie: I've got the feeling you need to talk to me about something.

Waited.

Kyle: All good. Was needed at home. Have fun. Talk later.
Allie: Need me to come over?
Kyle: No. It's prom night. Enjoy it.
Allie: K. I'll see you tomorrow.

I tucked the phone back into my purse, slid my heels on, and went to find my boyfriend. He was sitting with some of his football buddies and they were passing a bottle of whiskey to each other under the table. I came up behind him and put my hand on his shoulder.

"You ready to go?"

He leaned his head against my arm. "I'm ready. Are you ready?"

I knew his question was two-fold and I truthfully didn't know the answer to that one, but I told him what he wanted to hear. "Ready."

He jumped to his feet and grabbed my hand. "Later boys."

Austin had gotten us a room at the hotel next door, so as we walked over there, I tried to figure out what I was going to do by making a list in my head.

Pros and Cons of Having Sex with Austin
Pro:
I wouldn't go off to college a virgin
He says he loves me and I love him, too. Don't I?
We've been dating for six months, so it's not like he's a random guy
I've enjoyed the other stuff we've done together

Con:
Losing my virginity on prom night was a terrible cliche
Something didn't feel right about it

Well, that helped.

And by *helped*, I mean not at all.

Austin had checked us into the hotel earlier so everything we needed was already there. We rode the elevator up to the fifth floor and when he opened the door to our room, there was a trail of rose petals leading to the bed.

I turned to look up at him. "You did this?"

"I thought it'd make tonight extra special," he said, right before kissing me.

23

KYLE

Summer Before College - August

I'd officially been living in the Woodlawn section of the Bronx for a week, but I still planned to sleep at home some nights to help out. My school was halfway between my apartment and my house, so it didn't matter much where I stayed. The only reason I needed the apartment was for city residency and since I'd gotten a full scholarship for college, I was able to use my college fund to get it. Classes started in a week and all of my friends were leaving for their respective colleges over the next few days, so there was a big party that night on the beach.

After parking in the lot, I walked up to the beach and as soon as my feet hit the sand I spotted Allie. She was hard to miss given how gorgeous she looked in her teal bikini top and jean shorts. I hadn't seen her in two days because she'd been busy packing and had spent some time alone with her mom and also with Austin. Thinking about her leaving the next day made me nauseous and I'd been dreading having to say goodbye to her for weeks.

"Kyle," she shouted as she ran over and hugged me. *Fuck, I'd miss holding her.*

"Hey, Al." I forced myself to let go and Shawn tossed me a beer. I looked around for her boyfriend. "Where's Austin?"

Her eyes darkened for a brief moment before she pointed down the beach. "Over there."

I wondered what that was about. If my girlfriend was leaving to go halfway across the country from me in less than twenty-four hours, nothing would be able to pry me from her side. Perhaps the impending long distance was too stressful.

In my living room the night before, I'd drank a six-pack and came to the decision that I couldn't let Allie leave for college without telling her how I felt. When Austin had cut in on us dancing at prom, I'd taken it as a sign to keep my mouth shut. She was happy with him and the last thing I wanted was for her to resent me for trying to screw that up. But something had changed over the last couple of weeks. I'd gotten the feeling that things weren't going so well for them and that got me thinking again about telling her.

I'd probably always regret it if I let her leave for Michigan thinking I only loved her as a friend. Sweat pooled on my lower back—more from the nerves than the heat—so I took my t-shirt off and tossed it aside. I glanced over at Allie and caught her looking at my abs. It had only been for a second, but she'd looked. Choosing to interpret that as maybe the attraction between us wasn't one-sided, I willed my nerves to chill out.

The party ended up being more fun than I'd expected it to be. We all danced barefoot on the beach and it was surreal knowing it would likely be the last time so many of us would be together until our class reunion. I'd only allowed myself to have two drinks—enough to calm my nerves, but not enough to cloud my head. Allie had limited herself as well since she had to leave the following day. A few hours into the party, we were pretty much the only sober ones.

Allie hooked her arm in mine. "Come sit with me." She dragged me over to a quiet spot away from the others and my stomach flopped because I knew that her plan was to say goodbye to me, which meant I couldn't stall any longer. We sat in the sand and stared out at the waves.

She let out a small laugh.

"What?"

"We've come full circle."

"What do you mean?"

She grabbed a handful of sand and let it slip through her fingers. "We played together in the sand on the day we met and now here we are sitting in the sand on the day we say goodbye."

I didn't respond because I didn't think I'd be able to get words out and keep my emotions in check.

She sighed and leaned her head on my shoulder, so I put my arm around her back. The thought of not being able to touch her for months made me physically ill.

"I think I made a mistake," tumbled from my mouth.

"What kind of mistake?"

"Letting you go to college without me, for one."

She tilted her head to look up at me. "Pelham is a small public school, I bet Michigan would be able to help you out of that contract if you still want to pursue hockey."

I swallowed. "That's not what I meant. I've made peace with my choice. I really do want to be a firefighter. My dad loved it and I'm sure I will, too."

"What do you mean then?"

"I don't know if I can handle being separated from you."

She put a hand on my thigh. "It's definitely going to suck, but we'll talk a lot, I'm sure. And I'll be home for Thanksgiving."

"I know."

"What's for two?"

"Huh?"

"You said, 'for one,' so I assume there's something else you think is a mistake."

This was my chance. Either I took it or I kept my mouth shut and let her go off to move on without me, because surely that was what would happen. We'd grow apart eventually. Once she left me behind, there was no way we'd ever be as close as we were right then.

She must've felt me tense because she lifted her head and turned her body around so she was sitting with her legs crossed facing me. "What is it?"

I took a deep breath and blew it out hard.

"This is going to be big, isn't it?" Her eyes widened.

I nodded.

She reached for my hand. "Tell me."

"You remember sophomore year. *That* night." I didn't have to say anymore because she nodded slowly.

"Yeah, of course."

"And you remember the conversation we had after when we decided that us dating would be a mistake?"

"Yeah..." she dragged the word out.

"I think making *that* decision was a mistake."

Her lips parted and then closed again.

I shut my eyes and took another deep breath before opening them again. I needed to see her face when I said the next part. "You are the most important person in my life, Allie, and you know that I love you." I swallowed. "But I'm also *in love* with you. I have been for years."

She blinked rapidly.

"I tried not to be, but I am."

She let go of my hand and rubbed her palms on her knees.

"And I couldn't let you leave without you knowing that." My pulse drummed in my head. "Please say something," I practically begged.

"I, umm..." She sighed. "Kyle, I..."

My heart cracked.

She shook her head back and forth and muttered, "Fuck."

"It's not—"

"Why now?"

"What do you mean?"

"If you've been in love with me for years, why did you choose *now* as the time to tell me?" A hint of anger laced her voice.

"Because we'd agreed our friendship was too important."

"And it's not important now?" She gestured exaggeratedly with her hands.

"Of course it is."

"Then why was it too important to say anything before, but *now* it's okay?"

I ran a hand over my jaw. "I told you. I couldn't let you leave without you knowing the truth."

Her hands flailed. "But what are we supposed to do about it, Kyle? I'm leaving for Michigan *tomorrow*. And I have a boyfriend for fuck's sake."

"I know and I'm sorry. We don't have to do anything about it if you don't want to, I just needed you to know."

"It doesn't work like that, Kyle. This affects our friendship drastically."

"It doesn't have to." I reached for her hand but she pulled away. "Allie, nothing has to change. If you tell me you're in love with Austin and you don't want to be with me then I will accept that and we can just stay best friends."

She chuffed. "You're delusional. Of course this changes things. We can't go back to five minutes ago and forget this conversation ever happened. I can't just ignore what you've said."

I tugged on my hair. "Tell me what you need me to do, Allie."

"I needed you to be my *friend* and now I don't know what to do."

"What do you mean?"

She got up on her knees. "I need to go."

"Allie, please don't." I reached up to stop her from standing, but she shook me off.

"I can't do this right now."

I jumped up and grabbed her by the shoulders so she couldn't get away. My voice shook and I swallowed. "Please don't go, Al. Not like this."

She bit her quivering lip.

"It's fine if you don't want to be with me, I promise you." It would kill me, but I'd find a way to get over her eventually. "I'll never stop being here for you. As a friend."

She squeezed her eyes closed. "Let me go, Kyle." Her words were a punch to the gut.

Reluctantly, I released her and as she turned away from me and disappeared down the beach, my heart cracked in two. Overwhelmed with the need to scream or punch something, I ran back to my car and got inside before covering my mouth with my forearm and screaming at the top of my lungs.

Some time later, I found myself sitting on the old swing at our spot wallowing in the pain. My intention had been to go back to my apartment, but my car had taken me to the park instead. It was the one place in the world where I knew I'd always be able to go and feel Allie's presence. And I desperately needed that.

I wasn't sure how I'd expected her to react to my confession, but I hadn't fucking anticipated it going that badly. I'd pushed her to turn her back on our friendship and that hurt nearly as badly as losing my dad had. That might seem extreme, but she'd been a big part of my life for nearly as far back as I could remember. Hell, I'd known her longer than I had my youngest brother. I rested my elbows on my knees and lowered my head to my hands.

"I had a feeling I'd find you here."

My head shot up. I must've been so deep in my despair I hadn't heard her walk up.

She had put on a tank top, but her feet were still bare. She dropped her bag in the sand and as she sat on her swing, she sighed. "I'm sorry for the way I reacted."

"You don't have to apologize."

Her being there was enough.

"Yes, I do. It's flattering when someone tells you they're in love with you and I acted embarrassingly ungracious. It's just that you shocked me, and the past few days have been really rough. I'm emotional and I'm stressed out and I needed to process everything."

"That's totally understandable." I desperately wanted to hug her to convince myself that she was truly there and not a figment of my wishful thinking, but I didn't.

She sighed. "I'm not happy that you chose tonight to tell me how you feel."

"Sorry—"

She put her hand up. "I don't want an apology. I just wish you'd been honest with me sooner that way we would've had more time to figure this out."

I cursed myself for all of the times I'd wanted to tell her but had chickened out. "You're right. I should've, but I tried to get over you and by the time I realized that wasn't gonna happen it was too late—you were with Austin. I was gonna let it go, but the closer it's gotten to you leaving, the more I realized I couldn't." I sighed. "I would've regretted it the rest of my life if I let you get on that plane tomorrow without at least trying."

"Kyle—"

"I meant what I said before. If you want to be with him, I'll respect that. If you don't see me as anything more than your best friend, then I'll respect that, too. But you understand I had to try, right?"

"Yeah, I do, but I still have the same concern that I had sophomore year. Our friendship is important to me."

I had one final shot and this was it. "It is to me, too, but I realized something. Our friendship is a relationship. We've been dating for years; we just don't have sex. Everything else though…" I took a deep breath. "Allie, we've got it all and you can't deny that."

Her bronze eyes, while locked with mine, seemed deep in thought.

I had to convince her. "We talk or see each other every single day. If one of us needs something, the other comes running, no questions asked. When we're going through hard times, we go through them together. We go on dates all of the time; we just don't call them dates. And most importantly, we love each other."

She gave me a lopsided grin.

My heart rapped against my ribcage. "Can you honestly tell me you've felt a connection with another guy like the one we have?"

She shook her head. "Not even close."

I smiled at her admission. "If that's true, then why couldn't we work? We've basically been doing the hard part of dating for a long time and we might argue every once in a while, but we've always worked it out. I can't see how changing our labels and throwing sex into the mix would change that."

She bit her lip. "I leave for Michigan tomorrow."

"I know. And I get that long distance is going to suck, but I have faith in us. I'm willing to try it if you are."

"I broke up with Austin."

I was taken aback by that. "You did?"

She nodded.

"When?"

She kicked at the sand. "Half-hour ago."

"Are you okay?"

She lifted and dropped one shoulder. "I think so. It was

inevitable. We've been fighting for weeks and we were both kidding ourselves if we thought we'd be able to handle the distance."

I hated myself for being disappointed that she hadn't broken up with him for me.

"That's one of the reasons I've been so stressed out lately. I think I've known for a while that things with Austin wouldn't work out."

"I'm sorry, Allie."

"Don't be. Actually, I should be thanking you."

"Thanking me? Why?"

"Because when you told me that you were in love with me, I believed you."

"Good because it's true, but I'm not following."

"I don't think Austin was in love with me. Maybe he thought he was, but he wasn't. Not really. Not like you." She sighed and I could tell by the way her face scrunched that she was thinking. Allie continued, "And also because my first thought was the fear of losing you because dating could destroy everything. My relationship with Austin was an afterthought." She got up and stood in front of me, resting her hands on my thighs. "But also because when you put *us* on the table..." She stared into my eyes. "I was intrigued."

A smile slowly crept over me and I reached for her hips. "You were?"

She bit her lip. "I *am*."

A warmth flooded my body and I smirked. "Should we try another experiment?"

She laughed. "Why not. At least we had the conversation first this time."

Keeping hold of her hips, I stood, towering over her. "You sure?"

Her hands slid over my forearms. "No, but isn't that what the experiment is for?" She gazed hungrily at me.

I leaned down and she rolled up onto her toes, but I paused

before our faces could meet. "I want to make you a promise," I whispered. "Friends first. Always."

She laced her fingers behind my neck and echoed, "Friends first."

I closed the gap and when our mouths met, everything about it felt right. My arms wrapped around her back and I pressed her body against mine as I slipped my tongue between her lips. She whimpered as she met mine with hers and we deepened the kiss. Keeping one arm wrapped around her back, I brought a hand up behind her neck and fed it into her hair. My fingers tangled with her strands as I held her head in place and kissed her with a fervor that had been building up for years. We breathed each other in, strengthening our connection, and I knew then that I'd be hers for as long as she'd have me.

We took our time kissing, exploring, and savoring each other. Her little moans shot directly to my dick and I was nearly completely engorged. Given how close our bodies were, I knew she had to feel what she was doing to me. As badly as I wanted to take things further, I didn't want to push it. I'd kissed her because I wanted her to feel what I knew. I needed her to get on that plane confident in what we could be.

It killed me to pull away, but I forced myself to do it. It took us both some time to open our eyes, but when we did, the lust in hers matched mine.

"Kyle?" she whispered.

"Hmm?"

"Can we go to your apartment?"

I pursed my lips in an effort to maintain some semblance of control over my rationality. She'd just broken up with her boyfriend an hour ago and I wouldn't be her rebound. "I don't know if that's a good idea. You and Austin—"

She put a finger over my lips. "Take me to your place." She grabbed my hand and tugged me toward my car.

"Where's yours?" I asked, seeing the lot empty

"Sold it yesterday since I'm not taking it with me."

I opened the passenger door for her. "Oh. How'd you get here then?" I didn't like the idea of her having walked from the beach so late at night.

"Lila dropped me off."

I reached for her hand and held it the whole way to my apartment. Nothing had ever felt more right.

We made it to my apartment in record time. I hadn't wanted to waste a single precious second. After parking on the street, I led her to the simple brick building that housed my new home. We walked up the three flights and once we were inside, I didn't know what to do with myself. I don't think Allie did either because she just kind of stood there in the middle of my living room with her hands tucked into her back pockets, while I leaned against the door.

I broke the tension. "So..."

"So," she echoed.

"Do you want to watch a movie or something?"

She giggled, which made me smile. "No, to the movie." She sashayed toward me. "Yes, to the something."

I held my breath as she placed her palms on my chest and my nipples hardened.

"We have some more experimenting to do."

I brushed her hair behind her ear and left my palm pressed against the side of her head. "We don't have to," I whispered.

She got up on her toes and placed a tender kiss on my lips. "No, but I want to."

I grasped her head with both hands and tilted her toward me as I bent to meet her in the middle. There was nothing tentative about that kiss. We devoured each other like we'd been starving for it. Her hands migrated down my body. She slipped them up the front of my shirt, fingering my abs. Then she swept her palms around to my lower back and tugged me toward her.

I spun us around and pressed her against my wall, pinning

her with my body. I rubbed against her and she moaned as she arched her spine, letting me feel her boobs on my chest, as she brought her hands further up my back beneath my shirt. Taking the cue, I pulled away long enough to discard my shirt before diving back in. Her nails scraped against my shoulder blades and my cock hardened to the point of being almost painful. Reaching between us, I adjusted myself so I wasn't squished in my shorts. To my surprise, her hand replaced mine and she gripped my shaft over my zipper making me gasp.

While she stroked me, I cupped her breasts and brought her earlobe into my mouth, biting down on the fleshy part. Her moans egged me on and I ground into her palm while I squeezed her nipples. Her boobs felt bigger than I'd remembered. They overflowed my hands and I desperately needed them bare against me. Reading my mind, she discarded her tank top and I immediately reached behind her to untie her bikini, freeing her from the material. My hands were calloused and rough, which only made the softness of her smooth skin more exquisite.

She fingered the button on my shorts and glided the zipper down, allowing them to fall from my hips to the floor. I kissed her neck and along her collar bone, nibbling as I went, which made her jolt and elicited a particularly pleasurable sound all the way from her diaphragm.

After kicking my sandals aside and stepping out of my shorts, I grabbed her ass and lifted her into the air. Taking the cue, she wrapped her legs around my waist and her arms around my neck. I kissed her hard and then pulled away so I could see where I was going while I traversed the new territory to my bedroom. Allie's fingers weaved into my hair and she licked along the edge of my ear.

Once in my room, I laid her down on the bed and covered her body with mine while we kissed some more. She left her ankles hooked behind my ass, pressing me against her center and I could feel the heat beckoning through our clothes. While grinding my hips, the head of my dick poked through the opening in my boxers. It rubbed against the scratchy denim, so I had to lift myself off of her. Noticing that I was free, she reached down and wrapped her hand around me.

"Fuck," I growled through my teeth.

She applied the perfect amount of pressure and it felt incredible, but knowing it was *Allie* touching me took the pleasure to an entirely new level. I stared down at her and drank in the sight of her creamy skin—from her flat stomach to her ample breasts, which peaked with the most perfect pink nipples. I rubbed the pads of my thumbs over them and she bucked beneath me from the sensation, so I did it again, getting the same response.

I bit down hard on my lip because I needed to show restraint, but I'd waited four long years to be with her and my desire was much stronger than my resolve. With one hand, I undid the three buttons on her shorts and she lifted her hips for me so I could drag them off her. Once discarded, I reached for the ties on the sides of her bikini bottoms and pulled them loose, leaving her naked on my bed. Taking a moment to appreciate that, I let my eyes wander the length of her. Every inch of her was perfect. From the dip in her throat, to the swell of her boobs. The slightest hint of abdominal muscles poked through her soft skin, leading me from her torso to the neatly trimmed apex of her thighs. She was every bit a woman.

"You are so damn sexy."

She pressed her palm against the center of my chest and let it graze over my abs. "So are you."

I licked my lips. "If we keep going..."

Her fingers brushed my cheek. "I want this, Kyle. I want you."

I exhaled. "You sure?"

She nodded. "Yes."

I smirked before kissing her and brought a hand between her legs to tease her slit, which was slick with need. Her hips rose, causing my fingers to slip between her lips. I'd planned on teasing her, but I couldn't endure that torture, so I slid a finger into her wet hole. She was tight and my cock twitched at the thought of how good she was going to feel wrapped around me.

Pulling my mouth from hers, I trailed kisses down her torso until my tongue found her swollen bud. She gasped as I lapped at her pussy, tasting her sweetness and savoring the slick, softness of her. Her breathing grew rapid and I knew she was close because she bucked against my face, riding my finger and my tongue. I increased the pressure and that did it. She tumbled and fell with a whimper, trapping my head between her thighs. It was sexy as fuck.

After easing my finger out, I kissed up her body until I reached her mouth. She didn't hesitate to taste herself on my lips.

"Mmm." She dipped her fingers into the waistband of my boxers and grabbed my ass.

I lifted away from her and gazed down into her eyes. The love reflected in her intense stare was all the reassurance I needed to know she wanted this as much as I did.

"Are you still on the pill or do I need a condom? I'm clean." I'd always used a condom, but with her, I didn't want to. I wanted to feel every bit.

She smiled. "We're good."

After kicking off my boxers, I hovered over her, with my tip pressed against her entrance. My breathing quickened and judging by her parted lips and soft whimpers, so did hers. I was nervous, excited, anxious, but most of all I was happy, truly happy, for the first time in a long while.

Our eyes locked and her lips pursed as she gave me the smallest nod. I reached between us to help guide my dick inside of her. I went slow, wanting to savor every sensation, and fuck she was tight. Almost too tight. Her eyes widened and I whispered, "Just relax. You know I'll take good care of you."

She bit her lip as I thrust forward, pushing past her resistance. The gasp that came from her lips was not from pleasure and her hands pushed up on my chest as she sucked in a sharp breath.

I froze. "You said you weren't a virgin."

She panted and her eyes were wide with uncertainty. "I lied."

Oh fuck, oh fuck, oh fuck. "Why?"

She bit her lip.

"Allie…" I was afraid to move. The last thing I wanted to do was hurt her.

Her chest heaved up and down like she'd run a marathon. "I know I shouldn't talk about another guy while we're...you know...but I—I couldn't do it. Before."

I felt the relief from her confession deep in my core.

"I really thought something was wrong with me, but now I know." She swallowed. "I couldn't do it because you're the only one I should give my virginity to."

I nearly exploded inside of her at that admission. I exhaled as I leaned my forehead on hers and closed my eyes. "Do you have any idea how much I love you?"

Her lashes fluttered. "Show me."

I sighed. "I'll go slow, but tell me if you need me to stop."

She threaded her hands behind my neck. "Okay."

I eased my hips back an inch and then rocked forward a couple. She was tense and I wasn't a small guy. I knew it would take a bit to get her acclimated to me before I could bury myself all the way in.

"I'm going to kiss you and I want you to focus on kissing me back. Try to relax, okay?"

She nodded.

My lips closed over hers and I gave her all the passion I had in me. As she got lost in the movement of our lips, her pussy relaxed a bit more and I eased forward, deepening our kiss to distract her. The warmth of her around my cock was comforting. She was so fucking tight—no way I would be able to last long. Shaking from the restraint I was showing, I clenched my ass to remind myself to take it slow. Her nails scraped against my shoulder blades. I was almost fully seated inside her and I craved to know how she'd feel when I was balls deep.

I whispered into her mouth, "Wrap your legs around me."

She did. When her ankles crossed behind me, I bit down on her lip and thrust forward, sinking all the way in. My eyes rolled into my head.

I released her lip rom my teeth. "Holy...fuck."

She whimpered.

"You okay?"

"More than okay." Her bronze eyes sparkled. "Kyle...this is..."

I kissed her softly. "Tell me."

"I feel so...stretched...full."

I pinned her eyes with mine. "Is it bad?"

"No. Surreal."

I kissed her again. "I'm gonna move now."

She nodded.

I retreated halfway, then thrust forward again. It took a few pumps, but the tightness subsided as her muscles softened and I was able to move inside of her more easily. When she moaned, I knew we'd gotten past the hard part. I snuck a hand between us and rubbed her clit.

"Kyle," she whimpered against my mouth and I stopped.

"Did I hurt you?" I asked as I lifted off of her.

She laughed. "No. It feels really good."

I grinned. "Yeah, it does." I went back to flicking her bud as I thrust inside of her, bringing her to the brink of ecstasy. The pressure of my own release was building quickly. She was too tight...too wet...too perfect.

"Oh. My..." she squealed as her orgasm took over. Her legs

pinned me in place and the walls of her pussy squeezed my cock. I tried to fight it but the attempt was useless.

"Allie," I exclaimed as I came inside my best friend—the person who meant the most to me in this world. We'd crossed the point of no return and I didn't regret it for a second.

24

ALLIE

After

$\mathcal{I}$ woke to Kyle snoring softly beside me and I was suddenly very self-conscious of the fact that I was naked. My best friend was *in love* with me and I'd had sex with him.

I'd had sex. Period.

Holy shit.

The room started to feel extra small and my lungs struggled to get air. Taking care not to wake him, I slid out of bed and found my swimsuit bottoms and shorts on the floor. After gathering them up, I tiptoed into the living room. I was sore between my legs—a reminder that I hadn't dreamed up what had happened. Once I slipped my bottoms on, I found my tank by the door, but I struggled to locate my bikini top in the dark. I vaguely remembered Kyle tossing it across the room. Panic was welling inside me by the second, so I decided to fore-go the top and simply slid on my tank before grabbing my bag and slipping out of the apartment.

As I hustled down the hall, I dug my phone out and called

for a taxi. New York City cabs couldn't leave the city limits, so I had to call a car service in Westchester. Thankfully, they had a taxi in the area so I didn't have to wait long. Standing on the sidewalk at four a.m. in the Bronx probably wouldn't have been smart. Stepping out into the fresh air helped some, but I couldn't help the feeling that I was on the verge of hyperventilating.

The ride home took all of ten minutes and the entire time I couldn't help but dwell on the ache between my thighs. It was like my vagina had its own memory of what I'd done. The way Kyle filled me would be something hard to forget. Once home, I snuck inside, kicked off my sandals, and tiptoed up to my bedroom.

I dropped my bag beside my desk and the photo wall I'd been working on since middle school caught my eye. I ran my hand over the glossy images. There were photos of us all as a group, some of me with Melissa and Lila, some of me with the guys I'd dated, some from cheer, but the vast majority were of me and Kyle. My favorite one was of us from freshman year. I was perched on his lap on the bleachers after a football game and we both had these goofy smiles on our faces. We'd been so young then and it reminded me just how huge a part of my life he was. I loved everything about our friendship, but it would never be the same after what we'd just done.

I perched on the edge of my desk, squeezed my eyes shut, and sighed. Earlier, having sex with Kyle had seemed like a good idea, but after was a different story. In the moment, it had been perfect. It had been everything I'd wanted for my first time and then some. And it happening with Kyle was something I'd treasure forever because, like I had told him, it had felt right that I'd waited for him, but that didn't help ease my confusion any. I was leaving for Michigan in a few hours and our friendship was hanging in the balance.

I got up and walked toward my bed. There was a picture of Austin and I from prom on my nightstand. It reminded me of how exorbitantly stressful the past month had been. Austin and I had fought constantly. My inability to have sex with him had really screwed with his head. Mine, too, if I'm being honest. But the ease with which I'd given myself to Kyle had cleared that up. Except...

Now what?

The reality of being separated from Kyle had been hard enough before, but with everything that had transpired, I didn't know how to wrap my head around the implications of it all. It's not like we'd gotten drunk and made a mistake—that I think we would've been able to get past—but he was *in love* with me. And I wasn't sure if I was in love with him, too. Sure, I loved him, but was I *in love*? Did I even know what that meant?

I sat on the edge of my bed and ran my fingers through my tangled hair. There was no way I could move forward like the night hadn't happened. Feelings were involved. Deep feelings. But I'd also had a boyfriend—who wasn't Kyle—mere hours before he made love to me...

I was a fucking mess.

I eyed my suitcases standing in the corner and my mouth went dry. Leaving behind everything I knew was terrifying enough, but adding in the whole *what are we?* drama only made me more stressed and more scared and more...overwhelmed.

I was pissed at myself for thinking with my hormones and doing something so monumental when we were facing the longest separation of our entire friendship. Jumping into a new relationship on the same day I was jumping onto an airplane was incredibly stupid. Kyle might think we could handle it, but I had my doubts. Nothing about us dating would be simple. We'd have to learn how to turn fourteen-years of friendship into something more, all while having hundreds of miles between us.

I fell back and covered my face with my hands. "How could we be so stupid?" I whispered into the empty room.

The clock ticked toward five in the morning. I wasn't planning on leaving for the airport until ten, but if I waited until then, Kyle would inevitably show up at my door and I couldn't handle that. Not yet. Since my bags were already packed, I had no reason to delay.

I got up and went into the bathroom to shower. I still had the sticky salt air on my skin from the beach, not to mention the wetness between my thighs—mine and Kyle's. As I washed my skin, I couldn't help but remember what it had felt like to have Kyle touching me everywhere. Ironically, his big, rough hands had been gentle with me. It had been as though I could feel his love for me simply from the warmth of his caress.

I was sore where he'd stretched me and when I closed my eyes as the warm water cascaded over my head, I got a vivid picture of his crystal-blue eyes staring down at me while he filled me so completely. Tears stung my eyes, but I washed them away.

After my shower, I gathered my hair into a bun and tugged on jeans and a hockey tee that Kyle had given me a few years before from one of the teams he'd been on. Once dressed, I went downstairs and made coffee before going back up to wake my mom.

"Mom?" I whispered by her bedside.

She groaned.

"Mom, wake up."

She opened one eye. "What is it, Allie?"

"Can you take me to the airport?"

Her arms stretched over her head. "What time is it?"

"Around six."

"It's a little early to go now," she said with a yawn.

"Please?"

She blinked a few times. "Excited to get to school, huh?"

"Uh, yeah." I'd go with that assumption.

"All right. Let me get ready."

While I waited in my room for her, I decided to write Kyle a letter, so I pulled out note paper and took a seat at my desk.

Dear Kyle,

Please don't hate me. I realize running away after what happened between us may seem cowardly, but I need some time to think. Last night was...incredibly special. Don't think that I'm distancing myself because I regret it. No, I'm distancing myself because I'm confused and I know that the only way I'll be able to get un-confused is by taking the time to consider the magnitude of what happened.

The idea of leaving for college has been much harder on me than I've let on. One thing that has made me feel more secure about it though has been knowing that even though we'll be apart, you'll still be there for me. After last night though, I'm scared that will change. I can hear you arguing with me right about now, but that's why I'm writing you this letter instead of having this conversation.

I need to figure this one out on my own first. If we rush into dating for the wrong reasons, it will never work. I'm not saying that I don't want to be with you, but I'm also not saying that I do. It wouldn't be fair of me to keep this going until I can honestly answer that question for myself. And the only way to do that is to get a little distance so I can live in my feelings for a while until I have a clear answer.

I'm sorry and I hope you know that my intent is not to hurt you, which is why I need to figure this out before we take this somewhere that only leads to more pain. I love you, Kyle. Now I need to see if that love means something more—or if it could.

Hugs,
Allie

I folded the paper and stuffed it into an envelope, then scribbled his name on the outside. Right before sealing it, I reached for my favorite photo of us and pulled it off the wall, adding it to the envelope.

After wrestling my suitcases to the car, I put the letter on the coffee table in the living room and sipped my coffee while I waited for my mom. The sun had risen and I bounced my leg, worried that Kyle would be getting up soon.

"All ready to go, Allie?" Mom asked from the bottom of the stairs.

She went out to the car first, but I hung back to survey everything one last time. I knew I'd be back in a few months, but that place had been the only home I'd ever known. The idea of making a new home for myself elsewhere was hard to contemplate. I sighed as I gripped the door knob and tugged it closed behind me.

I got in the car.

"You have everything?" Mom asked.

I nodded.

She backed out of the driveway.

"Mom, Kyle's going to come by. Will you make sure he gets the letter I left out on our coffee table?"

She smiled. "Of course. Saying goodbye to him must be hard."

We drove past the playground and I had to bite the inside of my cheeks to keep myself together. "You have no idea." I rested my head against the seat and closed my eyes.

25

KYLE

Freshman Year of College - September

*T*wo weeks—fourteen whole days—that's three-hundred-and-thirty-six hours...

That's how long it had been since Allie had left, and it felt like a goddamn lifetime because not only hadn't I seen her, but I hadn't spoken to her either. At all. Fucking torture.

I sat down at the dining room table for Sunday dinner and I didn't even get a forkful of the corned beef into my mouth before her name came up.

"How's Allie liking school?" Jenna, Dylan's girlfriend, asked. They'd been together a year and my brother was head over heels for her. Being near them made the ache in my chest that much worse.

I managed a shrug.

Instead of letting it go, Dylan pushed. "What's going on with you two?"

"Nothing," I snapped, which was the perfect truth. Not for my lack of trying either. When I'd woken up in an empty apartment that next morning, I'd known something was

KAYE KENNEDY

wrong. I had sped over to her house only to have Mrs. Dupree hand me a letter and tell me that Allie had taken an earlier flight. My heart had sunk. I'd gone to the playground, but since it had been a nice morning there'd been a bunch of kids there. Instead, I'd driven around for several hours hating myself for having opened my damn mouth.

Calling her had proved futile because she'd refused to answer. After ten days of calling, I'd finally given up. Her letter had said she needed space and while I knew I should respect that, it was the last thing I wanted to do. But I did it anyway. If I still didn't hear from her after a week, then I'd try again. At least that was the theory. Who knew if I'd last that long.

Dylan scratched the knife on his plate while cutting the beef. "You've been a moody prick since she left."

I glared at him.

Ryan—my twelve-year-old brother—said, "He's mad because he loves her and she left."

Jesse laughed. "Allie and Kyle are just friends, Ry."

"Looks like he loves her to me," Ryan replied.

I narrowed my eyes. "And what would you know about love at twelve?"

He smirked. "I know that you're not denying it."

"I don't have to explain myself to you."

"Whatever is going on can you fix it? Because I really like Allie."

Yeah, me too. "Drop it, Ryan," I threatened.

My mother swooped in and changed the topic by turning the attention to Jenna and cheerleading. I couldn't have been more grateful.

Three weeks. I'd made it three weeks without talking to Allie and it was a damn miracle because I was so ornery that I seriously wondered how long it'd take for me to get put in jail for

166

road rage, or assaulting a dick who took too long in line at the store, or straight up murdering anyone who looked at me funny.

I tapped my pen on the desk in the back of my calculus class because I needed to do something physical with the hostile energy flowing through me. In the past, whenever I got in one of my moods, there was always one person who could make it better, but this time she was the cause of my reproachable demeanor so I was basically fucked.

I checked my phone for the umpteenth time since I'd broken my silence streak in a text to her that morning.

Kyle: I was really hoping I'd hear from you by now. I get that you needed time, but I fucking miss you, Allie. Please don't do this to us.

Nothing. Not a damn thing.

I got that she was confused and overwhelmed and all that shit, but what I didn't get was why it was taking so long for her to figure it out. Or why she couldn't at least talk to me about it. Or even not about it, just talk to me. Period. All I wanted was to hear her voice.

After class, I headed to the rink. Since hockey didn't start for a couple more weeks, I'd joined an intramural league at school. It was basically all of my new teammates trying to stay fresh until we officially started our season. And it wasn't exactly optional. The team captains made sure all of us freshman got on the roster. Coach tended to stop by, as well.

I laced up my skates and checked my phone a final time before putting it in my locker.

On the ice, I was a fucking beast. No one could touch me and they sure as hell couldn't get by me. One dude came racing down the left, so I sprinted toward him at full force and checked him into the boards. It was a hard enough hit that he bounced off and landed on his ass.

"What the fuck, Hogan?" he shouted, while another guy helped him to his feet.

"Defending my goalie," I stated matter-of-factly as I skated away. It wasn't my fault that I was leagues better than most of them.

"Eighty-three, in the box. Now!" My coach glared at me.

Fuck me. I hadn't realized he'd been there. I took my time skating across the ice.

"He's your damn teammate. Save it for the real games, Hogan," he scolded.

I grunted as I parked my ass on the bench.

Twenty-six days.

Nothing.

Seriously considering going to Michigan.

Angry as fuck.

26

ALLIE

Freshman Year of College - September

I was a cold-hearted bitch. School had started three weeks ago, which meant that I'd gone four weeks without talking to my best friend and it was killing me. With a textbook clutched to my chest, I walked across campus to my psychology class. There was a couple holding hands on the walkway in front of me and it made me nauseous. I needed to get over myself and call Kyle.

It had been so long and I feared he'd be angry with me beyond repair, but I missed him desperately and I needed to at least try. Resolving to call him that afternoon, I let out a sigh. I'd beg for his forgiveness and pray he still wanted to be my friend. As for the other stuff...well, I'd follow my gut since clearly my attempt to rationalize had gotten me nowhere.

When I'd left New York, my intention had been to take my first week, while getting acclimated to my new home, to think about what to do. I'd blocked his number so that I wouldn't be tempted to talk to him because I knew if I saw him calling, I'd pick it up and then he'd be all charming and I'd throw all reason out the window. Definitely not healthy for either of us.

But when that first week had come and gone and I hadn't gotten any closer to figuring it out, I'd started seriously doubting myself. It hadn't helped that my roommate was a total wackadoo. She was a self-proclaimed witch who did spells and made potions. She even had a cauldron. A fucking *cauldron*. The creepiest part though was the voodoo doll looking thing made out of human hair. I'd literally been too scared to fall asleep for fear I'd become her experiment. To make it worse, she slept with a CPAP machine that kept me up all night because it was like sleeping next to a vacuum cleaner, so by the end of that first week I'd become a zombie.

I sank into my seat in the middle of the giant lecture hall and pulled out my notebook. Being in a class with a hundred students was taking some getting used to. College hadn't been what I'd expected. On my first day of classes, my English professor had assigned us a ten-page paper due the following week.

"Welcome to college," he'd said with a sadistic grin. My other classes weren't much lighter on the workload. I knew college would be hard, but I hadn't anticipated the workload.

My psychology professor took his place at the front of the class and began reading from his slide show presentation on various research methods. I leaned my elbow on the desk and put my chin in my hand.

"Hey, can I borrow a pen?" the guy next to me asked.

I dug into my bag and fished one out for him.

"Thanks." He smiled at me and I gave him an awkward grin back. The guy was cute with his short dark hair, tan skin, and chin dimple; under different circumstances, I probably would've flirted with him, but the thought of that sickened me.

Ugh, I need to talk to Kyle. I leaned my elbow on the desk and put my chin in my hand as I daydreamed about what it would've been like had we gone to Michigan together. Desperately, I wished that the guy beside me was my best friend. After three weeks in Michigan, I'd been so stressed out that I'd woken up nauseous and with the start of a migraine pretty much every day.

As the professor droned on, my eyelids grew heavy. It would be a miracle if I managed to stay awake. Between studying and the lack of sleep in my dorm, I really didn't know how I was functioning. Four times in the first two weeks alone, I'd been woken up at closing time in the library by Security Steve. Not only was I not getting my studying done, but pretty much the only sleep I was getting occurred in a wooden chair with my head on a textbook. Definitely not great for my back or my neck.

Oh, and then the second week, Tyler had called to tell me that he was re-deploying to Baghdad. I'd almost broken down and called Kyle then, but I still hadn't come up with a good answer for him and frankly, I was embarrassed. Knowing full well ignoring him was childish, I'd done it anyway.

My stomach cramped, making me wince. That morning, I'd been blessed with my period so I was also crampy as hell. It was nearly two weeks late, so there was a part of me that was grateful it had finally come. I'd mostly assumed I'd been late because of the stress and all the changes, plus I'd also screwed up with taking my pills a few times, so I figured that had something to do with it, too. Besides, who gets pregnant the first time they have sex?

Halfway through the lecture, I really wasn't feeling well. While the birth control pills helped some, I still had pretty bad pain and bleeding two or three times a year. The professor asked a question and the girl behind me answered it, but I couldn't make out their words. My skin was clammy, I was lightheaded, and my cramps were becoming severe. I whimpered.

"You okay?" the guy beside me leaned over and asked.

I pursed my lips and nodded. The last thing I wanted to do

was draw attention to myself, so I had to get back to my dorm before I turned into a writhing mess. Not quite the image I wanted to start the semester off with.

My symptoms escalated quickly. Of course, I had a seat in the middle of a row, which meant sneaking stealthily out would be impossible, but I had no choice. I closed my notebook and didn't bother to waste time shoving it into my bag. I stood, feeling instantly wobbly on my feet. After four steps, I collapsed on top of another student's desk.

When I came to, I was in the back of an ambulance and vaguely coherent.

"Miss, can you hear me?" the pimply-faced medic asked.

I gulped.

"Can you tell me what happened."

I opened my mouth to speak, but nothing came out. The cramping was excruciating. I rolled to my side and pulled my knees up as I grabbed my stomach. Tears fell and I reached a hand out to Kyle, but he didn't take it. My lip quivered and I moaned. "Ky…"

"What?" the medic asked.

Right, Kyle's not here. I sniffled. I needed him—fiercely.

"Is it your stomach?" The guy pressed on my abdomen and I wailed, nearly blacking out from the torture.

He said something, but the pain prevented me from under-standing, though I thought he'd mentioned my appendix. Whatever it was, I'd never been in more agony in my entire life. While I writhed on the stretcher, my heart broke, too. Pushing Kyle away had been my own doing, so I had no right to be upset, but I was devastated.

I was rushed into the Emergency Room on a gurney and was immediately taken into one of the curtained bays. The pain made everything blurry and I heard voices murmuring. *Ultra-sound. Blood panel.* I was hardly aware of anything being done to me. A woman spoke slowly right beside my ear, but I only

caught   a   few   words.   "Pregnant...
Burst...Surgery...Emergency."

Then I was being wheeled around again. Shortly after, I was sedated and no longer felt a thing. Not my stomach. Not my broken heart.

I woke up groggy and a woman hovered over me, half of her face hidden behind a surgical mask.

"Welcome back, Allison," she said.

I blinked several times. "What's happening?"

"You're waking up from surgery. Try to relax and I'll go get the doctor."

Surgery? Right. I fainted in class and then I was taken to the hospital and the pain...wait. The pain was gone.

A woman in a white coat walked in. "Allison, I'm Dr. Stein, I performed your surgery this morning."

"It's Allie." As I became more lucid, my breathing quickened and my eyes widened. "What surgery?"

Dr. Stein looked to be about my mother's age and she had a kind face and a soothing voice. "Did you know you were pregnant, Allie?"

My brows shot up. "Pregnant?"

"Yes."

"But that's not possible. I have my period. Besides, I'm on the pill and I've only ever had sex once."

No. She must be wrong.

She gave me a sad smile. "Were you taking the pill consistently at the same time every day?"

I thought back to how hectic things had been before I had left. "I might have missed a few."

She nodded. "You experienced an ectopic tubular pregnancy, which means that the embryo implanted inside your fallopian tube, causing it to rupture. Blood was leaking into your abdomen, which is why you lost consciousness and it also caused the vaginal bleeding you mistook for your period."

Pregnant? Queasiness overtook me again.

The doctor continued, "I performed what's called a laparoscopic unilateral salpingectomy. I made a few small incisions. Here, here, and here." She pointed to several places on her abdomen. "I tried to repair the tube, but too much damage had been done, so I had to remove it."

"Remove it?" I swallowed.

She nodded.

"So now I only have one?"

"That's correct."

My mouth felt like it was stuffed with cotton.

"While I was in there, I also noticed you have endometriosis. Did you know that?"

I grimaced. "My doctor suspected that, but I didn't know for sure."

"The only way to diagnose is through surgery. Your pregnancy allowed me to find it, so I removed some scar tissue and scraped the lining. It should lessen your pain."

Finally, some good news. "Thank you."

"There's more for us to talk about, but first is there someone I can call for you? Maybe the baby's father?"

Holy shit. Kyle would have been a dad...

I would have been a mom...

Disappointment churned within. I clenched my jaw and tried to keep from crying because, while we were too young to become parents, if I had to choose a father for my child, Kyle would've been it. Without question. "No. I'm a freshman at the university, so I don't really have anyone here. I'm from New York." The weight of Kyle's absence crushed me again.

She pulled over a stool and sat beside me. "Allie, you need to know that this is going to affect your fertility going forward."

I jolted from the shock, but the incision pain kept me from

moving further. Having children was important to me. Very important. I wanted to be a teacher because of how much I loved kids.

"When a woman ovulates, her ovaries alternate releasing an egg each cycle, which means that instead of every twenty-eight days, you'll only be fertile every fifty-six days."

I did some quick math. "So you're saying I'll only be able to get pregnant fifty-percent of the time?"

She nodded. "That's correct."

I bit my lip. Fifty-percent wasn't great, but it wasn't horrible.

"Although we also need to factor in your endometriosis."

"Oh." My chest hurt.

"Allie, with one tube that brings your chances of conceiving down to between two and five percent."

My eyes filled with water and my body went numb.

She placed her hand on my arm, but the touch barely registered. "There are things we can do. Medications, fertility treatments...and when you're ready to try and conceive again, you can work with your doctor to find the best course for you."

I bit my lip and sniffled. "Okay."

"I know this is a lot to process, but right now, let's focus on getting you better. Try to rest and I'll come check on you later. I'm very sorry for your loss."

All I could manage was a nod. Once she left, I let the tears fall. I'd lost a baby. My baby. Mine and Kyle's baby. A baby I hadn't known about...hadn't been nurturing...

But it was too late. Our baby was gone and it was all my fault.

PART II

THE PRESENT

27

KYLE

$\mathcal{I}$ wiped the sweat that had accumulated between my helmet and my forehead. Thanks to a manhole cover explosion, we'd spent the entire afternoon extinguishing underground fires and evacuating two city blocks. It was unseasonably hot for the end of September and the power grid had overheated causing the explosion. With these kinds of fires, we have to deal with three-hundred-pound steel disks turning into projectiles, which could easily kill or injure people. Plus, they give off high levels of carbon monoxide, so people are at risk of getting sick or worse from the poisoning.

My firehouse was on Columbus Avenue on the Upper West Side of Manhattan, so when we had incidents like this, we had to clear out multiple high-rise buildings filled with thousands of people. In order to put out the fire, we needed to cut the power, but in order to cut the power, we had to get the buildings evacuated first or the elevators wouldn't work. Despite the risk, people are *never* happy about having to evacuate and they tend to take their time doing it. These incidents take several companies and dozens of firefighters out of commission for hours.

I was a lieutenant in Engine 11 (E11) and, as an engine

179

company, our job was to put the fire out, so for three hours we camped out next to a flaming manhole, dousing it with water every so often. Definitely one of the more boring parts of the job. Lots of standing around and waiting all while citizens complained about road closures, traffic, and having to leave their homes, offices, or hotels.

As we were re-packing the hoses onto the rig, a woman shouted to get my attention. "Hey, there's some guy who needs help over here."

I pointed to one of my men. "Draper, with me for a med assist." We followed the woman down a side street and into an alley where there was a guy precariously wobbling on the ledge outside a third-story window. I hit the transmit button on my radio. "Dispatch, this is E11 I've got an EDP on a building ledge near the 10-25 we were covering. Is there still a ladder company on scene?"

"Standby E11."

I looked up at the guy. "Hey, man. What are you doing up there?"

Catching sight of me, he hollered, "Oh, you a hero! Me, too. We both heroes." *He has to be on something.*

"Yeah? Why are you a hero?"

"Can't say. Is a secret," he slurred.

My radio squelched and the dispatcher said, "L64 is on its way to you E11."

"10-4," I acknowledged. Ladder 64 was my brother Dylan's company, but he wasn't working that day. We often went on runs together since we were both on the Upper West Side. "Draper, go to the street and flag them down," I ordered before turning my attention back to the guy. "So you're a secret hero?"

"Yeah, dawg. I'm a superhero."

I got back on my radio. "E11 to dispatch. Can you also roll an ambulance to our location?" The likelihood of me talking the emotionally disturbed person (EDP) down would be slim since he was clearly hallucinating. This would end one of two ways. The ladder company would manage to get him down or he would fall. Either way, he needed to go to the hospital.

"10-4, E11."

"A superhero, huh?"

He laughed maniacally. "Wanna see?"

"No. You don't want to show me your powers then it won't be secret anymore."

"You right, you right."

Dodged a bullet there. I figured since he was dangling on what appeared to be a ten-inch wide decorative ledge that somewhere in his mind he thought he could fly.

"Since we're both heroes, though, I'd love to talk to you about how maybe we can work together," I said in an effort to build rapport and trust so that when we tried to grab for him he'd be more willing.

"You want me to work with you?"

"Sure, man."

"A'ight, dawg. Yeah we can do that."

The ladder truck pulled up and I heard the scraping of metal as they retrieved a ladder from the back. I shouted up to the guy. "My name is Kyle. What's yours?"

"Spiderman."

Ah, hell. Well, I was right about the flying.

"Spiderman, one of my friends is going to come up and talk to you, okay? He's cool. He's a hero, too."

Two guys from L64 carried a thirty-five foot extension ladder in my direction. I put my hand up signaling for them to stop.

Spiderman spotted them and shouted, "Need help? You gotta rescue someone?"

"Spiderman, those are my friends. They want to come up and talk to you, but they need a ladder because they don't have superpowers." I waved the guys over.

One of them, who I recognized as Keith Hart asked,

"Where do you want us, Lieutenant Hogan?"

I pointed to the left of the ledge. "Put it up there. I'll keep talking to him."

Spiderman said, "Nah, dawg, I'll come down and talk." He lifted his hand like he was going to shoot out a spider web.

"No," I shouted, but he ignored me and lurched off the building.

We all hopped back to get out of the way, then there was the tell-tale splat of a body hitting pavement. I squeezed my eyes shut and mentally prepared myself for the carnage. I knelt by his side and he laughed.

How the hell did he survive a thirty-foot fall? "Draper, where's the med kit?"

"It's on the rig, Lieutenant."

"Go fucking get it," I snapped.

While he ran back to the engine, I did a quick evaluation of the patient. He'd shattered both legs and had multiple compound fractures where the bones poked through the skin. He was also gurgling blood. I got on my radio, "Dispatch, we've got a 10-45 code 2." That let them know we had a life-threatening injury. "Spiderman, why'd you do that? We were going to come up."

"I like to fly, dawg. Web must a missed."

Draper returned with the other guys in our company along with a backboard. As an engine company, we also responded to medical calls so we had equipment on our rig, and we were all required to be Certified First Responders (CFRs) that way we could properly care for a patient before the EMT/Paramedics arrived on the ambulance.

"Eger, stabilize his head," I directed one of my guys. He pulled on medical gloves, got on his knees behind the guy's head and positioned his hands to hold it still so we could get a cervical collar on the patient.

I pulled a pair of blue medical gloves out of the med kit for myself and unwrapped a collar before guiding it around his

neck. The man kept trying to move, which made things difficult. "Spiderman, I need you to stay still." It was unbelievable
that he didn't seem to be in any pain. "Can you tell me what
you took?"

He chuckled, coughing up blood.

I patted his pockets and found a bag with a yellowish-white
powder. "Did you do bath salts, Spiderman?" I held up
the bag.

"That's mine," he lurched, but we managed to hold him
down.

Thankfully, the ambulance arrived and the medics took
over, so we headed back to the rig. I pulled Draper aside.
"When I say we're going for a med assist, what do I mean?"

"Um, medical assistance?"

"Is that a fucking question, Draper?"

He straightened his back and stood like I'd ordered him to
attention. "No, Lieutenant."

"And what do you think we need for a *medical* assist?"

I saw his jaw tick. "The medical bag."

"Damn, right. So why didn't you grab it when I told you
where we were going?"

"I'm sorry, Lieutenant."

"Sorry wouldn't cut it if we were going to an imminent
emergency and you had to waste time running back to the rig,
now would it?"

"Won't happen again."

"Better not." I turned my back and opened the front
passenger door to my officer's seat.

We got back on our rig and returned to quarters. Because
we'd gotten called out for the manhole fire as we were about to
sit down for lunch, we were all starving. As we were backing
into the firehouse, we got called out on another run.

The guys grumbled in the back.

"You signed up for this shit," I reminded them, as we
zoomed down the block.

. . .

The cold lager was exactly what I needed after the twenty-four hour shift I'd had. I reclined on the chair in my brother's living room as I sipped from the amber bottle, feeling some of the stress evaporate. Every once in a while, I stopped by Dylan's apartment for a beer after work since he lived close to my fire house. This was one of those nights that called for it.

My sister-in-law, Autumn, was cuddled up on the couch with her cat on her lap and Dylan had his arm around her. They were disgustingly perfect for each other. Sure, I was happy for my little brother, but I could only handle so much of the love before it made me want to poke my own eyes out. All of my brothers were happily paired off. Dylan had gotten married that summer, Jesse and Lana's wedding was in the spring, and I knew it was only a matter of time before Ryan asked Zoe to marry him.

Again, stoked for them, because I loved my brothers, but I found my limit getting lower and lower every time we were all together. Love was more damn pain than it was worth, and I hoped my brothers would never have to experience that heartache. Their women were cool, and they were all well-matched, but sometimes even being perfect for each other wasn't enough. Love wasn't always enough.

Autumn looked up from her phone. "Jace and Britt are back from Vegas and they want to stop by." Jace was Dylan's best friend. They both worked together at Ladder 64 and Britt was Autumn's best friend from college. The two of them had started dating after Dylan and Autumn's wedding.

"Cool." Dylan took a sip of his beer.

I nodded. Just what I wanted; another happy couple to hang out with. While I'd thought Ryan settling down had been shocking, finding out that Jace Palmer was serious about a girl had damn near floored me. He was as big a playboy as they'd come.

"They're in a cab and should be here soon," Autumn added.

I remembered Autumn's best friend Britt from the wedding. Had to give it to her, she was fun. If I really thought about it, it wasn't all that surprising that she and Jace had shacked up. I grabbed a handful of popcorn from the bowl on the coffee table and tossed it back in one bite.

"What the hell was that ref?" Dylan shouted at the television.

Sunday nights were for football and hockey. Dylan had a massive TV that was perfect for watching the games. There was even a split screen feature so we could watch two channels at the same time. Super clutch. Toronto was facing off against St. Louis, and while I wasn't particularly invested in either hockey team, I was still all about it. I missed my hockey days.

For football, it was still early in the season, but Dallas was crushing our New York team, which was exactly why Dylan was giving the ref an earful as though the guy could actually hear him. Autumn wasn't all that interested in sports, but she made an effort because Dylan liked it. She was cute like that.

When they broke for commercial, Dylan went to get us another round of beers. Just as he handed me mine, there was a knock at the door.

"It's open," Dylan shouted.

Jace and Britt let themselves in. They were practically skipping from new relationship bliss.

Fuck me.

They squeezed into the chair and a half that bookended the other side of the couch, opposite me.

"How was Vegas?" Autumn asked.

"Amazing"

"Incredible"

They spoke over each other, seeming a little too happy.

We all narrowed our eyes at them.

Autumn said, "Spill it, sister. I haven't seen you smile like that since," she paused looking to be in serious thought. "Ever."

185

Jace and Britt glanced at each other and giggled. Like fucking schoolchildren. Then, they held up their left hands, each of which sported silver bands on a very significant finger. In unison, they announced, "We eloped!" And then he kissed her like they were alone in the room.

They might as well have been, given how deathly quiet the three of us were. The pit in my stomach that had been growing larger ever since my brothers started settling down made its presence known with a twist. I winced.

They finally came up for air.

Autumn pointed at them. "You're messing with us."

Britt shook her head. "Nope. Jace proposed and I said yes."

Jace added, "Then we found ourselves a wedding chapel on the strip and made it happen."

Autumn pounced to her feet and jumped up and down. Britt met her mid-air and they hugged each other while they squealed at a decibel that I never needed to hear again.

Dylan stepped over the coffee table and wrapped an arm around Jace. "Congrats, brother."

I got up for the obligatory congratulations as well. "You're a crazy SOB, Palmer."

He bumped my outstretched fist. "It's all her, man. She does things to me that make no damn sense, but I've never been so happy."

My stomach gave another twist. "This calls for champagne. I'll run to the liquor store and get some."

"Great idea. Thanks," Dylan replied.

I was out the door within seconds and once it closed, I pressed my back against the wall in the hallway and sighed. Even Jace Palmer got his happily ever after. *What the hell?*

I rode the elevator down and took some much-needed breaths of fresh air once I was out on the sidewalk. I couldn't get out of that apartment fast enough and I was proud of myself for coming up with an excuse to leave as quickly as I had. After pulling my phone from my pocket, I typed *liquor store* into my GPS and walked the three blocks to my destination.

I was half tempted to stop at each bar I passed on the way to get a shot of Irish whiskey, but I resisted the urge. Stumbling back to Dylan's apartment wouldn't be a good look. I told myself that if I still felt like I needed a shot on my walk back, then I'd stop for one. Just one.

The bell jingled when I opened the door to the liquor store and I raised my chin at the guy behind the counter before going in search of the champagne. Foil tops poked out two aisles down, so I made my way over there, assuming that they were champagne. As I turned down the aisle, my eyes caught sight of a familiar head of chocolate-colored hair and my feet froze to the tile.

As involuntarily as my breath, her name slipped out of my mouth, "Allie?"

She glanced up from the chardonnays and her bronze eyes widened as she turned toward me. The bottle she was holding slipped from her hand and her foot broke its fall, preventing it from shattering. It had to have hurt, but she didn't even flinch. She simply stared at me with her mouth agape as the bottle rolled under the shelf.

My blood drained to my feet as every last feeling I'd had for her since we were four came rushing back like they'd never left. Sixteen years ago. When she did.

I didn't know if I should run away and scream, or run to her and pull her into my arms.

I wanted to do both, so I didn't do either.

We stood in the wine aisle, neither of us making a move beyond staring in silence.

I was ten feet from the one that got away, and the sight of her told me what my heart already knew: she may have gotten away, but I had never let her go.

28
_____

ALLIE

*I*nstantly, my palms began to sweat and a chill ran up my spine. *This can't be happening.* I'd been living in Manhattan for a month and out of the three million people who crammed onto that island on a daily basis, I somehow managed to enter the same liquor store as the one person I'd hoped to never see again. Life could be cruel.

I glanced up and turned toward him. My mouth hung open, but I struggled to come up with words. Kyle Hogan. My childhood best friend who I'd selfishly abandoned sixteen-years before. The wine bottle fell from my hand and hit my foot, but the pain hardly registered.

In many ways, he looked the same. He was still a big, muscular guy with those captivating crystal blue irises. His hair was cropped short in a military style and he had lines around his eyes that showed every one of his thirty-four-years.

I fought the urge to run into his arms and tell him how much I'd missed him and how sorry I was because certainly he hated me. "Kyle," I managed to choke out. "Hi."

He blinked several times as though he was trying to figure out if I was an apparition. I was having the same thought. As I stared into his eyes, I got a glimpse of what was beneath his

Burning for You

rugged exterior, and I saw the boy who'd loved me in our youth. He was my biggest *what if?* in life. The boy who might have been my forever…if only…

"Allie," he repeated.

"H-how are you?" I asked. It was a platitude I almost immediately regretted.

He shrugged. "What are you doing here?"

"I, um, I live here."

"Oh." There was a tinge of hurt in his tone. He folded his arms across his chest. My gaze dropped to his biceps, which swelled beneath the hem of his t-shirt sleeves. He'd managed to get even more muscular than he'd been at eighteen.

"I moved back from Michigan a few weeks ago."

He nodded. "I see."

Yup, he definitely hates me.

I pointed to the emblem on his shirt. "So you're a fireman?"

He nodded. "Lieutenant."

I smiled. "That's great."

"Yeah." He took a couple steps forward. "You living around here?"

I hooked my thumbs in the belt loops of my jeans. "Two blocks away. You?"

"I own a house in New Rochelle, but I work on Columbus Ave."

An entire island and I picked an apartment right by Kyle's station. *Fucking life.* "Oh, so did you just finish work then?"

"Earlier. Dylan lives around here, so I was at his place."

Fucking life times two. "Yeah? How's he doing."

"Good. He got married this past June."

I grinned. "That's great." It was weird to imagine the sixteen year old boy I knew being all grown up and married.

"Yeah. His firehouse is in this area, too."

Of course it is. "So, you're both firemen?"

He nodded. "Jesse and Ryan, too."

My brows arched. "All four of you?"

189

He nodded.

"Wow, that's wonderful, Kyle."

He stared at me and as uncomfortable as it was, I couldn't look away. There was a heavily guarded pain in his eyes that I recognized because I saw the same distant emptiness in my own when I looked in a mirror.

I bit my lip and his gaze dropped to my mouth.

"Allie..." his voice trailed off, but that one word—my name —said a million things. He wanted answers, and I couldn't blame him for that, but I wouldn't put him through that pain. I'd carried the burden on my own for close to two decades and I was content with my decision to shield him from that.

I swallowed.

He sighed.

I held my breath.

He said, "It's nice to see you. You look great."

Trying not to dwell on the fact that I was in my gym clothes, I exhaled. "Thanks. So do you." I had to get out of there. "I, um, I've gotta go, but it was good to see you, too."

He reached into his back pocket and retrieved his wallet, pulling out a business card. "I'd love to get together and catch up." He extended the card to me. "If you want."

When I took the card, my finger brushed against his and we both flinched. His card had the FDNY emblem on front with *Lieutenant Kyle Hogan* imprinted in the middle. I grinned with pride over his success. "Sure."

"My cell is on the back."

I flipped it over to find the numbers scrawled across the back in his familiar abysmal handwriting.

He stepped back. "I hope to see you soon, Allie."

I nodded and began to walk down the aisle toward the door.

He stopped me. "You're forgetting your wine."

I spun around to see him holding the bottle I'd dropped, so I went back to him. "Oh, right."

He held out the bottle and I noticed there was no wedding ring on his finger. I reached for the other end and both of us held on for a few seconds too long. My heart raced from the sensation of being near him again after all this time. He let go and stepped back.

"Thanks."

"You're welcome."

I clutched the chardonnay to my chest and scurried to the register where I paid for my wine before high-tailing it out the door. The entire walk home, I wondered if that encounter had really happened or if I'd been daydreaming. Seeing Kyle again was surreal, to say the least. There had been so many times over the years where I'd come close to contacting him, but I'd always chickened out because I was embarrassed about how I'd behaved. Plus, after disappearing the way that I had, I figured he'd never take my call. Months turned into years turned into a decade and a half.

I'd moved on. Gotten married. Gotten divorced. But the memory of Kyle was always in the back of my mind. I'd thought of him often and wondered how his life had turned out. I couldn't dwell on it long though before the familiar sense of self-loathing kicked in.

Back at home, in my tiny one-bedroom apartment, I put the wine in the fridge, having lost the craving, and curled up on my living room couch. I squeezed my eyes closed and repeated the mantra that my therapist had practically beat into me. "I am enough. I am enough. I am enough." Eventually, I fell asleep.

My mother had invited me for lunch on Saturday, so I drove up to Mamaroneck to the house she shared with her new husband. Well, not exactly new. They'd been married twelve years. Since I'd moved to Michigan, I'd only been back to my hometown maybe ten to fifteen times. My ex-husband, Kevin, wasn't big on New York so we'd mostly stayed in Michigan, which is where he'd grown up.

Mom's husband, Jerry, had two kids of his own. One was in college in Florida and the other was some tech genius in Silicon Valley, so it was just the three of us. Mom wanted to go to the Farmer's Market, so we drove to the parking lot on the beach where the market was held every Saturday. The last time I'd been there had been the night Kyle had told me he'd been in love with me. I rubbed my lips together as I got out of the car.

While Mom got lost in conversation with one of the bakers, I wandered. There were various pop-up tents housing all sorts of makers. Most of the items were food, but there were a few artists selling their wares, as well. I stopped to look at a pair of dangly earrings.

"Allie Dupree?"

I spun around to the smiling face of Ann Hogan. "Mrs. H?"

She held her arms open. "Well don't just stand there. Come give me a hug."

So I did and it felt damn good. When I'd left for Michigan, I hadn't just lost Kyle, I'd lost my family in the Hogans. "It's great to see you, Mrs. H."

She pulled away. "Please, dear, you can call me Ann now. I'm no longer your principal." She had quite a few more wrinkles than I'd remembered, but there was a comforting familiarity in her iconic blue eyes that she'd passed on to her boys.

I grinned. "How are you?"

She tucked her fabulous silver hair behind her ear. "I'm well. Retired. Enjoying life."

"I bet."

"Are you here visiting your mom?"

I nodded. "For the day, yes. I actually moved back to New York. I'm living in Manhattan."

"No kidding. What are you doing there?"

"I'm a kindergarten teacher."

She beamed. "That's wonderful, dear. And your husband? I remember your mother mentioning that you'd gotten married."

I shifted my weight on my feet. "Divorced, actually."

"Well, I'm sorry to hear that. Do you have children?"

I winced. "That's okay. It was for the best. And no, I don't."

There was pity in her eyes. "I would've thought you'd have fifteen little ones by now. I remember when you kids were little and you used to play with my boys. You were always so wonderful with them." Ann smiled. "It's no wonder you're a kindergarten teacher."

I gave her my standard response for whenever the subject arose. "It's the perfect way to get my kid fix, but then I can send them home to their parents for the tantrums while I enjoy a glass of wine and some peace and quiet."

Like everyone always did, she laughed. "The best of both worlds."

"It is," I agreed, despite the fact that I would've cut off my own leg if it meant I'd been able to have children of my own.

A forlorn look filled her eyes. "You've been missed, Allie."

I knew full well she hadn't been referring to just herself, but I played dumb. "I've missed you, too. Mrs. H. I mean, Ann." Her name felt weird to say.

She sighed. "I know you're seeing your mom today, but if you're free next Saturday, I'd love to have you over for dinner. Take pity on this retired widow. " She winked. "I'd enjoy the pleasure of your company."

I swallowed the lump in my throat. "Sounds great. I'll be there."

"Splendid. I trust you still know how to find my house."

"Blindfolded and barefoot," I jested.

She "grinned. Five o'clock?"

"I'll see you then."

She gave me a goodbye hug and went on her way.

I'd surprised myself by agreeing to dinner, but seeing Mrs.

H again made me happy and I hadn't felt that in a very long time.

"Oh, and Allie?"

I spun around. "Yes?"

"He never married." Her knowing eyes stared at me for a beat before turning away in search of fresh apple cider from the orchard vendor.

I stood in the middle of the row watching her weave through the crowd. Unsure of what to make of her statement, I sighed. I thought back to the previous weekend when I'd run into him at the liquor store. Several times throughout the week, I'd tried to text him, but I could never bring myself to hit send. He'd said he wanted to get together and catch up, which a part of me wanted to do as well, but there was a bigger part of me that didn't want to dredge up the past. More than anything, I wanted to believe that Kyle had gone on to live this amazing life with the family and the career he deserved because if he didn't, then my protecting him would have been for nothing.

29

KYLE

I flipped the burgers and closed the lid on the grill, then reached for my beer and took a sip. We were having an impromptu lunch at my mom's. Since it was a Monday, Autumn was at work and Zoe was on shift at the hospital, but everyone else was there. It'd been a while since we'd had a family meal that was just the boys. Well, Jesse's fiancée, Lana, was there, too, but she was basically one of the guys. Plus, she brought the beer since she owned a brewery, so she was always welcome. We tried to do a family meal every week, but it was tough with our schedules. In the FDNY, we were constantly rotating shifts, but when we were all off, we tried to schedule family time. It meant a lot to Mom.

Dylan joined me on the patio. "You okay, bro?"

"Yeah. Should be done in about five minutes."

"Good because I'm starving, but that's not what I meant."

I cocked my head. "What did you mean?" I hadn't seen him since the previous week when I'd run out to the liquor store and had never come back.

"The way you disappeared the other night. Just wanted to make sure all was good."

"Fine." I brought the bottle to my lips to cover my lie.

"What was the deal the other night then?"

"Told you. I ran into someone." After seeing Allie, I'd gone straight home. There'd been no way I could've put on a face and pulled it off like my world hadn't just been shook if I'd gone back to Dylan's.

He perched on the edge of the table. "Right. But it's not like you to just bail like that."

"Sorry. She was prettier than you."

He raised a brow. "The someone you ran into was a she?"

I ran my hand over the stubble on my jaw. "Yeah."

He grinned. "No shit."

Ryan came outside with the buns. "No shit, what?"

"Kyle ditched me last weekend for a woman."

Ryan placed the buns down on the ledge beside the grill. "No shit is right."

"Don't be idiots. I date." I used that term very loosely. On occasion, when the urge struck, I'd take a woman out before taking her home. I hadn't had a girlfriend since college and even that hadn't been all that serious. As I got older, the women who were still single were looking for something serious and I'd lost my desire to get married a long time ago, so I stopped dating. It worked for me.

They both laughed like assholes.

Jesse slid open the door and stuck his head out. "Ma, wants to know how long—what's so funny?" He stepped onto the patio.

I shook my head as I took another swig of my beer.

"Kyle says he dates," Ryan said with a smirk.

"Oh, yeah?" Jesse returned with a smirk of his own.

I looked from one to the other and back again. "What's going on?" They were up to something.

Jesse pulled out his phone. "Glad to hear you're finally putting yourself on the market."

I pursed my lips.

Jesse continued, "Because we made you a dating profile

and you are very popular, bro." He turned his phone so I could see. Sure as shit there was a photo of me in my tux at Dylan's wedding right next to the heading: *Kyle, 34, New Rochelle, NY, Firefighter.*

"You did what?" I asked for clarification, because surely my brothers weren't that stupid, as I reached for the phone, but he snapped it back.

"You've got quite a few matches."

My jaw clenched. "You son of a bitch."

Ryan said, "Don't be mad. This is a good thing."

"How the hell do you figure?"

"You just said you're dating. Think of this as our way of helping," he replied.

"I don't fucking need help. Delete that shit."

"Sorry, bro, but my wedding is this spring," Jesse said as he swiped his finger across the screen. "Maybe if you start now, you'll have a date for it."

Dylan was laughing his ass off, hovering over Jesse's shoulder along with Ryan.

"That one. Yes." Ryan pointed to the screen.

I opened the grill and tossed the buns on. "You've got until the burgers are done to delete that crap."

"I wouldn't be so hasty, Kyle. Some of these women are pretty cute," Dylan responded.

I wasn't the online dating type. If my hand wasn't doing it for me, I'd go to a bar and wait for an opportunity to present itself. Afterward, we'd both go our separate ways. It worked for me. No expectations. No drama. No risk.

"Yeah, check this one out." Jesse turned his phone toward me.

I had to admit, the blonde was cute, but she was on a dating site, which meant she was likely looking for something I couldn't give her. "Not happening." I'd done my lone wolf routine for too many years to change it.

Jesse's phone made an obnoxious musical ding. "Oh shit. You matched."

I opened the buns on the platter and topped them with the patties. "That better not mean what I think it does."

The phone dinged again.

"She thinks you're cute," Ryan announced.

My jaw ticked again.

"Pull up her profile," Dylan instructed. Then, he read over Jesse's shoulder. "Her name is Skye. She's twenty-nine, lives in White Plains, and she's in sales."

"That's not a name, it's a thing." I turned off the grill, picked up the platter, and went inside while Dylan was reading off something about Jamaica being Skye's favorite vacation spot.

Mom and Lana were already at the table when I placed the burgers down in the middle and took my seat. My brothers followed closely behind. A vibration in my pocket drew my attention, so I checked it. Ever since I'd given Allie my number, I found myself going back to my old habit of desperately waiting for her to call. I hated myself for it, but it was out of my control. When I'd given her my card, I'd been afraid this would happen, but after all these years, I couldn't have just let her leave.

I was disappointed when Jesse's name was displayed on the screen. He'd texted me a photo of Skye along with what I assumed was her phone number and the words: *CALL HER.* I shoved the device back into my pocket.

Jesse swung his arm around his fiancée and gave me a smug grin. Ignoring him, I reached for a burger.

"So, yeah. I'm this close to eloping," Lana said to my mom, clearly continuing a conversation they'd been having before we'd come in.

"Just tell me when, beautiful," Jesse said.

I bit into my burger. The last thing I wanted to talk about

was weddings or dating because I was trying *not* to think about Allie.

Lana sighed. "I know, but I really want a wedding, too. I just want it to be *my* wedding and not my mother's." She took a sip of her beer and then corrected, "I mean our wedding."

Jesse kissed her forehead. "It will be. When she's here visiting in a few weeks we'll make that clear to her."

"Speaking of visiting," my mom interjected. "You're never going to believe who I ran into at the Farmer's Market on Saturday."

"Martha Stewart?" Dylan guessed.

"No, not this time." She gave me a pointed look and I knew who she was going to say before she said it. "Allie Dupree."

All eyes went to me but Lana's. I must've disappointed them though because I didn't look shocked.

Lana asked, "Who's that?"

"An old friend," I tried to play it off like I wasn't considering catapulting from my chair to my car.

Really digging in the knife, Jesse added, "She was practically our sister. Then she went off to college and we never heard from her again."

"Really? Why?" Lana asked.

He shrugged and said, "No idea." He looked at me.

Before my brothers could get on me about that—again—Mom continued, "She was up here visiting her mother, but she lives in Manhattan now."

"No way," Dylan commented. "How is she?"

"She looked great and she's a kindergarten teacher."

"Huh," Ryan said, "I can see that."

So could I. She'd always been great with kids. Having suddenly lost my appetite, I put my burger down on the plate.

"Yeah, I can, too," Jesse added.

Mom stirred her iced tea with her straw as she looked right at me and casually mentioned, "She's divorced."

About ten years ago, I'd heard she'd gotten married. I'd

taken vacation days from work and had gone on a bender while holed up in my house for nine days straight. Not one for losing control, it had been extremely unlike me, but I'd learned over the years that when it came to Allie, all bets were off.

I reached for my beer. "That's unfortunate." At my core, I wanted her to be happy. That's all I'd ever wanted.

Mom added, "I don't think so. She said it was for the best."

I ran my tongue over my teeth.

Autumn's keen perceptive abilities must have been rubbing off on Dylan because the way he looked at me with his lips parted and his eyes wide, it appeared as though he'd just figured something out. To his credit, he stayed quiet about it.

"Well, good for her," I said as I got up from the table. "Excuse me a minute." I went down the hall to the bathroom, put the lid down on the toilet so I could sit, and hung my head in my hands. No matter how hard I'd tried to shake Allie over the years, I couldn't. I'd love her until the day I die.

30

ALLIE

*W*hile waiting for my class to arrive on Wednesday I sat at my desk, staring at my phone. My message screen was open with Kyle's name across the top banner. The cursor blinked in the empty box. There'd been several failed attempts to reach out to him ever since I'd seen Mrs. H that past weekend. Her words had been echoing in my head non-stop: *He never married.*

I suppose some might hear that and take it at face value, but I knew better. His mom wouldn't have told me that if it hadn't had a deeper meaning. What she'd really been saying was: *He never married because he wanted you.* It broke my heart because for a long time I'd wrestled with that myself. I closed my eyes and sighed. After losing his baby, I'd fallen down a deep, dark hole and by the time I got out of it, it was too late.

Seeing him again had been a shock to my system. Physically, my body reacted...positively, because good lord did he age well. Emotionally, it stirred up all sorts of feelings that I'd tried to keep buried deep. The most overwhelmingly confusing part though was that even though I knew I should stay away, I wanted to see him. I wanted to explain. I wanted to apologize and beg for his forgiveness. I wanted him back in my life. But I didn't deserve that.

"Hi, Ms. Pierce." The first little face bounced into my classroom. Being a divorced teacher was a daily reminder of my failure. One day, I'd get around to changing my name back. I put my phone away, another message left unwritten, and plastered on a smile.

We usually started the day with group reading, but we were having a special guest for reading time that day and he wouldn't be there until later, so we started with math. At ten o'clock, right on schedule, there was a knock on our classroom door. When I opened it, I nearly fell over.

It was Fire Prevention Week and Hot Dog the Dalmatian, who was the FDNY's fire safety mascot, was visiting each kindergarten class with a firefighter to read a story about fire prevention. My kids all squealed upon seeing the guy in the big Dalmatian costume, but I stood there like an idiot staring at the firefighter who'd come with him.

"Um, hi." Kyle glanced down at the paper in his hands. "Sorry, I'm looking for Ms. Pierce's class."

I nodded. "That's me."

"Oh."

"Ms. Pierce, Ms. Pierce is the doggy our special guest?" Ariella, one of my students asked, snapping me back into teacher mode.

I stepped aside to let them into my classroom and grinned broadly at my students as I mustered up as much excitement as I could despite the fact that my insides were twisted up in knots. "Okay, class. I want you to meet Hot Dog and his friend Lieutenant Hogan. They're here to read you a story about fire safety." I gestured to our reading corner and the kids scattered from their desks onto the floor by the big reading chair. I turned to Kyle. "What do you need from me?"

His smile lit up his face and I nearly melted into a puddle. "Do you have the book for us?"

"Yes. Right. Of course." I flitted about my desk like a flustered fool, finally finding it under the math workbook. I handed it to Kyle. "Here you go."

"Thanks." He escorted the guy in the Dalmatian suit to the reading corner, then addressed my class. "As Ms. Pierce said, I'm Lieutenant Hogan and this is my friend Hot Dog. We're going to read you a story about fire safety, sound good?"

The class erupted in a chorus of excited agreement.

While Kyle read the story about a Dalmatian family making their house fire safe with smoke detectors, creating an escape plan, and having a fire drill, I watched him transform from a man in his thirties who was a virtual stranger, into the boy I'd loved in my youth. Being the oldest brother, Kyle had always been a natural with children. He did the voices, made the kids laugh, and miraculously kept the attention of a bunch of five year olds for seven minutes.

Suddenly, another meaning behind what his mother had said hit me. If Kyle had never married, he likely hadn't had children, which was a damn shame because he'd make a great dad. That had been one reason I'd stayed away. I'd wanted that for him. The sadness gripped me. Hard.

I am enough. I am enough. I am enough.

"Ms. Pierce would you come help demonstrate stop, drop, and roll?" Kyle asked.

I felt like I'd been caught sleeping in class. "Sure." I stepped around the children to get to the reading corner.

I stood next to Kyle and waited for my instructions, but he never gave them to me, he just started speaking. "Oh, no, Ms. Pierce your clothes are on fire! Class what should she do first?"

"Stop!" they shouted.

Since I hadn't been moving, I did a little hop and then froze.

"Now what?" he asked.

"Drop!"

Immediately regretting wearing a skirt that day, I daintily got down on my stomach.

"Is she done, class?"

"No!"

"What should she do?"

"Roll!"

And so I did. Right into Kyle's feet. *Real graceful, Allie.*

Everyone giggled and wanted to try the procedure so they went through the movements as a class, which got out of hand real quick. I clapped twice as I chanted, "Silly silly."

The class clapped back and chanted "Quiet quiet." Then they returned to their spots.

Kyle grinned. "I'm gonna have to remember that for the firehouse." He winked.

I blushed.

After taking a class photo with our guests, I said, "Let's say thank you to Hot Dog and the lieutenant for coming to visit with us today and teach us about fire safety."

It was like a competition on who could say, "Thank you," the loudest.

I walked them to the door. Kyle hesitated for a moment, but with twenty nosy eyes and ears on us, the timing for a conversation wasn't optimal.

"Thanks again," I said.

"Thanks for having us."

The guy in the Dalmatian costume held his paw out for me to shake, so I did. Then Kyle did the same. My eyes lingered on his outstretched hand for a moment before I grasped it, feeling the sensation all the way in my toes. I don't think Kyle and I had ever shaken hands and I tilted forward a smidge on instinct like I was going in for a hug, but then I came to my senses and let go as I took three steps back.

And then they were gone.

. . .

When school finished, I walked to my gym for the Pilates class. After my divorce, I'd put on more than a few pounds, so I was religious about going to that class four times a week. I had twelve pounds left to shed to get to my goal weight. My ex-husband, on the other hand, got into the best shape of his life once we'd broken up. He'd met a woman ten years younger than me, knocked her up, and married her. Yeah...

I walked home after class to get more exercise in and then I took my time in the shower. My fingers lingered over the faint scars on my abdomen. Most people might not notice them, but I'd never not be able to see them. They were a constant reminder of how much I'd screwed up. How much I'd lost.

I wrapped myself in a robe and went to the kitchen to pour myself a glass of wine before making myself comfortable on the couch. I opened the messenger on my phone, pulled up his name, and typed.

Allie: That was quite the surprise today. My students really enjoyed it. Thanks.

I stared at the screen. Then I deleted it all.

Allie: It was good to see you today. My students wouldn't stop talking about your visit and honestly I haven't stopped thinking about it.

Delete.

Allie: I'm sorry it's taken me this long, but I'm apparently illiterate when it comes to writing you a damn text message.

Delete.

I sighed and leaned my head back. Of all the firefighters that could've come to my class that day, I'd got Kyle. What are the odds of that? It had to be some sort of sign. First, I run into him at a random store, then I see his mom, and then he shows up at my classroom. No way that's a mere coincidence. While I couldn't say I was a believer in fate, this message was hard to deny.

Allie: I miss you.

Send.

31

KYLE

*J*esse had called to tell me that he was in the city and he wanted to meet up with Dylan and me for dinner. Jesse worked in Brooklyn and lived in Long Beach, which was on the south shore of Long Island, an hour away from my house. Sometimes, we'd meet in the city because it was a good mid-point. Ryan lived and worked in Queens and he was on the roster that night, so he couldn't join us. I'd tried to turn the invite down, because I was feeling rather depressed after seeing Allie that morning, but Jesse was particularly insistent. That should've been my first clue that he was up to something.

When I was about to leave my house, my phone buzzed and I got a text message from a number with an area code that I didn't recognize. It simply read, *I miss you*. Whoever it was obviously had the wrong number so I slipped the phone into my pocket and headed out the door.

I parked at the restaurant, which wasn't far from where I worked, and thought for sure I had the wrong place. I double checked the text my brother had sent and it was definitely the right spot, but it was posher than our usual tavern-style haunt. That should've been my second clue. When I went inside, I told the hostess that we had a reservation under Hogan and she showed me to the table, which was set for two—not three. I took out my phone and keyed up the group message with Jesse and Dylan.

Kyle: Did one of you fuckers cancel?

I'd be pissed if they did when I'd been chastised for not wanting to go.

Jesse: Don't hate me.

My jaw clenched.
"Kyle?"
I looked up into the face of the cute blonde from that damn dating app. I was gonna kill him. Since it wasn't the woman's fault that my brother had duped us both, I did the polite thing and stood to shake her hand. "Uh, hi." I wracked my brain in attempt to recall her name. It was something trendy and ridiculous like Star. I pulled her chair out for her like the gentleman my mom had raised me to be, then said, "I'm very sorry because I know this is rude since you just got here, but I'm dealing with a bit of a family emergency. Can you excuse me for a moment?"
"Absolutely. Take your time."
I weaved through the restaurant to the restrooms in the back. Once there, I scrolled my old messages until I found the one Jesse had sent with the blonde's name. *Skye*. Then I texted the group.

Kyle: You're both dead.
Dylan: For the record, I said it was a bad idea.
Jesse: Give her a chance, Kyle. I think you're gonna like her.
Kyle: DEAD

After taking a piss, I went back out for my ambush date. I'd be nice, but I was going to rush through it as quickly as I could. As I walked by the bar, I did a double take upon noticing the brunette at the end. Allie. *You've got to be fucking kidding me.* My plan changed. When I got back to the table, I told Skye the truth about what my moronic little brother had done. I was mortified. She was embarrassed and left awkwardly after I made sure she had Jesse's phone number for scolding purposes.

I asked the hostess to hold my table while I went up to the bar. After taking a deep breath, I stepped in beside Allie and said, "Would you believe me if I swear I'm not stalking you?" I probably shouldn't have chosen the moment she'd been taking a sip of wine to surprise her because she coughed on it so badly that she had to drink water. "That seemed less creepy in my head."

That got a smile out of her. "What are you doing here?"

"It's a long story, but I've got a table that has a chair with your name on it if you'd like."

She bit her lower lip and I thought for sure she was going to say no, but then she said. "Okay. Just let me settle up with the bartender."

"Don't worry about that." I flagged the guy down. "Could you transfer the lady's tab to my table and can I get a lager on draft?"

"No, Kyle, that's not necess—"

"We can split it up later if that's why you want to argue with me." I had no intention of actually letting her pay for it, but she didn't need to know that.

The guy handed me my beer, then I led Allie to the table and pulled out her chair. As I took my seat across from her, she said, "Umm, Kyle, why is there lipstick on this glass?" She pointed to the water in front of her.

I stifled a laugh. "So, funny story..." I told her about what my brother had done.

Her grin put a huge smile on my face. "I've got to hand it to Jesse. That was clever."

"Oh, you think so, huh? Because I'm gonna strangle the moron." Well, maybe not anymore because his asinine plan had led me to an unintentional date with Allie. If I could call it that. I couldn't take my eyes off her. She had on black leggings and a tunic-style gray-knit sweater. If it was even possible, she'd gotten more beautiful than she'd been when we were younger. Despite the dim lighting, I spotted six sliver strands peppering her chocolate-brown hair and the lines around her eyes and on her forehead all told of a life lived. They also served to remind me just how much of that life I'd missed out on. Hell, we'd been apart more years than we'd been friends. That thought made me sick.

"Cut him some slack. He was trying to help you."

"Because I need help in the dating department, do I?" I regretted the question as soon as it came out of my mouth.

She shrugged. "I don't know."

Of course she didn't.

The waitress came over to take our order. Steak for me. Salmon salad for Allie.

"The girl I knew wouldn't be having salad for dinner."

"That girl had a much faster metabolism." She tilted her wine glass toward me. "We can't all be freaks of nature who get more fit as we age." Her compliment made me smile.

"You're still beautiful, Allie." And I meant it. Sure, she didn't have the body she'd had at eighteen, but she looked good with a little bit more meat on her bones. She looked like a woman. I liked it. A lot.

She took her time sipping on her white wine, then replied, "Thanks."

"So," I changed the subject, "it seems like you've got a great class, Ms. Pierce."

She flinched, but it was so slight that I'd almost missed it. "Yeah, I do. They loved your visit. It was all they wanted to talk about the rest of the day. They must've done stop, drop, and roll at least five more times before dismissal."

I blew past the compliment. "Being a kindergarten teacher suits you."

She shrugged. "I enjoy it. I'd planned to work with older kids, but I accidentally ended up in a kindergarten for my student teaching and it had me hooked."

It saddened me to know I'd missed out on those moments. "You've always been great with kids. Do you have any?" I hadn't heard about it if she had, but it seemed odd to me that she wouldn't.

"No." She pursed her lips and I sensed a story, but I didn't feel comfortable asking her about it. Not anymore. It'd been too long. She adjusted her spoon, lining it up perfectly with the knife on the white table cloth. "How long have you been a lieutenant?" Her abrupt subject change suggested my suspicion had been correct. At least I still had the ability to read her.

"Five years. I've got eleven total on the job."

"And is it everything you'd hoped for?"

"You know what? It is. I love it."

That earned me a smile. "I'm really happy to hear that."

"And I got to play hockey on the FDNY team for a while, so I got both of my dreams."

"No kidding."

Our food arrived and she placed her napkin daintily on her lap. Whatever life she'd been living had refined her. I could tell in her posture and the way that she kept her elbows off the table. Plus, the girl I knew hated wine. Her years in the Midwest had also given her a slight accent. She stretched her a's.

While I had my first bite in my mouth, she said, "I used to watch you play when the Pelham games were on TV."

I stopped chewing and covered my mouth with my hand. "You did?"

She nodded. "Of course."

My knee bounced a few times as I warred with myself over wanting to ask her why she'd disappeared on me. I was simply enjoying her company and I didn't want that to end, so instead, I asked, "So what brought you back to New York? Michigan finally get too cold for you?"

"It really is brutal. I'm not sure how I survived that long." She pushed a cucumber around on her plate. "I got divorced. Although I guess I should've started with I got married and *then* divorced. He'd grown up in Ann Arbor, so his whole family was there. After we split, I had nothing holding me there anymore other than my job and I needed a change."

"I'm sorry, Allie."

She waved me off. "Don't be. It's a good thing." She put a forkful in her mouth.

"So you decided on a familiar change, then?"

She finished chewing and replied, "Not exactly. I also applied to jobs in Boston and Baltimore. I wanted to be back on the east coast because I really missed the ocean, but I also wanted to be in a city, so I threw New York into the mix as well."

"What made you choose here?"

She picked up her wine glass. "Honestly, it paid the best. Divorce isn't cheap."

I nodded. "I work with a guy who's going through a divorce. He bitches about the cost almost every time I see him."

"Yeah, I get why some people stay in shitty marriages because of the financial burden. It was different with me and Kevin, though. He wanted to marry someone else, so..."

Kevin Pierce. I burned the name into my mind. The bitterness in her tone told me that he'd hurt her and I'd be glad to pay him back for that. "Seems like a stand up guy."

She laughed at my sarcasm. "Stellar." She broke off a flake of her salmon and speared it with her fork. "What about you?"

"Uh, well, I was here on an ambush date so there's that."

She laughed again. "And before that?"

I shrugged. "No one special."

She stared into her salad and asked, "Kids?"

"Nope." I'd given up on that dream quite some time ago.

She spun her wine glass on the table by the stem.

"How are your brothers?"

"They're good. Tyler turned the military into a career and became an Army Ranger. He's stationed in Savannah, Georgia but they deploy frequently."

"Wow."

"Yeah. I worry about him pretty much daily, but he loves it and he's obviously good at it. As for Brandon, he stayed in Houston after college and got married. He and his wife have two girls."

"You're an aunt." I grinned.

"I am. How about your brothers? You said Dylan got married, right?"

"He did. His wife, Autumn, is great. Like I said, they live here on the Upper West Side." I took a sip of my beer. "Jesse's engaged to Lana. They're getting married this spring and they live in Long Beach. He's a lieutenant as well. In Brooklyn."

"Both of you made lieutenant? That's amazing."

I nodded. "Yeah, he's damn good at it, too. I'm proud of him." Though I wondered if he knew just how proud I was. "You'd love Lana. She owns a brewery in Island Park called Hop Toddy. She actually brews it, too."

"That's so cool."

"Yeah and it's pretty good."

"What about Ryan?"

He'd always been her favorite.

"He lives and works in Queens. He and his girlfriend, Zoe, have a place in Forest Hills. She's a nurse, but is planning on going to medical school soon."

"It's great that you're all so happy."

I shrugged. Happy wasn't a word I'd use to describe my life.

When we finished eating, I excused myself to go to the restroom, but I actually went to pay the bill in order to avoid having her argue with me over it. She wasn't happy about it when she found out, but she thanked me. I hated for the night to end, especially before I'd had a chance to ask her why she'd cut me out, but it was getting late and I had work early in the morning, plus she had to get some lesson plans done.

"Can I drive you home?" I asked her once we were on the sidewalk.

"I'm only two blocks away. I can walk it. No need for you to fight the traffic in the opposite direction of where you've got to go."

"Let me walk you then." I offered her my arm and prayed like hell that she'd take it.

She did.

I'd desperately missed holding her close.

It took hardly any time at all to get to her apartment, which was in a quaint, four-story brick attached home. She paused at the ornate metal gate and released my arm. "Thank you, Kyle. Tonight was a really wonderful surprise."

I smiled down at her. "Thanks for saying yes."

"Well, good night." She went to open the gate and I had a sinking feeling that this might be my one and only chance, so I had to take it. I couldn't risk her vanishing on me again and never knowing the truth.

I put my hand on top of the gate. "Wait. Allie, what happened back then? Why'd you cut me out?"

She took a deep breath and stared at her door. "Trust me, Kyle, you're better off not knowing." She pushed open the gate and headed up the stoop.

"That's it?" I called after her. "Fourteen years of friendship and that's all I get?"

She fingered her keys. "Know that I'm sorry. I take full responsibility and I've spent every day beating myself up over it ever since." She slipped the key in the door. "Goodbye, Kyle."

She slipped inside before I could say anything else, leaving me standing there alone on the sidewalk with even more questions than I'd had before.

As I drove home, her words replayed in my head. We'd had a very nice night together and it had given me hope that we could at the very least rekindle our friendship, but when she'd said goodbye, I'd gotten this dreadful feeling that it was permanent. The pain and anguish from all those years ago had returned with a vengeance. By the time I got home, I was holding on by a thread. Once inside, I pulled a pillow off the couch and screamed into it at the top of my lungs. Even though I hadn't heard from her in sixteen years, even though I knew she'd gotten married, I'd always held out hope that one day...maybe...

But after that goodbye, I realized she would never be with me. It didn't matter that I'd been in love with her for twenty-years. I finally had to let her go. I eyed the framed photo of us on the bookcase beside my living room fireplace. It was the photo that had been with the letter she'd written me that day she'd left. Despite the passing years, I could never bring myself to get rid of it.

On an impulse, I grabbed the frame and chucked it against the far wall, splintering it into pieces and shattering the glass. I stared down at the wreckage on the floor and muttered, "Now you know how I feel." I shuffled upstairs and collapsed on my bed. Then I did something I hadn't done in years. I cried.

32

ALLIE

*A*ll day I'd been feeling terrible about how I'd left Kyle hanging, but that was a conversation I needed to prepare for in advance. And it certainly wasn't one I'd have on the sidewalk in front of my house. When I hadn't gotten a text back from Kyle the night before, I'd gone to the restaurant to cheer myself up. Running into him had been a happy coincidence, and I'd excused him for not texting me back since he'd been on an ambush date, but I was surprised that I'd made it to three o'clock in the afternoon without hearing from him after how we'd said goodnight. While I recognized that I hadn't left things in an inviting manor, I half expected him to at least send me an angry message.

After dismissing my students, I loaded my bag with the big envelope that contained the handmade cards they'd colored for Kyle and Hot Dog, and I took the subway to Columbus Ave. Finding Kyle's firehouse was easy, but getting into it was another story. I knocked on the door, but no one answered and when I peered through the window, I found it empty. There was a coffee shop across the street so I decided to go wait there until I saw them come back, but before I could cross, the massive red truck came around the corner. When it pulled up, two guys hopped out and blocked traffic so the truck could back into the building.

Once they'd done their job, one of them jogged over to me. "You need something, miss?"

"I'm looking for Kyle Hogan." He'd mentioned that he was working that day.

The guy pointed at a second truck that was pulling up. "He's on the engine."

"Okay, thanks."

He tilted his chin and went inside.

Kyle got out of the passenger's seat and made his way over while the other guys backed the truck in. He looked sexy in his gear with his coat slung over his shoulder and his chest bulging beneath his suspenders. That was the moment I fully understood why women had firefighter fantasies. His expression, however, was cold.

"Allie."

"I'm sorry to just show up like this, but my students made thank you cards for you and Hot Dog." I tugged the envelope out of my bag and handed it to him.

"Thanks."

I took a deep breath. "I also wanted to invite you over to my house for dinner tomorrow night. You were right. You deserve an answer. But it's a long one and it's not going to be an easy conversation, so I think we should—"

"I'll be there."

I nodded. "Thanks. Six o'clock?"

"Sure."

I did something I had no business doing, but I couldn't stop myself. I reached out and hugged him. It was quick and he couldn't hug me back because of the gear he was holding, but when I stepped away he looked a bit less angry. "See you tomorrow," I uttered before scurrying down the block.

I'd woken up so nauseous that day that I'd considered calling in sick. Miraculously, I'd only heaved once during the day, and since I'd been too nervous to eat, nothing came out. I attempted to go to Pilates after school, but I only made it through the first ten minutes before I had to run to the bathroom and dry heave again, so I left and went to the grocery store. Not wasting time, I headed directly to the frozen section and grabbed a pre-made lasagna from the cooler. I'd originally planned on making something nice, but my nerves were firing on all cylinders and I didn't trust myself with a knife.

When I got home, I put the lasagna in the oven and changed into my softest pair of black leggings and my favorite sweatshirt from college. I probably should've dressed to impress, but I was so on edge I needed to get comfort anywhere I could. I cuddled up on the couch and stared at the back of the door for forty-five minutes until the door bell rang. Taking several deep breaths, I shuffled to the intercom and buzzed Kyle in. My apartment was on the second floor, so it didn't take long for him to knock.

After one more breath, I opened it. "Hi."

He looked good in his jeans and the hunter green flannel. "Hey." He smiled.

I stepped to the side, letting him in, then closed the door.

"I brought wine. I think this is the same one you got that night at the store." He placed the chardonnay on my coffee table.

"That's very sweet of you. Thanks. Would you like some?"

"Sure."

I left him in the living room and went down the hall to my efficiency-style kitchen and retrieved two glasses and a corkscrew.

"Allow me." He held his hand out for the corkscrew and I gladly gave it to him.

While he opened it, I placed the two glasses on the table

and sat on the couch. He poured them out and handed me one before joining me on the couch. I thanked him and took a gulp.

Neither of us said anything and I knew that it was on me to do so, but I was terrified. I took another sip.

He put his glass on the table and turned to me, his hands folded in his lap. "Allie, it's just me. Yes, we're older and we've been...estranged, but we used to be able to tell each other anything, remember?"

I gave him a lopsided grin. "I remember." I sighed and fidgeted with my half-empty glass. "When I tell you this, I need you to promise that you'll listen to the whole story before you judge me, okay?"

"I'm not going to judge you and I promise I'll listen."

I'd had two days to prepare how this conversation would go, but I might as well have not bothered because my brain was mush. I took one more sip of my wine before putting it down. "I guess I should start at the beginning."

33

KYLE

*I*n all the years I'd known Allie, and all the things we'd gone through together, I'd never seen her in such a state. It killed me to know that whatever it was she had to tell me had been a big enough deal to still affect her like that all these years later. Suddenly, my nervousness doubled. I'd already been anxious going over there, but mostly I'd been glad that I'd finally be getting answers. Then I'd seen her in her comfortable clothes and with the worry lines on her face and I had immediately become concerned.

"I guess I should start at the beginning." Her knee bobbed up and down, so I put my hand out to steady it. She turned her body toward me and I removed my hand from her leg as she bent one knee and tucked it beneath her. "As I'd said in my letter the morning after we..." She sighed. "I was confused and I needed to distance myself from you to figure it all out. That had nothing to do with you and everything to do with me." She took a breath. "My plan was to spend my first week at school really considering it so that we could then make the best decision for us. But then I had a nightmare roommate and school started and it was really hard and I wasn't sleeping. I won't bore you with all the details, but the next thing I knew, a month had gone by and I woke up one day and decided I was going to get over my shit and call you to beg for forgiveness."

Her gaze went to her hands folded in her lap. "I hadn't been feeling great, but I assumed it was from the stress and then I got what I thought was my period, but halfway through my psych class the pain became excruciating, so I got up to leave. But I collapsed."

Even though it had happened sixteen years ago, my heart lurched.

She bit her lip. "I don't remember much because I was in and out of consciousness, but when I woke up after surgery..." All of a sudden the color drained from her face.

"Allie, you okay?"

Her whole body shook.

I immediately reached for the pulse point on her wrist, but she pulled away and blurted out, "I was pregnant."

My jaw hung slack. *We had a kid?* No way I'd heard her correctly.

But then she said, "It was an ectopic pregnancy and my fallopian tube had ruptured."

My body started going numb.

"They did surgery to remove my tube."

I covered her hands with one of mine. "Oh, Allie."

"I realize now that the pregnancy was never viable, but back then, I was convinced it was my fault I'd lost the baby." She finally looked up at me. "Our baby." Her lip quivered.

I pulled her against my chest and held her like I'd used to do when we were young. "I'm so sorry."

We stayed like that for a while and I tried to process what that had been like for her. She must've been terrified and it killed me that I hadn't been there to help her through it. That she hadn't let me be there...

She pulled away, but kept a hand on my leg and I kept one on hers. She continued. "There's more."

My stomach turned over.

"While the doctor was performing my surgery, she found out that I have endometriosis, which explains why I've always had such terrible uterine pain."

Shit.

Her lips pressed bitterly into a hard line. "So there I was in the hospital bed, after living through one of the most stressful months of my entire life, being told that I had been pregnant, lost the baby, lost my fallopian tube, and I had endo." She huffed. "Then, the doctor delivered the fatal blow when she told me that my chances of getting pregnant in the future were between two and five percent."

How she was keeping herself together was shocking because my eyes were watering. "I'm sorry," I uttered because I honestly couldn't find any other words.

"It's not your fault. I mean, if I'm being honest, back then I definitely blamed you a little bit. Mostly I blamed myself, but there was certainly a part of me that was mad at you, albeit misdirected."

I grabbed her hand and cradled it between mine. "That's completely understandable. I just wish..." I sniffled. "Fuck, Allie, I wish I'd known so I could've been there for you." As my tears fell, her eyes glazed over. "It kills me to know that you were going through all of that without me." I kissed the back of her hand and pressed it against my wet cheek.

"It destroyed me," she whispered. "And I didn't want it to destroy you too."

I hugged her again because I had to. Despite all of the agony and anguish she'd gone through, she was protecting me. And that right there was why I'd loved her for twenty years, no matter how much I'd tried not to.

When we finally pulled away from each other, we both had wet faces and red eyes.

"I'm sorry, Kyle. So very sorry. I wanted to call you many, many times, but I couldn't bring myself to do it because how was I supposed to tell my best friend, the guy I loved—was in love with—that *I'd* lost his baby."

My baby. Chills shot up my spine. There were so many things I wanted to say in response. "First, please don't ever again feel like that was your fault. Ectopic pregnancies aren't caused by anything you did."

"I know, but at eighteen I couldn't see it that way."

"But please tell me you get that now because it's honestly killing me to think that you believe that."

She nodded.

"Second." I rubbed the back of her hand. "You were in love with me?"

She bit her lip. "Yes."

I squeezed my eyes shut for a moment.

"I didn't realize it until the doctor called you my baby's father." Her lip quivered and her jaw tensed. "And it clicked for me that I wanted that with you. Not at eighteen, but eventually."

"That's all I've ever wanted, Allie. *You're* all I've ever wanted." I swallowed. "But how could you feel that way and then not reach out to me?"

She sighed. "The only answer I can give you is I was eighteen and traumatized. Then, after so much time passed, I was embarrassed by my behavior and I was convinced that you hated me because..." Her voice cracked. "I hated myself."

"I could never hate you," I whispered.

"But you need to understand that I was a kid and I was scared and I was angry and I was grieving. I'd lost a child—a piece of you and me—a child that would've been treasured and loved beyond belief. I was feeling guilty and worthless." The emptiness in her eyes was haunting.

My breath hitched. "You're not worthless."

"I was depressed. It was ugly and irrational, but I'd convinced myself that I was unlovable. That even if I had told you, you wouldn't want me anymore."

"I really can't stress this enough, Allie. That could never happen."

"Except it had happened. First my father left. Then Brandon went off to college and I barely saw him after that. Tyler went into the military. I can count on my fingers the number of times I've seen him since then. My mother had a new family." She wove her fingers into her hair at her scalp. "Then, I couldn't even hold onto our baby. And I...I knew that if you left me I'd never recover from it. So, I was the one who left. I'm not saying it was right, but—"

"I get that."

"Really?" The desperation on her face broke me.

"Yes. I do. I don't like it, but I understand."

She sighed and it looked like a thousand pound weight had been lifted off of her chest.

I bit the inside of my cheeks. "You don't still feel that way though, do you?"

"I haven't finished the story yet."

My brows arched in disbelief. "There's more?" I didn't now how much more my heart could take, but then I realized that she'd lived through it and, for that, I had more respect for her than anyone else I knew.

"My husband had been my professor my sophomore year."

That took me aback. "Oh."

"He's nine years older than I am, so we got engaged shortly after I graduated. As soon as we got married, we started trying to get pregnant."

I hated the thought of her being with another guy, but I tried to push that aside.

"You know how badly I wanted kids."

I nodded.

"We tried for a year with no luck. Then we tried IUI. I had to inject myself with ovulation induction medications and then go to the doctor to be inseminated. After three rounds, one took." Her legs shook again. "I miscarried at nine weeks."

"Allie," I whispered soothingly.

"We tried it again, but it didn't take. After that, we decided to continue to try naturally while we saved up for IVF, which was fifteen-thousand-dollars."

"Damn."

"It took nearly two years, but we did it. And I got pregnant with twins."

I held my breath.

"I lost them at eleven weeks."

"Fuck, Allie."

Her whole body was shaking, so I put an arm around her and leaned back so she could rest on me while she continued telling me her story. "As I'm sure you can imagine, it destroyed me. I felt utterly worthless. And Kevin blamed me, too. Our marriage fell apart because he resented me for taking those years away from him...for not giving him a child."

I wanted to strangle the motherfucker. I turned her around so she had to look at me. "I'm going to say this again." I stared straight into her eyes. "You are not worthless."

She grunted and started counting on her fingers. "My father, my mother, Brandon, Tyler, four babies, my husband." She shook her head. "Here I am at thirty-four all alone because none of those people thought I was worth sticking around for."

I leaned my forehead on hers and whispered, "You have me. You've always had me. And you always will."

She sighed and pulled her head back. "So there you have it. My life story. It's ugly and grim and—"

"It's you."

She scoffed. "Lucky me."

"No, I'm serious. All of those things have made you who you are today and you should be damn proud of that. Honestly, Allie I am astounded by you and beyond impressed, even a little intimidated because I don't know if I could go through all that and be as strong as you are."

She cupped my cheek. "You could, Kyle, but I would never want you to have to."

"Do me one favor, Allie?"

"What's that?"

"Let me decide what I do or do not want to be around for from now on, okay?"

She smiled. "I can do that."

I kissed her forehead.

She leapt from the couch with a gasp and fled from the room. I was on my feet and on her trail. "What is it?"

I found her in the kitchen sitting on the floor laughing her ass off.

I smiled. "What?"

"I thought...lasagna...burning," she got out amongst her laughter.

It was contagious so I started laughing as well.

She pointed at the oven. "I...never turned...it on."

I sat beside her on the floor and we both laughed entirely too hard. Partly because she'd been defrosting the lasagna in a cold oven, but mostly because we needed to release. When we finally caught our breath, we leaned our backs against the cabinets, sufficiently spent.

I turned to her. "Should we order a pizza?"

She grinned. "That sounds perfect."

34

ALLIE

*A*s I drove the familiar stretch of I-95 up to Mamaroneck for dinner with Mrs. H, I reflected on the night before with Kyle. It had been one of the most difficult conversations of my life, but it had gone better than I'd anticipated. After more than a decade of imagining that moment, I'd fully expected him to be disgusted with me. But I should've known better. Kyle was nothing like Kevin.

All day, I'd felt lighter and happier than I had in an unfathomably long time. I also felt completely foolish because if I hadn't been so blinded by my grief and anger, Kyle would've supported me through it and, while who knows where our lives would've led, one thing I was certain of, it would've saved me a lot of heartache. Spending time alone with Kyle after so many years apart had been wonderful. I'd always known there'd been a Kyle-shaped hole in my heart, but that night really dialed in on how much I'd missed my best friend.

After such an emotional evening, we'd left things open ended with a "see you soon" promise. I hadn't mentioned the dinner with his mom. Not sure why. I suppose I worried he wouldn't trust me around his family yet. Kyle was fiercely protective of them and when I left, I'd hurt them, too. I needed to make amends with each of them, which was what I'd planned to start doing that night with Mrs. H.

I pulled up to what could only be referred to as my second home. It was the same two-story, white brick colonial with black shutters that had been the backdrop for so many of my memories. As I pulled in the driveway, I counted four cars, which was four too many assuming Mrs. H's was in the garage. I laughed to myself because I should've expected her to pull something like this. Family had always been paramount to her and for a long time I'd been a part of that family. Before I could back out and pretend like I'd had an emergency and couldn't make it, a tall, handsome man with shaggy blonde hair came out the kitchen door. He cocked his head in surprise and started heading toward me. I turned off my car and got out, wiping my sweaty palms on my jeans.

"Do you need directions or something?" he asked.

I covered my mouth with my hand. He may have grown up, but he still had that baby face. "Ryan?"

His brow furrowed. "Do I — ?"

"I'm Allie."

His jaw dropped. "Holy shit, Allie?"

I surveyed him. The last time I'd seen him, he'd been twelve and a whole lot shorter. He had to be six-and-a-half-feet tall and his muscles rivaled his big brother's. I craned my neck and said, "My goodness you are all grown up."

He laughed and opened his arms. "Come here. It's good to see you."

I hugged him and replied, "Good to see you, too."

When we parted, he asked, "Does everyone know you're coming?"

I shook my head. "I don't think so. Your mom invited me, but she left out the part about it being a family affair."

He smirked. "Sounds about right. I've got to grab something from my car, but then I'll go in with you."

"Thanks."

He retrieved a woman's pink sweater from the front seat of his BMW and then I followed him to the house. He opened the door to the empty kitchen and went straight to the living room where he announced, "You guys are never gonna believe what I found outside."

"Your sense of humor?" a man's deep voice guessed.

I stepped into the room and gave a small wave. "Hi everyone." It was quite intimidating having all of their shocked eyes on me. I tucked my hands into the pockets of my black puffy vest. Mrs. H and the boys were there, but there were also three women I didn't recognize. My gaze went straight to Kyle and after he picked his jaw up from the floor he gave me a smile that lit up his entire face and that made some of my anxiety melt away.

Mrs. H stepped forward and pulled me into a giant mom hug. "Allie, I'm so glad you could make it."

Dylan came over next. "Well, this is a great surprise." He gave me a quick hug. "It's good to see you, Allie." He looked so much like the teenaged boy I remembered.

"Yeah, you, too."

Jesse greeted me next. I almost didn't recognize him because he was a far cry from the fourteen-year-old kid I'd last seen, but his blue-gray eyes were a dead giveaway. He looked so much like his father.

Then, Kyle was there. I leaned into his hug like it was my lifeline.

"What are you doing here?" he asked curiously.

"Apparently your mom hasn't lost her ability to orchestrate a surprise. I thought it was just going to be me and her." I glanced over at Mrs. H who had her face twisted in a perplexed manner. Guess Kyle hadn't told her that we'd already seen each other because she appeared to be slightly disappointed like maybe she'd been expecting some big, emotional reunion. I unzipped my vest.

Kyle shook his head and chuckled. "Well, I'm glad you're here." He took the vest from me and draped it over the back of a chair. "Come meet the girls."

An adorable pint-sized brunette wrapped her arms around me. "I'm Autumn. Dylan's wife."

"Nice to meet you. And congratulations, Kyle told me you got married over the summer."

Dylan draped his arm over her shoulders. "We did." He beamed with pride and my heart swelled for them.

Another set of arms were around me. These belonged to a tall, stunning woman with curly auburn hair and emerald eyes. "Nice to meet you, Allie. I'm Jesse's fiancée, Lana."

"Congrats to you as well." I looked from her to Jesse and back. "You own a brewery, right?"

She grinned. "Yeah, I do."

"That's fun. I'd love to check it out."

"Stop by whenever. I'll give you the family treatment."

Jesse laughed beside her. "That means you'd better be ready to be put to work."

Lana slapped his arm. "Quit it, you."

He shrugged. "Did you or did you not give me a job the first day I was there."

She poked his chest. "You volunteered."

"Yeah, yeah."

Ryan stepped between us clutching the hand of a cute blonde. "Allie, this is my girlfriend, Zoe."

She released his hand and hugged me. "Ryan has told me a lot about you."

"Oh, has he?" I pinned him with my eyes and he grinned. "Did he tell you that I used to change his diapers?"

The room erupted in laughter.

Mrs. H added, "I was almost convinced that when Ryan said, 'Mom,' for the first time he'd say it to Allie. She used to tote him around on her hip and push him in the stroller like he was her baby doll."

I shook my head and giggled. "What can I say? At least you made one cute kid, Mrs. H."

That comment yielded mock outrage from the other guys and hearty laughter from the women.

When we sat down to dinner, Mrs. H, raised her wine glass. "I'd like to make a toast to finally having all of my kids at the table." She looked directly at me and my heart leapt. "Welcome home, Allie. To family."

"To family," everyone echoed before clinking glasses and digging into the shepherd's pie. If home had a flavor, that would be it for me.

During dinner, I found out a little bit more about everyone's lives and I noticed one common theme: they all seemed incredibly happy. That was what life should be like. If I hadn't made the foolish choice to walk away from Kyle, I could've had a chair at that table for the last sixteen years, too.

Once dinner wound down, I took a few steadying breaths and cleared my throat. "I'd like to say something to all of you." I glanced at Kyle who gave me a reassuring grin. "I need to apologize for the way I left. None of you deserved that. We used to joke that I was the Hogan sister." I grinned. "And I've missed all of you terribly. Please know that my leaving was about me and not a reflection of anything you'd done."

Kyle squeezed my thigh under the table.

"I'm sorry for hurting you and I hope that we can start over."

Mrs. H replied, "Oh, honey, you'll always be a member of this family and don't forget it."

"Yeah, Allie," Ryan added. "Although now you've got to share us with these other sisters, but you'll always be the O.G."

I smiled. "That's fine by me."

Once we'd cleaned up and said our goodbyes, Kyle walked me to my car, but before I could get in, he looked at me with a twinkle in his eye and asked, "Feel up for a walk?"

"Always." I didn't have to ask where we were going.

231

It had been nearly two decades since I'd sat on that swing set. My hips didn't quite fit into the seat the same way they used to. The last time I'd been there had been the night Kyle had told me he was in love with me. They'd since taken out everything but the swings and had replaced it all with a new, brightly-colored jungle gym.

I pumped my knees and lifted slowly into the air, savoring the feel of the wind on my face. "Wow, this brings me back, " I uttered.

"Yeah, me, too." He kicked his feet in the sand. "I still come here every once in a while."

"You do?"

He nodded. "I came here a lot that first year." The sadness in his voice made my gut pang. "I've always felt close to you here. Even after all these years. I come here and it's like I could sense you next to me."

"That's actually really beautiful, Kyle."

He shrugged. "I went there, you know."

"Went where?" I asked as I slowed my swing to a stop.

"Michigan."

"You did."

He nodded.

"When?"

"Columbus Day weekend. We'd gotten two days off that week from hockey, so I booked a flight."

"I—I had no idea."

"I'd remembered the name of your residence hall, so I found it and waited outside for hours." He huffed. "In retrospect, I'm surprised no one called campus security on me for being creepy."

"What happened?" If I had known, I wouldn't have been strong enough to refuse to see him. It might have fixed everything...

"Eventually you came outside and I remember you looked

so incredibly beautiful. It took my breath away." He ran his hand over his jaw. "I got up from the bench, but before I could get to you, some guy walked up and put his arm around you. You laughed and..." He hung his head. "The thought of you dating..." He sighed. "I went back to the airport and came home."

I wracked my brain trying to recall the moment he may have been talking about, but the only person I could possibly think of was this guy, Andre, who had been my R.A.—my very gay R.A. He'd known about what I'd gone through, so he'd looked out for me that whole semester. "Kyle, I never so much as looked at another guy after you."

He cocked his head. "What?"

I wet my lips and rubbed them together. "Even with Kevin. He pursued me and it made me feel like maybe I wasn't entirely worthless, so that's why I eventually agreed to go out with him. But it took him an entire semester and then some to wear me down."

"Are you serious?"

I nodded. "Very much so." I bit my lip. "In retrospect, his behavior was borderline predatory. I was his student and he'd leveraged that power dynamic to his advantage."

He sneered. "Fair warning: if I ever see this guy I'm gonna kill him."

I snickered. "Get in line." I took a deep breath as I decided to let him in on my last secret. "I told you he re-married, right?"

He nodded.

"She's pregnant. That's the real reason I left Michigan. She's a fifth grade teacher at my old elementary school. I couldn't handle seeing her every day."

"Fuck, Allie. It keeps getting worse."

"Tell me about it."

"Your bravery is something else."

I shook my head. "I wouldn't go that far."

"It's true. Trust me, I know a thing or two about being brave."

The thought of him running into a burning building made my chest tighten. "If you compare me to you, I'm going to leave," I threatened.

He rolled his eyes. "What I do takes bravery, sure, but the emotional trauma that you've endured requires a whole other level of resilience." He held out his hand and I put mine into it. "You're an incredible woman, Allie."

There was only so much praise I could take before becoming overwhelmingly uncomfortable and he was bordering that line. "Thank you," I said, squeezing his hand. "We should go. It's getting cold out."

He released my hand and we walked back to the house. At my car, he said, "I'm really glad you came tonight."

I nodded, surprising myself. "Me, too."

He reached into his pocket and retrieved his phone. "I, umm, forgot to get your phone number last night."

I squinted. "I texted you the other day."

"You did?"

I shook my head feeling foolish. "I probably should've told you it was me when I did though, huh?"

He chuckled. "That would've been helpful."

I pulled out my phone, opened the unanswered message from the other night, and simply put a heart in the message box before hitting send. "I assumed you didn't reply because you were on your ambush date."

His phone dinged and his eyes widened. "That text was you?"

I nodded.

"Well, damn." He took a step forward and tucked a strand of my hair behind my ear, letting his hand linger for a moment. "I've missed you, too." His eyes were intense and I could've stood there getting lost in them forever, but then he let me go and took a step back. "See you soon?"

I nodded. "Definitely."

As I drove back into the city, a part of me that I thought had been beaten to death and buried, poked her head out. And she smiled.

35

KYLE

I didn't want to jinx it and call it a real date, but Allie and I were having a Friday date night. Since dinner at my mom's that past Saturday, she and I had been texting non-stop. I hummed along to the alternative rock song playing on my sound system in the kitchen as I pulled the produce out of the bins. I laughed at myself because Kyle Hogan didn't hum. All week, I'd been walking around with a constant smile. It must have been freaking out the guys in my firehouse. I wasn't an idiot, I knew they all thought I was a hard ass because, well...I was, but I'd been pig-in-shit level happy all week and none of them knew how to act around me. It had been an unexpectedly welcome break from my usual bitter and brooding attitude.

The onions were making my eyes water as I diced them for the quesadillas. Allie had always liked those—hopefully she still did—so I figured I'd try my hand at making some. At work the night before, I had been texting Allie and decided to go out on a limb, so I'd asked her to come over for dinner that night. I was going all out.

Without a doubt I loved her, but at the same time, I wasn't the same eighteen-year-old kid she'd known all those years ago, just as she wasn't that girl anymore. While I wanted to say that I was still *in love* with her, it would be naïve of me. We were well settled into adulthood and we'd missed out on so much. In a way, we had to get to know each other all over again, but I had high hopes I could be in love with the present version of her, too.

While the onions and peppers cooked down, I went into the living room to assemble the other part of my plan. I pulled all of the cushions off my sectional and made a big pillow pile on the floor, then covered it with blankets. When I grabbed the remote off the bookcase, I eyed the photograph of Allie and me as teens. It made me smile. I'd gotten a new frame for it the day after she'd told me about why she'd vanished.

I couldn't begin to understand how difficult her life had been the past sixteen years, but I could only imagine that those things had toughened her. Hopefully, she wasn't too hardened to consider opening her heart for me because I honestly didn't think I could handle falling for her again simply for her to push me away.

After cuing Netflix up on the television, I went back to the kitchen and grabbed a beer from the fridge. I popped off the top, then stirred the vegetables. Once they'd finished cooking, I assembled the quesadillas with the veggies, cheese, and the shrimp I'd cooked earlier, that way when she arrived, all I had to do was toss them on the griddle for a few minutes.

Just as I finished washing the last dish, my doorbell rang. When I opened the door and saw her standing there in yoga pants and a sweatshirt I grinned. I'd told her to dress comfortably and I loved that she'd taken it seriously.

"Hey," I said as I pulled her in for a hug.

"Your house is adorable."

I grinned. "Thanks. I bought it in foreclosure and it was a mess, so I re-did it."

"Yourself?" she asked as I took her coat.

"Yeah. My brothers helped, too. And some guys from the

firehouse." It had been a fun project. "It was about a year before I could move into it because I'd taken it pretty much down to the studs, but it was worth it."

"I can't wait to see it." She followed me from the foyer to the living room and she froze when she saw what I'd done. Her jaw dropped and she put her hand over her heart. "No you didn't!"

I laughed. "Thought it could be fun. Like old times."

The smile on her face was priceless. "It's so perfect."

"Come on, I'll show you around." We started in the kitchen. "Can I get you a drink? I've got beer and I picked up some of the wine you like."

She parted her lips as if to speak and then snapped them closed again. She reached her hand out. "Do you mind if I try your beer?"

It was a standard lager, nothing special, but despite being perplexed, I held the bottle out for her. "Go ahead."

Tentatively, she brought the bottle to her lips. After sipping, her expression was one of pleasant surprise. "I think I'll have a beer, please."

I grabbed a cold one from the fridge and popped open the top for her. "Here you go."

"Thanks. I haven't had a beer in years."

"Really?"

She nodded. "Kevin wasn't much of a drinker. He'd have wine every now and then, which is how I became a wine drinker."

"I wondered because you used to hate wine."

"Now you know." She took a sip of the lager. "This is good."

I laughed. "Well, enjoy. There's plenty more."

I tossed the quesadillas on the griddle and then gave her the tour, finishing up back in the kitchen.

"You've done a wonderful job on this place, Kyle."

I flipped the quesadillas and shrugged. "I like it. It's home."

She leaned against the counter beside me. "It feels good here."

"Yeah?"

"Yeah."

I put the quesadillas on a plate. "Wanna go pick a movie while I finish these up?"

"I'll never turn down an opportunity to control the remote." She smirked before sauntering into the living room.

I cut up the quesadillas and put them on a plate with salsa and guacamole. When I brought them in the other room, I immediately flashed back to being a teenager at the sight of Allie curled up with a blanket on the pillow pile. I handed her a plate then took a seat beside her. Without a word, she spread the blanket out over my legs, too. Just like old times.

To my surprise, she picked a psychological thriller. I asked, "This isn't going to be too scary for you?"

She grinned, but her bronze eyes seemed sad. "My life has felt like a bit of a horror movie, so I guess they're not so scary anymore. I still don't like the blood and guts and things jumping out of the dark, but some thrillers are okay. I like the mystery."

We ate the quesadillas while we watched and when we were finished with dinner, I paused the movie to clear the plates and brought back popcorn from the kitchen. Her eyes were fixed on the photo of us.

She bit her lip. "You kept it."

I nodded.

"All these years..." She sighed.

I sat back down and placed the popcorn in front of her. "You're the best."

I smiled. "It's not a movie night without popcorn, right?"

"Absolutely."

Allie scooted closer so we could share the bowl. By the end of the movie, she had her head on my shoulder and I would've done anything to make sure the moment never ended. But, of course, the movie couldn't go on forever.

As the credits rolled, I asked, "Wanna watch another."

"Sure," she replied without lifting her head. "You pick."

I chose a critically acclaimed flick I'd been wanting to see.

About a quarter of the way in, Allie asked, "Are you lost?"

I laughed. "Completely. Apparently critically acclaimed is code for slow, confusing, and boring."

She sighed. "This is nice." She snuggled closer.

"Yeah, it is."

"Thanks for inviting me and setting all this up. It means a lot."

"I'm really glad you came."

"Me, too."

She lifted her head and looked up at me with serious eyes. "I knew I missed this, but I hadn't realized how much."

That made me smile. "I've missed it, too."

"I know we aren't kids anymore and we've got our own lives, but tonight..." She pressed her lips together. "I don't know. It almost feels like nothing has changed."

"I know exactly what you mean."

She grinned, drawing my attention to her lips and I couldn't look away. She'd always had lush lips and I tried to recall what they had tasted like back then. My gaze lingered and the tension built up between us. Her lips parted slightly and I caught a glimpse of the pink tip of her tongue. Her chest rose and fell more rapidly as her breathing quickened. Foolishly, I bit down on my lip as though it would stop me from kissing her. In response, her tongue curled upward and grazed the tiniest section of her upper lip.

Unable to resist, I leaned forward, bringing my face mere inches from hers. When she didn't turn away I edged closer, stopping just before the point of no return to ask for permission. "Allie?"

"Yes," she whispered.

Our mouths connected and I moaned almost immediately from the contact. As did she. Allie wasted no time opening up for me and I sought out her tongue with mine, tasting the salt from the popcorn we'd shared. My hands cupped her face, holding her in place, while I devoured her. Her palm flattened on my chest and she curled her fingers, bunching up my t-shirt. I traded her top lip for the bottom, savoring the fullness of it as I caught it gently between my teeth.

Allie must've liked it because she grasped the back of my neck and tugged me closer. I snaked an arm behind her lower back and guided her to lay down, then I perched myself on top of her, deepening the kiss. My hand glided along her collarbone and up her neck, hooking the heel on her jawline and landing my fingers around her ear. She whimpered as I ran my tongue along her lips.

I could've easily made love to Allie right then and there on the pillows piled on my living room floor, but my heart told me to hold off, so I eased up, bringing us to a panting stop. Because if I gave myself to her again, I needed to trust that without a doubt she'd still be in my bed when I woke up the next morning and we weren't there yet.

When she opened her eyes, they were darkened with desire and I desperately wanted to continue what we'd started, but as it was, I was destined for blue balls.

I brushed the hair from her face and lightly kissed her nose. "Well, Allie Dupree, looks like we've still got it."

Her bronze eyes gleamed. "I'd say so."

Staring into the face of my oldest friend, I grasped the importance of that moment. For whatever reason, we were being given a second chance and I was determined to do everything in my power to make sure that this time, it lasted.

"What are you thinking" she asked.

"Remembering how you were my first kiss."

She giggled. "If you can call it that."

"Yours were the first lips to touch mine. It counts."

Her smile eased. "You were my first everything. First kiss. First time. First love. That'll never be taken away from us."

Fuck, I loved the sound of that. "No, it won't."

"I really like that."

So did I, but it wasn't enough because I knew, in that moment while holding her, that I wanted to be her last everything, too.

36

ALLIE

yle and I walked into The Monterey Club for happy hour, which according to his sister-in-law, Autumn, was one of the best in the city. After chasing around five year olds with finger paint for most of the morning, a good happy hour was exactly what I needed. I followed Kyle to a table by the bar. Dylan and Autumn were already there, so I hugged them hello. There was another couple there as well.

As we sat down, Kyle introduced us. "Allie Pierce, this is Britt and Jace Palmer."

Hearing my married name on Kyle's lips made me cringe every time. "Nice to meet you both." I nodded.

Autumn jumped in, "They're celebrating a month of wedded bliss."

"Wow, congrats."

"Thanks," Britt said, clutching her husband like true newlyweds.

"So how do you all know each other?" I asked.

Dylan answered, "Jace and I are on the job together."

Jace added. "We went through the academy at the same time, then ended up rookies in the same house, so I didn't have much choice but to be friends with his goofy ass."

"Friends? I tolerate you, at best." Dylan retorted.

Autumn shook her head. "Don't let them fool you. They have a serious bromance going on." She pointed to Britt. "We went to NYU together."

Britt nodded. "She's my bestie." That made me smile because the only thing I missed about Michigan was my friends. Although we'd hardly spoken since I'd moved, so maybe they weren't as good of friends as I'd thought they were.

I pointed to Dylan. "So your best friend," I pointed to Autumn, "married your best friend."

"That's right," Dylan replied.

"That's so sweet."

The waitress came over and Kyle ordered a beer, then asked me, "What would you like?"

"Umm, I'll have what you're having." Hanging out with Kyle the last few weeks, I'd realized how much I'd missed beer. Kevin couldn't stand the smell and wouldn't let me have any in the house, so I had stopped drinking it all together.

Kyle held up two fingers to the waitress before she walked away.

Autumn smiled at me. "Allie, what were these two like as kids? I want all the juicy details."

The guys groaned.

"Typical boys. Everything was about hockey with them. They were both quite good."

"Yeah?" Autumn asked. "I thought their stories were more hyperbolic than truth. You know, like the six-inch fish they caught was actually six-feet-long."

I laughed. "Well, some of them may be, but they're not lying about their talent." I pointed my thumb at Kyle. "He easily could've gone pro if he'd wanted to."

"Huh," Autumn replied. "Skiing, too?"

"Skiing?" I asked.

"Yeah, Kyle was on the FDNY ski team for a bit."

Kyle responded, "I took it up on a whim. One of the guys on the hockey team with me had crossed over. He invited me to one of their competitions as a last-minute replacement for a guy who'd been injured. Skiing is actually a lot like skating."

Dylan finished, "Who knew he'd end up being so good they'd ask him to join the team."

I grinned. "I'm not surprised."

The waitress brought over our beers and I savored the first sip.

"Tough day?" Kyle asked.

I shrugged. "Long."

"What do you do?" Britt asked.

"I'm a kindergarten teacher."

She held up her martini glass. "Cheers to you, sister. I'm out on that."

Everyone laughed.

Jace kissed her temple.

"Could you imagine?" Autumn interjected.

Britt sipped her cosmo. "Nightmare."

Autumn replied, "Yeah for the kids." She turned to me. "Britt's the department editor for the sex and dating section of *Contemporary Magazine.*"

I raised my brows. "Wow."

"So the idea of her working with children is quite laughable," Autumn said.

A little while later, we'd all switched seats so that the guys were together on one side of the round table and us women were on the other.

Autumn took a sip of her mocktail. According to Kyle, Autumn couldn't drink alcohol because she'd had a lung transplant as a child. She stirred her straw in the glass. "So, Allie, I've got to ask. Are you and Kyle dating?"

I glanced over at Kyle who'd been deep in conversation with the guys. As though he could feel my stare, he turned to me and grinned. I smiled back. We'd seen each other a couple of times since the movie night at his house, but we hadn't talked about we were doing. We were kind of just going with the flow. He'd kissed me several times, but that's as far as it'd gone. Kissing him...well, it was a million times better than I'd remembered.

I reached for my beer. "Umm, we haven't put a label on it or anything."

"Girl, whatever you're doing, keep it up. I've never seen Kyle like this. The first time we met, I was convinced he hated me because he was so moody. He actually smiles now. It's wild."

I rubbed my lips together. "Really?"

"Yeah," Britt added. "He could be broody as fuck."

My stomach twisted. I hated that the decisions I'd made as a naïve teenager had led to him becoming so bitter.

Autumn continued, "The other night, Dylan said he finally felt like he had his brother back and that it's all your doing."

Britt responded, "Jeez, Autumn. No pressure or anything."

She put up her hands. "Just saying."

I neared the end of my third beer. "The Kyle I knew was actually a lot of fun." Sure, after his father had died, he'd become vastly more serious, but I'd assumed with time, that would've passed. Apparently not.

Both girls raised their eyebrows and Autumn said, "Interesting."

I finished my beer. They'd apparently all gone straight to my head because the next thing I said was, "It's my fault for leaving. I broke his heart. He told me he was in love with me and I ran away."

"Damn," Britt replied.

Autumn reached for my hand. "We all make mistakes."

I sighed. "I'm hoping I'm not too late to fix mine."

"If it's meant to be," Britt said, "then there's no such thing as too late. Sometimes people deserve second chances." She glanced at her husband with a smile and I wondered what the story was there.

"That's true," Autumn added. "And from where I sit, I'd be willing to bet that Kyle has never stopped loving you."

Britt leaned forward. "Oh, that would explain a lot."

I tapped my fingers on the table. "You think?"

They both nodded and Autumn declared, "Definitely. It's clear in the way he looks at you."

I eyed him in my periphery. Seeing him happy made me smile. When I returned my attention to the women they were both staring at me with mischievous grins. "What?" I asked.

Autumn folded her arms on top of the table. "You look at him the same way."

"I don't know..." I protested, but it was weak.

Britt replied, "Take it from someone who lives and breathes love and dating: the two of you have it bad."

"But, that's oh so good," Autumn finished.

I picked up my beer glass, forgetting that it was empty, then put it back down. Of course I loved Kyle. I'd never stopped loving him despite everything that had happened. Two people couldn't possibly be as close as we'd been and not retain at least some of those feelings for life. But was I *in love* with him? And there it was. The question that had gotten us into trouble all those years ago. We'd come full circle, but this time I was determined not to let history repeat itself.

37

KYLE

$\mathcal{T}$he night tour at the firehouse had been a long one. We'd run our balls off mostly for bullshit medical calls. One woman had actually called the fire department because her kid had a splinter...at one in the morning. Just when you thought you'd seen it all on this job, something happened to prove you wrong.

I pulled the lever on the recliner in the lounge and cradled my coffee as I leaned against the headrest, resting my eyes.

"Hogan, can I ask you something?" Lt. Bryce McNamara asked from the chair beside me. He was the Ladder lieutenant on shift that tour.

I didn't bother to move or open my eyes. "What's up?"

"Would I be completely insane for wanting Alicia back?"

I opened one eye and glanced at him from my periphery. "Is this like a hypothetical or are you seriously considering it?"

"She was my wife, man."

"Right, but she cheated on you."

He sighed. "We've been through a lot together, though. Trauma creates some strong bonds."

I opened both eyes and lifted my head. "Where is this coming from?"

He cracked his knuckles and said in a near whisper, "I miss her, man."

"She left you for another guy, Mack."

"We were together for nine years. You ever love someone for that long? It doesn't just go away. Feelings don't dissolve the second the divorce papers are signed." They'd had a particularly nasty divorce that had finally ended a few months prior.

"Believe it or not, bro, I know exactly what you mean."

He eyed me quizzically. "You do?"

I nodded.

"How'd you get over it?"

I bit the inside of my cheeks. "I haven't."

"Fuck, man."

"But lucky for me, I'm getting a second chance."

He jolted to the edge of his seat. "Hold up. Are you for real?"

My grin was response enough.

"Shit, well that explains a lot."

I cocked my head.

He laughed. "The guys have a poll going on which stripper from Sapphire you'd managed to charm. You've gotta admit, man, you've been walking around here like a new man lately."

"A fucking stripper? Are you kidding me?"

"It was either that or a badge bunny."

I shook my head and snorted. "Hell, no."

He shrugged. "Considering you don't date, those were the best options."

Our conversation ended abruptly when the tones went off, calling us to a 10-75, which was a full response for a confirmed fire. We leapt from our chairs and sprinted to the pole. After sliding down, we each headed to the officer's seat on our respective rigs. More information came through en route telling us we were going to a fully involved fire in an attached home. Attached homes were a bitch because one house on fire could quickly multiply since they shared walls with others.

"Fuck," I exclaimed before turning around to address my men. "We've got high wind gusts tonight boys, let's not lose a whole city block."

From two avenues away, the dark smoke was visible in the blue sky along with a faint orange glow. As we pulled up, I got on my radio to announce our arrival on scene. "Dispatch, E11 is 10-84 at 326 West 87th."

"10-4, E11."

Neighbors were screaming that people were still inside. Our house was first on scene, which meant that Mack or I had to be Incident Commander until a higher ranked officer arrived. He pointed at me and shouted, "I'm going in, we've got people trapped." As a ladder company, their job was to locate victims, so it made sense for me to hang back to direct the scene.

I assessed what we were dealing with and immediately got on the radio. "Dispatch, we need a second alarm at 326 West 87th. Confirmed people trapped. We've got fire out the windows in three houses and we've got flames threatening to jump the alley." For a 10-75, four Engines and three Ladders would respond along with the chiefs, but from my assessment, that wouldn't be enough. Calling for a second alarm would essentially double the number of responding units as well as send additional support personnel.

I hollered to my nozzleman, "Hit the alley on the four-side and protect the exposure." For clarity purposes, we referred to sides of buildings by a number: one through four. The one-side was the front and it went around clockwise, meaning the four-side was the right of the building.

The winds whistled down the alley and I knew we were in trouble. I ran to my rig. Valenti, the chauffeur had hooked up to the hydrant and was priming the pump while my nozzleman, Eger, was piling hose lengths onto his shoulder.

"This bitch is gonna jump the alley. Hurry the fuck up," I ordered, pushing them to move quicker.

The radio squelched. "L171 to Incident Command."

"Go 171," I replied.

"We've got a twenty-pound propane tank on the first floor on the one side of the middle involved home. Tank looks like it's been converted into a heater."

"Motherfucker." That wasn't good. "10-4 171. All personnel at 326 West 87th evacuate. We've got a 10-80. Moving to exterior operations." The 10-80 code let them know we had a hazmat incident. As I updated Dispatch, Engine 13 pulled up.

Four of the five L171 guys that had gone inside scrambled out of the building. I got on the radio to my unit. "E11 shut down the line and move to cover the 10-80. E13, hook up and cover the alley on the four side."

I ran to the guys on L171 to find out where their fifth man was. With their gear and masks, it was nearly impossible to tell who they were unless I read the names on the back of their bunker coats, so I asked, "Who's missing."

"Lt. Mack," one of them replied.

I hit my transmitter. "IC to L171 lieutenant. Confirm evacuating." Then, I turned back to the men. "What house did he go into?"

The guys pointed to the one on the far right.

"You sure?"

"Yes, lieutenant."

"Which window is the propane tank closest to?"

The guy who I assumed had transmitted the message pointed to the one beside the front stoop in the middle house.

"All right. Evacuate the houses, starting with the one across the alley." I gestured to the one I meant, then I ran to my nozzleman and pointed at the window. "You get water into that window like it's a carnival game, understood?"

"Yes, lieutenant."

"But don't get too close, stay on the road," I warned.

Still no sign of Mack. "Dammit." I transmitted again. "IC to L171 lieutenant. Confirm evacuating."

Engine 13 was moving into place to cover the alley and Ladder 64 arrived on scene. Back on the radio. "L64 standby as FAST. We have one firefighter unaccounted for." The company assigned as FAST or Firefighter Assist and Search Team was solely dedicated to performing search and rescue for firefighters in distress. Dylan was on L64, but I wasn't sure if he was working or not.

A civilian wailed in the distance, "My husband is inside."

I didn't have time to think about how my call to evacuate was leaving civilians trapped inside the inferno. As an officer, it was my job to make those tough calls and with the threat of a propane tank indoors, I simply couldn't risk doing a search and rescue.

I tried Mack one more time. "IC to L171 lieutenant. Status!"

Engine 19 arrived on scene.

"IC to E19, stretch a line to the front and help E11 cover this tank," I ordered.

Still no sign of Mack, I made the call. "L64 prepare to go in as FAST to the third house in search of L171 lieutenant, Bryce McNamara."

"Fuck," I spat through my teeth. I realized I'd screwed up and jumped on the radio. "E13 shut down the line in the alley and cover the middle involved house from the one side." That would put all three operating hose lines on the middle unit housing the propane tank. Since Mack was trapped in the unit on the right, between the alley and the house with the propane tank, if I kept hose lines operating on both sides, it would essentially sandwich the fire, forcing it into the unit where Mack was trapped. I prayed the damage hadn't already been done. I'd given Engine 13 their orders before I knew which unit Mack was in and I should've called them off then, but it was fucking hectic and I'd screwed up.

I had to risk the fire jumping the alley because it was more important to keep the propane tank stable so it didn't BLEVE (explode) and cause a much bigger problem. Especially with guys inside. Once Engine 13 was in place, I issued an order, "L64 go," while praying that I wasn't sending them to their deaths.

I stood back and watched as four firefighters breached the house. One of the names on the jackets read, *Palmer* and another, *Hogan*. My stomach turned over.

Battalion Chief Richards finally arrived on scene and I ran over to meet him and get him up to speed so he could take over as Incident Commander. "Chief, we've got confirmed fire in these three houses and it's threatening to jump the alley." I pointed to the middle house. "There's a twenty-pound propane tank on the one side of that house. All three Engines are in place to prevent a BLEVE." I gestured to the house on the right. "Engine 171 lieutenant was conducting a primary search of that unit. He has been out of radio communication since the evacuation order. Ladder 64, acting as FAST, is in there now."

"Nice work, Lieutenant. Stick by me." He got on the radio and called a third alarm, requesting even more units. The fourth engine arrived and they were put on exterior attack of the far left unit. I stared at the door that Dylan and Jace had run into and nearly held my breath in anticipation of seeing them exit. If there was a BLEVE while they were inside...

No, I couldn't go there.

Chief Richards hit his transmitter. "L64 status report."

"Nothing yet."

I pressed my palms together and brought my hands up to my chin as we waited.

And waited.

And waited.

After what felt like fucking forever, we got a report. "L64 to IC."

"Go L64."

"L171 lieutenant located with two civilians. Exiting now."

"10-4," the chief acknowledged.

I rocked on my heels.

A minute later, bodies shoved through the doorway, emerging from the thick, black smoke. I counted helmets. All were accounted for. *Thank you, Dad.*

Then there was a loud boom, sending glass, brick, and wood flying.

"Was there only one tank?" Chief Richards asked.

"That's all that was reported."

He scratched his face. "All right, we're moving to interior." He hit his transmitter and began assigning companies.

I rushed to Dylan who was crouched beside Mack. "What happened?"

Mack, out of breath, coughed out. "House is filled with garbage. A pile of crap...fell over trapping me...in the back with the two vics." He pointed to his radio. "Fucking stopped working."

We'd gotten damn lucky. That could've been a serious disaster. I looked up and saw the flames licking the eaves on the building across the alley. "Dammit." I got on my radio, "The fire has jumped." Then I ran back to the chief.

It had taken us four hours to get the fire under control. In the end, five homes had been affected, three civilians had been seriously injured, and four had been treated for smoke inhalation. I was supposed to go on a date with Allie that night, but I was in a piss-poor mood, so I'd texted her and canceled. Even though I'd showered before leaving the firehouse, by the time I got home, I felt like I needed another one. The smoke stench was burned into my nostrils. Once I felt clean...well, cleaner, I tugged on sweatpants, collapsed on my couch, and stared up at the ceiling.

It'd been one hell of a day. I tried not to dwell on the fact that I could've burned Mack alive had I not thought to call off the engine in the alley, but then my mind went to the knowledge that I'd sent my friend and my brother into one of the most dangerous situations I'd ever had to make a call on...no, wait, it was definitely the most dangerous call I'd ever had to make as a lieutenant. And then there was—

My doorbell rang. *Who the fuck is bothering me?* I ignored it.

It rang again. "Goddammit." I got to my feet and opened the door. "What the—"

Allie smiled up at me. "I know we canceled, but you seemed down, so I brought you dinner and thought I'd try and cheer you up."

I ran a hand over my cropped hair. "I'm not really in the mood."

She put a hand on her hip. "I know, Mr. Grouch, that's why I'm here." Stepping around me, she let herself in. Back in the day, she'd call me that whenever I'd gotten in one of my moods, but I wasn't a kid anymore, and I wasn't upset over a stupid hockey game or failed test.

After shutting the door, I found her in the kitchen, unpacking Chinese food containers.

"Allie, I appreciate what you're trying to do, but I just want to wallow in my misery."

"Go sit. I'll bring dinner in for you."

"I'm not hungry."

She let go of the noodles she'd been spooning onto a plate and turned to face me. "All right, let's talk then."

"Don't wanna talk either."

She crossed the room, grabbed my hand, and led me out to the couch. "Sit."

I did with a sigh.

Allie sat beside me. "What has you so down?"

"Allie—"

"What happened at work?"

"You're a persistent pain in the ass."

She smirked. "I'm one that cares. Spill."

"We're not kids anymore, Al," I warned."

"I know that, but I used to be really good at making you feel better, so what harm can be done in trying?"

I shook my head. "That was then."

"And I'm here now." Each time she pushed, my frustration built.

"I didn't ask you to be."

"That's the thing with our friendship, Kyle. You never have to ask."

I leaned my head back, closed my eyes, and pinched the bridge of my nose.

"Talk to me."

"No."

"Fine. Wallow away. I'm just going to sit here and—"

My limit was hit and I shouted, "Stop."

She flinched.

"Just fucking stop."

She responded in a soft tone, "Kyle, I—"

"I know what you're trying to do, but fuck, Allie, you lost that damn right when you turned your back on me. You're not my best friend anymore. You can't just barge in and try to fix me like you used to. It no longer works that way."

Her mouth hung open.

All of my anger from the day was suddenly on a fast track in her direction. Recalling the conversation I'd had with Mack earlier, something clicked. He wanted to go back to his ex-wife, even though she'd betrayed him, simply because of the shit they'd gone through together and the years they'd shared...

What would stop Allie from having those same feelings and leaving me? Again. My heart wouldn't survive that.

I lashed out. "I'm not going to open up and bare my soul like I did when we were kids just for you to turn-tail and disappear on me again."

Her head drooped. "Okay. I deserved that."

ALLIE

$\mathcal{I}$n the past, the things Kyle would sometimes say when he was in one of his moods usually rolled right off my shoulders because there'd been no truth to them. But this time was different. This time, the things he said were warranted.

I sighed. "I realize my track record is shitty, and you have every right to feel this way, but I promise you I'm not going anywhere. I've learned from my mistakes and I won't do that to you again. I promise."

He sneered. "Words, Allie. Just words."

"What do you want me to *do* then?"

"I don't know if there's anything you can do."

"There must be something—"

"And I don't know if I want you to." He got up and paced. "Do you have any idea what my life's been like since you left? Miserable. Fucking miserable, Allie. I loved you with everything I had and you shit on that like I'd never meant a damn thing to you."

"I loved you—"

"Don't! Don't say it. I've tried to move on. Trust me, pining over you for decades wasn't something I'd had any control over. I've dated. I've done my best to try to fucking forget you, but you left this goddamn gaping hole in my heart and no matter what I did, or who I tried to be with, nothing filled it." He grimaced and I felt his pain in my chest.

Heavy breaths made his shoulders rise. "And now that you're here and I can have you, I want to jump at the chance, but that doesn't change the fact that you wrecked me, Allie. No, you fucking destroyed me, and I don't know if I can trust you again."

And there it was. My biggest fear.

He rubbed his jaw. "You should go."

I didn't have the will to argue, so I got up from the couch, retrieved my purse and went to the door. With my hand on the knob, I exhaled and said, "I'm sorry." I went out to my car, and drove away.

The trip home was agonizing. I knew it had been too easy that night I'd told Kyle the truth about why I'd vanished. Everything he'd just said to me was what I'd feared and when we'd gotten through that initial conversation without any of that, I'd been so relieved. But I'd had a false sense of security.

The worst part was, I couldn't blame him for any of the things he'd said because they were valid feelings and I'd brought that wrath upon myself. I knew full well how Kyle could get when he was in a mood and I should've seen that coming. Of course we couldn't just go back to things as they were, despite how easy that had felt those past few weeks, because I'd ruined that. I'd destroyed his trust and it was my responsibility to earn it back.

And there was no guarantee that I would.

But I would try.

When I got home, I changed into my bathrobe as I ran the water in the tub. Soaking in the bath was one of the only soothing techniques my therapist had suggested that actually worked. I lit some candles, scattered my lavender scented bath salts, and ditched my robe before stepping into the hot water.

At first, it stung my cold skin, but once I was fully submerged, it felt fantastic.

After my miscarriages, I'd spent a lot of time in the bath tub. For some reason it made me feel secure in a time where I was anything but. I'd mentioned that to my therapist and she went off on how taking a bath could trigger memories of being in the womb. After that, I'd stopped taking baths because all I could picture were my babies—all four of them—in my womb that wouldn't keep them safe. It wasn't until I'd moved to New York that I'd been able to take baths again.

I breathed in the steam and tried to let the tension from my conflict with Kyle melt away. Despite how much I wanted to patch things up with him, I knew it wouldn't happen that night. He'd have to cool off first before we could have another conversation. I closed my eyes and pictured what my life could've been like had I made one decision differently when I was eighteen. This was something I'd done often over the years. If, after leaving the hospital, I'd called Kyle instead of choosing to alienate myself from him, maybe he and I would be married. In a perfect world, we would've had kids and we both would've been spared a lot of heartache.

The distinctive buzz of the front door disturbed my fantasy. The list of people it could be was two. One: a lost drunk person. Two: Kyle. I hastened to dry myself off and slip into my robe, then I sprinted to the door and hit the intercom button. "Who is it?"

"Me."

I buzzed him in. When I heard his footprints on the steps, I opened my door. The sullen expression on his face said it all. He held up the bag of Chinese food and said, "Hungry?"

I stepped aside, letting him in, then shut the door.

He placed the bag down on the coffee table and looked at me. "I'm sorry. I was a complete dick and you didn't deserve any of that."

I shook my head. "Yes, I did. Honestly, you'd let me off the hook too easily, so I'm glad you finally got all that off your chest."

"No, I've just had a shit day and I turned that on you. It wasn't fair of me and I'm sorry."

I sat on the couch and patted the spot next to me. He crossed the room and took it.

Crossing my legs, I said. "Okay, so maybe you didn't have to yell, but I'm glad you told me how you feel because now we can deal with it."

He leaned back and rested his head. "I've missed you, Al. All these years I've felt like a fool for holding on, but you're as much a part of me as I am myself. Having you back..." He trailed off and sighed. "It's all I've ever wanted. Losing you was the hardest thing I've ever gone through, which I realize sounds asinine in comparison to your struggles, but it's the truth and the thought of opening myself back up to being hurt like that again...hell."

I placed my hand on his thigh. "You're not a fool and that's not asinine because honestly, Kyle, I've been miserable without you, too." I rubbed my lips together. "All I can offer is that I've spent years in therapy dissecting this. Subconsciously, I cut you out to punish myself, but in doing so, I had also punished you and that was the very last thing I wanted. Hurting you was never my plan; it was a side effect of what I was doing to hurt myself." I sighed. "Saying sorry will never be strong enough, and you were right—I need to prove it through my actions. If you let me, I'm willing to try and do that."

His crystal eyes held a glimmer of hope.

"I'm done running from us, Kyle."

He brought his hand up to my cheek. "I want *us* back."

I gave him a half-smile. "Me, too."

Leaning forward, he whispered, "I love you, Allie. I've loved you since I was fourteen and I know this is going to take some work, but I want to try. You're worth the risk."

I released a breath. "I think I've loved you that long, too, but I didn't know what those feelings meant back then. I'm not a scared kid anymore though." I pierced his eyes with my gaze. "I know exactly how I feel now—exactly what I want. You. It's always been you."

"I'm yours." He claimed my lips and proved it.

My fingers gripped the t-shirt covering his chest, bunching it up as I pulled him closer. His tongue probed my mouth and I met him halfway, tasting the spearmint flavored candy he must've had. The minty sensation made my lips tingle and I wanted more. The hint of stubble on his chin rubbed against me—a reminder of the rugged man he'd become.

His hands skated along my neck, holding me in place so he could direct our kiss. It had come as no surprise that Kyle liked to be in control; he'd been that way with every aspect of his life and I wondered how that would translate to the bedroom. Surely, as adults, sex would be very different than that one and only time we'd done it that fateful night. While it'd been about a month since we'd rekindled out relationship, we still hadn't ventured into the bedroom. We'd been spending more time focusing on rebuilding our friendship, but the way he was kissing just then told me that was about to change.

My hands found the hem of his shirt and dove underneath, relishing in the ripple of his abs that told of many hours in the gym. I had a feeling I was about to reap the benefits of his hard work. When my hands made it to his pecs, he pulled away just long enough to remove his shirt, then he went back to devouring my mouth.

He wrapped his arms around me and tugged me forward, guiding my legs so that I was straddling him. The only thing separating me from his hardening bulge was his sweatpants and I lowered myself to feel more. Kyle's hands slipped under my robe, nudging it off my shoulders. His calloused hands were rough against the smoothness of my chest. He gripped my hips and rocked them, making me feel how hard he was for me and I moaned at the sensation. With one hand, he loosened the belt, letting my robe fall open before cupping one of my breasts and grazing over the nipple with his thumb.

Pulling his mouth from mine, he nibbled along my collar bone while I fondled his biceps. His tongue trailed from the dip in my throat down the valley between my peaks and I leaned into him. He gripped my breasts, pushing them together, burying his face in between while he tweaked my nipples, sending a jolt to my core.

His mouth closed over one nipple, his tongue flicking at it. I tossed my head back, moaning appreciatively, and he repeated it with my other breast.

Without warning, he stood and I hooked my ankles behind his back, but protested, "I'm too heavy." I certainly wasn't the hundred-and-ten-pound cheerleader I'd once been. Sixteen years had added forty pounds.

He lurched his head back and pinned my eyes with his hard stare. "Not even close. You're perfect."

I bit my lip, wanting to believe him, but I didn't, then Kyle tugged it from my teeth with his thumb and said, "Don't you dare." He'd always had an uncanny ability to read my mind. "You're beautiful, Allie."

A tinge of discomfort shot up my spine. It'd been a long time since someone had called me beautiful. Toward the end of my marriage, the resentment my husband had felt for me had eliminated all elements of attraction and appreciation he'd once had.

Kyle cocked his head. "You really don't believe me do you?"

I blinked.

"I'm going to prove it to you. I'm going to make you feel beautiful again."

He carried me to the bedroom and took care as he placed me on the bed. I wiggled free of my robe as he removed his pants. Standing before me, a perfect specimen of a man, he gripped his impressive length and stroked it. "See this?" he asked. "You did this. It's all for you."

My lips parted as my breathing quickened and he shoved apart my legs, kneeling between them. He bent forward, hovering over me, and grasped my wrists, pinning them above my head with one hand, then stared me dead in the eyes and said. "I'm gonna worship you, Allie." He reached over and turned on the lamp on my nightstand, lighting up the room in a faint white glow.

Instinctively, I tried to free my arms to cover myself up. "No," I protested.

"Yes," he growled. "I want to see you. Watch you come apart for me." He took his time kissing down my body, paying attention to every dip and every ridge, only releasing my wrists when he could no longer reach them. "Keep your hands there. Don't even think about hiding yourself from me," he ordered, as he kissed the pooch on my abdomen.

I sucked it in and he got to his knees. His hands roamed over my stomach and my breathing grew erratic. "My beautiful, Allie," he muttered. Somehow, his fingertips found one of the faint scars that my surgery had left behind. He pressed a finger over it, the focus in his eyes telling me that he knew the significance, while his other hand sought out another scar.

I squeezed my eyes shut and covered them with my forearm, unable to bear watching the recognition hit him, and willed myself not to cry.

He sighed. "Beautiful."

His hands migrated to my hips allowing me to breathe a little easier, then he scooted down so he was flat between my legs.

"Look at me, Allie."

Reluctantly, I removed my arm from my eyes and gazed down.

He stared up at me and said, "Watch me worship you."

Then his tongue connected with my swollen bud and my breath hitched.

Kyle lapped at the sensitive spot, making my core tighten. "Even sweeter than I remember," he purred.

I slammed my eyes shut again as he ravished me with his mouth. Abruptly, he stopped and gritted, "I said watch," he demanded in a low, husky voice that I felt in my core.

I opened my eyes and watched him bring me to the brink. Right before I fell, he eased a finger inside me and that was my undoing. My hips bucked and I cried out as wave after wave of pleasure overtook me. It'd been nearly a decade since I'd enjoyed sex and that orgasm was my unleashing.

Fuck, I need this. I need him.

He got to his knees and fisted himself, rubbing his tip over my slit, getting it slick with my cum. "You're mine, too, Allie."

I licked my lips.

He fixed his eyes on me, "Say it."

"I'm yours."

He exhaled a shaky breath. "Do I need a condom?"

I shook my head trying not to let the pain of knowing I couldn't get pregnant naturally ruin the moment.

He positioned the head at my opening. "It's been too damn long."

"Yes," I breathed.

He pressed and I gave, opening for him to penetrate me. The full sensation set my skin on fire as he gripped my hips and seated himself all the way inside.

"Oh, fuck," I murmured.

He released my hips, and bent forward so his face was just above mine. Those glistening blue spheres of his penetrated deep into my soul. "You," he whispered before leaning his forehead on mine. "It's always been you," he echoed my words from before, then added, "It will always be you." And then he set forth to prove it.

39

KYLE

*J*t'd been a few weeks since Allie had officially become my girlfriend. Well, in my mind at least. We never actually had that conversation, but that first night we'd had sex, we'd promised ourselves to each other and that had been good enough for me.

I'd gotten into the city early that day in the beginning of November, because there was something I had to do before work. I hit the doorbell at Frank's Jewelry and Watches and waited for it to buzz before I could enter. I'd passed that place every time I went to work, but the other day had been the first time I'd really looked at it. The sign in the window had caught my attention: *Give her a diamond that's as strong as your love for her.* That was all it took.

An older gentleman with balding gray hair and narrow glasses greeted me. "What brings you in today, sir?"

I walked up to the counter, my gaze dropping to the sparking gems in the case. "I need an engagement ring."

"I can certainly assist you with that. Congratulations on finding the one."

I grinned. "Thanks."

"Do you have an idea in mind?"

I shook my head.

"Not to worry. Tell me about her."

"What do you want to know?"

"Whatever you want to tell me."

I thought about it. "Uh, well her name's Allie. She's been my best friend since we were four."

He clasped his hands. "That's splendid."

I continued. "She's a kindergarten teacher. And as sweet as she can be, she's equally as strong."

His smile urged me to continue.

"She's got these beautiful bronze eyes. Brown with specks of gold that remind me of dripping honey. And her smile." I closed my eyes and pictured it. "She lights up a room."

"I can work with that," he responded as he retrieved one of the displays from the case. "It sounds like you want something ornate, but classy. A little mix of the old with the new."

I grinned. "Sounds perfect."

He showed me ring after ring and I found several elements that I liked in all of them, but there wasn't one that stood out to me as perfectly Allie.

After twenty minutes, the man suggested, "Perhaps we should design something custom."

"I think you're probably right."

He got out a sketch pad and started drawing. I was feeling overwhelmed. Picking out rings was more difficult than I'd anticipated. I expected to go in, point to one, and leave. Not so simple.

An idea took. I pulled out my phone.

Kyle: Hey are you busy?

Autumn: Nope. Just home cleaning. What's up?

Kyle: Could you come help me with something? I'm on Columbus and W 81st.

Autumn: Sure I can be there in 10
Kyle: Thanks. It's Frank's Jewelry
Autumn: Be there in 6!

I laughed as I slipped my phone back into my pocket. When the doorbell rang I turned and saw Autumn's broad grin through the glass as she waved excitedly.

Frank buzzed her in and she wrapped her arms around me. "How can I help?"

We showed her what Frank was working on and she gave him some feedback. Ten-minutes later, my bank account was several thousand dollars emptier, but my heart was certainly richer.

After swearing Autumn to secrecy, I went to work like I was floating on a cloud. All attempts to block a smile failed miserably. Cradling the clip board, I stared down at the check-list of things that needed to get done at shift change, but none of the words registered.

Mack patted me on the shoulder. "Dude, you're freaking the guys out with this happy thing you've got going on."

I laughed. "I'm really that much of a miserable bastard?"

He raised a shoulder. "You take this job very seriously."

"Too seriously?" It was less of a question since I knew the answer, but I asked regardless.

"It's part of your charm."

I chuckled. "Some charm that is."

As I went through my list, checking over the truck and the gear, I daydreamed of ways I'd ask Allie to be my wife. I knew it was sudden, but at the same time, it wasn't at all. In fact, it was long overdue. A smile crept across my lips as I imagined her face when I got down on one knee and promised her the world. She'd probably be shocked at first, but then her eyes would light up and she'd grin and probably shed a happy tear or two.

It would be the greatest moment of my life and it couldn't come soon enough. I'd ask her that day if I could, but the ring would take four to six weeks. At least it gave me plenty of time to come up with the perfect plan because Allie deserved nothing less.

40

ALLIE

*I*t'd been a long time since I'd spent Thanksgiving at the Hogan's. Brandon was in Texas with his wife's family, Tyler was supposed to come home, but he'd deployed last minute, and my mom was on a cruise with her husband. Of course, Mrs. H welcomed me with open arms. I truly loved that woman.

The whole family was there, plus a few. Zoe's sister Lauren, who lived near them in Queens, seemed a bit shy, but perfectly nice, and her blond hair matched Zoe's. I was jealous of their natural highlights.

I'd had a few grays pop-up since my divorce and had been considering dying my hair. I'd always left it my natural brown, but I wasn't ready for grays. Especially since, the past two months, I'd felt younger than I had in years, so I wanted to look it, too.

Mrs. H was sitting with Lana's dad and the two of them seemed to really be enjoying each other's company. I nudged Kyle. "Is there something there?" I pointed my chin at them.

He tilted his head. "You know what? I think you may be right." He rubbed his chin. "Hmm." According to Kyle, his mother hadn't dated at all since Mr. H passed. The way she laughed at whatever Mr. Murphy was saying suggested definite flirtation. Lana's dad was a battalion chief in the FDNY in Brooklyn and he actually worked with Jesse, but lived on Long Island.

Lana's brother, Declan, stepped to my side. "Are you thinking what I'm thinking?" He folded his tattooed arms over his chest.

Kyle nodded. "I think so."

Declan hummed. "Interesting." Declan was a firefighter in Brooklyn as well and, according to Kyle, he was also an MMA fighter. He looked the part, too. Kinda threatening with his huge arms, tattoos, and the scar in his eyebrow, but he seemed like a nice guy.

For a full house, it still felt intimate. The boys had set up a folding table beside the dining room table and we all crammed around it. As we ate, I observed everyone around me, and couldn't help but absorb the happy energy. Ryan teased Zoe about something, making her smile; Jesse shared food with Lana; Dylan held Autumn's hand on top of the table the whole meal. That's what relationships should be like. A twinge of sadness swirled inside me because I'd missed out on what could very well have been sixteen years of being that blissfully happy. Again, my fault, but still unsettling. At least I'd gotten it right eventually, though.

I caught Kyle smiling beside me and I smiled back.

"What's going through that pretty head of yours?" he asked.

"Honestly? That this is exactly where I belong."

He put his arm around my shoulder and pulled me close so he could kiss my forehead and then he released me. "Yes, it is."

As we finished up dinner, Ryan stood to start clearing plates, but Dylan stopped him. "Actually, Ryan, can you wait a minute?"

We all looked inquisitively at Dylan.

"There's something we've got to tell you all." He and

Autumn shared a smile, then they said in unison, "We're pregnant!"

The blood drained to my feet. I assume everyone was busy congratulating them, but I wouldn't know because I left the room; not actually left the room, but mentally I checked out. I was vaguely aware of Kyle's arm around me and I'm pretty sure he whispered something in my ear, but I couldn't be certain.

Over the years, plenty of friends and family got pregnant and every single time it was hard. Obviously, I was happy for them, but it also reminded me of how badly I'd failed as a woman. I willed myself to shake it off so that I wouldn't be incredibly rude. Everyone was on their feet hugging—the women all cried—except for me and Kyle. He held me close.

"I'm okay," I croaked out.

"You sure?" he asked, his voice laced with worry.

I nodded. "We should go congratulate them." I pushed my chair back and forced a smile.

Kyle stood as well and immediately wrapped his hand around mine as we went to hug Dylan and Autumn. The guys offered to clean up so we women could chat all things baby...great. We huddled together on the living room sectional, gushing over Autumn.

"When are you due?" Lana asked almost as soon as our butts hit the cushions.

"May thirtieth. Don't worry. I'll be huge, but good for your wedding in April unless this little one decides to come extra early." She rubbed her stomach. "But you stay in there and let Mommy take care of you, okay?"

I gulped the lump in my throat.

"Okay, good." Lana sounded relieved. "Not that I'm not excited about being an aunt, because I am super stoked, but this wedding has been stressful enough and adding a live birth on the altar would most certainly give my mother a coronary." She tapped her fingernails on the side of her pint glass. "On second thought, maybe we should plan it that way."

Everyone laughed and I tried to fake one along with them.

Zoe went into nurse mode wanting to know what Autumn was taking and when she was seeing the doctor, yada yada. As for me? I focused on breathing and keeping a smile on my face.

"We must discuss the baby shower," Mrs. H commented.

Lana groaned. "Another party to plan."

Lauren and Zoe high-fived and said, "We've got this."

"Well, while you talk details," Autumn said as she stood. "Allie would you mind helping me with something upstairs for a minute."

"Uh, sure." I put my wine glass on the table and followed her to Dylan's old bedroom. It still looked the same as it had in high school with the hockey and lacrosse trophies lining the shelves on the wall. It reminded me a lot of Kyle's old room next door, which also hadn't changed.

Autumn sat on the bed and said, "Sit with me a sec."

So I did. "What's up?"

"Are you okay?"

"Yeah. Why?"

She gave me a half-smile. "I couldn't help but notice the way that you and Kyle reacted when Dylan and I told everyone our news."

Damn. "Oh."

"I know we don't really know each other all that well, so feel free to tell me to mind my own business, but I just thought I'd check on you and see if you wanted to talk woman-to-woman." There was so much genuine kindness in her hazel eyes that I seriously considered it.

"I appreciate that. And I'm happy for you, honest. Kyle is, too. Our reaction wasn't about you at all."

She nodded, encouraging me to go on.

Surprising myself, I did. "Kyle and I were pregnant once, too."

Her brows shot up. "You were?"

"I was eighteen." I bit my lip and decided to go for it. I told her my story.

When I was done we both had wet eyes and she said, "Come here," as she pulled me into a hug. "I'm so sorry, Allie. And I'm sorry that this is triggering for you. If I'd known, I would've made sure to tell you privately beforehand so you weren't shocked."

That meant a lot to me. "It's okay. And I really am happy for you. Dylan is going to be a fantastic dad."

She pulled back and rolled the hem of her shirt between her fingers. "Since we're sharing things, I'm...I'm really worried about this pregnancy."

"How come?"

"I had a lung transplant when I was younger. Cancer."

I reached for her hand.

"That makes me high-risk, but there are also so many risks for my baby. Plus the death rate is three to four times higher for both of us."

I felt her fear. "I know it's scary. Losing a child is..." I searched for the right word. "Unbearable. But even after losing two babies, I tried again because the risk was worth it." I glanced at her stomach. "You just do everything the doctors say and take good care of yourself and that little one. The rest is about faith. You need to have faith that your body can do this." That's where it had all gone wrong for me. After losing the twins, I was done trying. It hadn't been about the money, although of course that had been a factor, it was because I'd lost faith in myself.

Autumn hugged me again. "Thank you for that."

I patted her back. "Of course. And I'm here for you if you want to talk about it, okay?"

She pulled back and wiped her eyes. "That's so sweet of you."

"I mean it." And, shockingly, I did. If I could help another woman avoid the pain and heartache I'd gone through, I would do it without question.

There was a knock at the door. "Come in," Autumn sniffled.

The knob turned and Kyle poked his head in. "Everything okay?" He noticed what I was certain was raccoon eyes from my wet mascara.

I gave him a lopsided grin. "Actually, yes. I told Autumn."

He glanced at his sister-in-law. "You did?"

I nodded.

Autumn got up and went to hug Kyle. She was so tiny compared to his giant frame. "I'm really sorry about your baby, Kyle."

It warmed my heart to see the soft expression on Kyle's face.

"I should probably go back down," she said. "I'm surprised Dylan hasn't sent a search party for me, yet. He's barely let me out of his sight these past few months. It's like he thinks this baby is a bomb or something." She smiled and rolled her eyes as she left the room.

Kyle sat beside me and squeezed my leg . "Are you really okay?"

I leaned my head against his shoulder and sighed. "I will be."

He kissed my hair. "I'll love you through it."

I smiled. "That sounds perfect." I sighed. "We should probably go back downstairs, too." I lifted my head and wiped the skin beneath my eyes.

Kyle smiled at me as he ran his thumb along my face from the corner of my eye socket to my nose. "All good."

"Thanks."

Back downstairs people were preparing to leave, so we gathered our things and said our goodbyes.

I hugged Kyle's mom and she squeezed me tight. "Thank you, Allie."

"What for?"

When she pulled away, she was teary. "For bringing Kyle back to us. It's been years since he's smiled and laughed like that at the dinner table."

I swallowed and gave her a half-smile. "Thanks for having me over tonight, Mrs. H."

"What did I tell you about calling me that. There's a chance you'll be a Mrs. H one day, you know." She winked at me.

I liked the sound of that. "It feels wrong calling you Ann, though."

"I suppose that makes sense." She tapped her lips with her forefinger. "What if you called me, Mom?"

I tried it out. "Mom?"

She beamed.

As did I. "I can do that."

41

KYLE

*T*he room stunk of blood, sweat, and beer. It was fantastic. Declan was ranked second in New York for his MMA weight class and that night he was going up against the number one guy. The place was packed with people who were chomping at the bit for the main event. The first time Jesse brought his future brother-in-law around, I knew he'd fit in and we thought of him as another brother. Over the past year and a half, I'd gone to several of his matches. The guy was a breathing lethal weapon. I thought I was a good fighter, but you couldn't pay me to get into a cage with Declan. Luckily, other people got paid to fight him and I got to watch.

Dylan had been checking his phone obsessively all night. We'd left the women together at home and I'd practically had to drag him away from his pregnant wife.

"Relax, bro. I'm sure she's fine. Plus, Allie's there," I shouted over the crowd.

"Can't help it." He shouted back. "I want this kid, but if anything happens to her..."

I squeezed his shoulder. "It won't."

Jesse and Ryan pushed their way into our row and handed us beers. "What'd we miss?"

"One guy hit the other guy and then the other guy hit him back," I jested.

"No shit," Jesse replied.

Declan's fight was the main event, so we had to wait through a bunch of other fights before he got in the ring.

Ryan leaned over Jesse's shoulder and yelled, "I want to ask Zoe to marry me."

Our heads swiveled.

"No shit, bro," Jesse teased. "What's taken you this long?"

"She's gonna start med school in the fall and she's got it in her head that we can't get married until she's done."

"How long will that take?" Dylan asked.

"Four fucking years. I'll be ancient."

"Thanks, dick," I responded.

"Shut up, Kyle. Until like a minute ago, you had no interest in even dating. You were fine being thirty-four and single," Ryan ribbed.

"Four years, you'll be what, thirty-two?" Dylan asked.

Ryan nodded.

Dylan replied, "Dude, that's how old I was at my wedding."

"Exactly. Ancient," Ryan replied.

"I'll be thirty-one at mine," Jesse added.

"I'm sensing a trend." I took a swig from my metal beer bottle.

"You could always ask her and have a long engagement," Dylan suggested.

I cleared my throat. "Speaking of engagements—"

"I fucking knew it," Dylan exclaimed. "When are you asking her?"

"How did you know?" I wondered.

Jesse stated, "Bro, you've been a completely different person since Allie's come home."

"Yeah, man. It's like we've finally got our brother back," Dylan nudged my shoulder.

"What do you mean?" I asked. None of them looked at me. "Hello?"

Jesse and Ryan both pointed at Dylan. He sighed. "Fine. When Dad died you got real serious about stepping up to fill his shoes. We figured it'd be temporary as time went on, but when Allie left..."

"You shut down," Jesse finished.

Ryan chimed in. "You've been an ass."

They weren't lying. I'd felt it happening, but it had honestly been out of my control. The months had turned into years and, well...

"So would you do us all a favor and marry her because you've actually been a lot of fun to be around lately," Dylan finished.

I ran a hand over my jaw. "I'm sorry, guys. I guess I've let my grief get the best of me."

"No need to explain that to me." Dylan had suffered after our father's death, too. Then, a year later he was in a car accident where his girlfriend had been killed. It took him finding Autumn to finally strip him of his survivor's guilt.

"All good, bro." Jesse squeezed my shoulder.

Ryan tipped his beer bottle toward me. "Seriously though, when are you gonna ask her? Because if I'm gonna ask Zoe, and Jesse and Lana are getting married, and Dylan and Autumn are having a baby, we should probably schedule this shit." That got a laugh from all of us.

"I don't know yet. Soon." I'd picked the ring up earlier that week and it was absolutely perfect. While I couldn't wait to give it to her, I wanted to wait until after the holidays. Everyone got engaged for Christmas and New Year's, and I wanted Allie to have her own special day. Or maybe I'd ask on my birthday in January so I wouldn't forget the date.

The music pumped up loud and we hopped to our feet as the announcer came over the speaker. "Now for the main event, please welcome to the ring middleweight champion, Carlos 'Turbo' Rodriguez."

We booed as loudly as we could over the crowd's cheers.

"And his challenger, 'Deck 'Em' Declan Murphy."

Declan sprinted into the ring and worked the crowd. After all the ceremony, the fight began and Declan had the other guy on his back within the first ten seconds. With his Brazilian Jiu Jitsu background, Declan was his strongest when he was on the ground grappling. His opponent had agility on his side, but Declan was patient and methodical. He got the guy into an arm triangle and we all hollered. The fight never made it to the second round.

When Dylan and I got back to his place, Autumn was sprawled out on the couch with her cat coiled up as though she were protecting the baby, while Allie was snuggled up in the chair and a half. Dylan nearly dove across the room and knelt beside the couch to give Autumn a kiss.

"How you feeling, sweetheart?" he asked.

"Great," she replied, and I could feel Dylan's relief.

Allie scooted over and lifted the blanket so I could wedge myself into the chair with her.

"Hi, my love." I rubbed Allie's cheek and gave her a kiss.

"How was the fight?"

"Great. Declan won." I glanced over at the television. "What are you watching?"

She gave me a mischievous grin. "*Legally Blonde*."

I groaned.

"Girls' night, girls' movies. Right, Autumn?"

"Exactly," Autumn exclaimed.

We stayed for another twenty-minutes or so until it ended and then said our goodbyes and walked over to Allie's. Being almost Christmas, it was cold and I held her close as we traversed the four blocks. I had to work the next night, so I had planned to stay over at Allie's. Lately, we'd been spending more nights together than not.

While I was brushing my teeth, I looked in the mirror and Allie was over my shoulder wearing a sexy-as-fuck negligee. "Hi," she purred.

I spun around and drank her in. The gown was long and made of black silk with lace edging the neckline. "Damn."

She gave me a teasing smile. As I raced to finish brushing my teeth, she wrapped her arms around my middle and her hands slid directly beneath my waistband. I spat out the toothpaste and gathered water into my hand to wash my mouth out with. My dick hardened at her touch. While I swished the water around, the fingers of her one hand wrapped around my shaft and her other hand cupped my balls. I spit the water out and watched her reflection as she bit her lip and jerked me off. She moved slowly, getting me worked up, and my lips parted as I hooked my thumbs into my boxers and pulled them down, letting them fall to the floor.

Her eyes were dark and filled with lust—I couldn't stop staring at her reflection next to mine. My fingers dug into the porcelain basin in an attempt to keep me from spinning around and grabbing her. I wanted to watch just a little while longer. She ran a fingertip over the tip and spread my pre-cum over my head before fisting me tightly and running her hand all the way to the base. Allie repeated that motion, but this time her other hand tugged my balls down and I hissed. "Fuck."

Her eyes never left mine and the confidence in them was so damn sexy. She was still a work in progress, but I was determined to make sure Allie knew how beautiful she was every single day for the rest of her life. My arms shook as I fought to keep my composure. As much as I was enjoying her show, I liked being in control, and Allie always let me. One more stroke and I was done with it. I spun around and grabbed her face, then kissed her with ferocity as I backed her into the wall, pinning her to it with my hips so she couldn't move.

I bit her lip, trapping it between my teeth, and she inhaled sharply as I flicked it with my tongue. Her fingernails dug into my ass and I pressed my hips into her harder, making her feel how damn stiff she'd made me. I released her lip and sucked as my hands found her wrists and wrapped around them. Lifting her arms above her head, I pushed them together and held them in place with one hand over her wrists so she was entirely at my mercy. With my other hand, I palmed her breast and she whimpered as I grazed over her sensitive peak. She arched her back.

I pulled my mouth from hers. "You want more, love?"

"Yes," she breathed out.

I pinched her nipple as I bit down on her ear lobe and she inhaled sharply, "Oh."

As sexy as she looked in that negligee, it needed to go because I couldn't get to her pussy. I released her and stepped back as I ordered, "Bedroom."

She scampered off and I slapped her ass while I chased her down the hall. Before she could turn around, I pushed her forward onto the bed so her ass was in the air and I tugged up on her bottom hem, bunching the silk until it piled onto her back. She wasn't wearing underwear, so I spread her legs with my foot to get a better view. Her folds glistened with her desire and I dropped to my knees to get a taste. While driving my tongue into her slit, I slapped her bare ass and she jolted, but she couldn't get away because my other arm was hooked in front of her bent waist. My tongue slid into her warm hole and I slapped her harder.

"Yes," she screamed while I fucked her with my tongue and brought my hand down on her other cheek. That time, she leaned into it, shoving my tongue further into her pussy and taking more of the sting from my palm. After slipping my tongue out, I replaced it with two of my fingers and bit her ass cheek with the intention of leaving my mark.

"Oh. Oh," she panted and I quickened the pace. Her pussy

tightened around my fingers and I could tell by the quickness of her breaths that she was getting close. Deciding to try something I hadn't done to her before, I licked the tender spot between her two holes and grazed my tongue upward over her asshole and into her crack. She clenched my fingers and screamed her release. Her legs shook and gave out so I had to hold her up until she was done coming. When she quieted, I removed my fingers, stripped her out of her negligee and flipped her over onto her back.

I brought my fingers up to her mouth. "Taste."

She parted her lips and I slid my fingers inside.

"Do you taste good, love?"

She nodded, bobbing on my fingers. Needing to see her lips wrapped around something else. I crawled onto the bed and perched on my knees beside her head. No command was needed, because she happily opened up and took me into her mouth. Watching her swallow my cock made my balls tense and I threaded my fingers into her hair to help guide her head.

As I fucked her mouth, she looked up at me with wanton eyes. She was so damn good at taking me deep and I held myself there for as long as she could take it. She cupped my balls and tugged them down making my eyes roll into my head. I needed to come, but not like that. Letting go of her hair, I retreated and positioned myself over her.

"Are you ready for me?" I asked.

"Fuck, yes."

Her pussy was so wet that I slipped right in and stretched her as I buried myself to the hilt. As badly as I wanted to make it last, her teasing had me fired up, so I hooked her legs over my arms and pounded into her.

"Harder," she screamed, so I gave the lady what she wanted.

She groaned. "Yes, more."

I took her faster, knocking the headboard into the wall, no doubt telling the neighbors exactly what I was doing to her, although her screams of ecstasy did that, too. The pressure built up my shaft as I impaled her with my cock.

"Touch yourself," I ordered, and her fingers found her clit. "Come for me again, love." I needed her to feel that good again, but I couldn't interrupt my pace, so I watched as she stroked herself, which only brought me closer to my release.

"That's fucking sexy as hell," I commented as I felt her walls tightening.

Her eyes snapped shut and I growled, "Look at me while you come on my cock."

She opened her eyes and they burned with desperation.

She was on the brink.

I drove into her even faster and my balls slammed against her ass as she fell over the edge.

"Kyle! Oh, fuck!"

I only got to enjoy the view for a moment because the pressure reached my head and I unloaded, collapsing on top of her.

When I opened my eyes, she looked as spent as I felt. Her hair was wet against her forehead and I brushed it aside before kissing her there.

"You're amazing, Allie."

"No, you are." She smiled up at me teasingly.

I bit my lip. "I fucking love you."

"I love fucking you, too."

I laughed, making my dick jolt inside of her.

"Round two?" she asked.

"Hell, yes."

42

ALLIE

*S*hortly after New Year's Eve, I'd started feeling lousy. It was almost like I had the flu. My body was sore and I was tired all of the time. When my kids had nap time in class, I put my head on my desk and joined them instead of working silently like I usually would. Kyle's birthday was later that week and since I'd missed every one of them after his eighteenth, I was going all out for his thirty-fifth. Lana had helped me arrange a surprise party for him at her brewery that weekend and I simply refused to be sick.

I suffered through the rest of the afternoon, then decided to face the music and went to the urgent care clinic after work. After waiting forever, they finally called me back and sent me to pee in a cup before taking me into an exam room. It was cold and reeked of disinfectant. I told the nurse what was going on, then she left and I waited again. Going to the clinic was always a last resort, but my doctor couldn't get me in for two weeks, and since I'd likely be better by then, I'd had no choice.

After another thirty-minutes, the doctor knocked and opened the door. "Hello, Ms. Pierce. I'm Dr. Mukherjee," he said in a thick accent. He took a seat on the rolling stool and read my chart. "I understand you've been experiencing flu-like symptoms?"

"Yes. It's been a few days now and it's not getting better, but it's also not getting worse."

"I see." He flipped the page on my chart, then closed it. "Well, Ms. Pierce it appears you're pregnant."

I nearly fell off the exam table. "B—but that's not possible," I stuttered.

"But it is, because you are." He gave me a goofy grin. "Congratulations."

The blood drained from my face and retreated from my limbs.

"Oh," he commented. "Not congratulations."

My eyes welled up. "Are you sure? Maybe my test results got switched with someone else's?"

"Doubtful, but we can confirm with a blood test if you'd like."

I rolled up my sleeve. "Yes."

While he grabbed supplies, I ran him through my medical history. He tied the rubber band around my bicep and said, "Often times women with endometriosis who have been treated throughout their twenties such as you have, end up conceiving in their thirties because it gets better." He pricked my vein and filled a tube as he released the rubber band.

I hadn't been aware of that. My lip quivered. "I can't go through this again."

He removed the needle and placed a cotton ball on my vein. "Since you conceived naturally this time, it is a very good sign of improvement." Opening the door, he called out to a nurse and handed her my blood before going back to his stool. "I recommend seeing your OB/GYN as soon as possible that way you can come up with a plan that will hopefully help you carry this baby to term."

While he droned on about neo-natal vitamins, all I could

think about was how painful it had been to lose my babies and I didn't have the strength to—

"Doctor." The nurse had opened the door and handed Dr. Mukherjee my sentence. Sweat dripped down my back and I felt clammy all over.

When he read it this time, he didn't smile as he said, "Pregnant."

I'm not sure how I managed to get home from the clinic. One minute I was listening to the doctor and the next I was sitting on the cold tiles of my bathroom floor with a stack of positive pregnancy tests scattered about. It looked like a Planned Parenthood had exploded in my apartment. My hand rested on my abdomen and I closed my eyes trying to forget about the other times when I'd gotten excited only to be left devastated and broken.

When Kyle and I had conceived before, I'd spent months afterwards fantasizing about what it would've been like to have his baby, and I wanted to be excited that we were getting a second chance, but after everything else...

That pain had been agonizing and I didn't want to go through it again myself, let alone put Kyle through it, too. How could I possibly let down the man I loved more than anything? The way he looked at me—with so much love—would change if I failed him. If I failed our child. Again.

I dropped my head between my knees and sobbed.

43

KYLE

*S*tanding at my locker, I grabbed the small black box off the shelf and opened it. Allie's engagement ring sparkled even under the dim fluorescent lighting. I'd been hiding it there so there'd be no way she would accidentally find it because I really wanted to see her face the first time she saw it.

"What's that?" Mack came up from behind me, so I showed him. "Damn, Hogan. You're gonna propose?"

I nodded with a grin.

"When?"

"My birthday. It'll be the best present I've ever gotten." I gazed at the ring for a moment longer before closing the box and putting it back on the shelf. When I looked over, Mack was staring at me like I was some circus freak. "What?"

"Man, who the hell is this chick?"

I cocked my head.

"She must be pretty incredible because she's really changed you. I had no idea you were capable of smiling and being nice."

"Fuck off," I jested.

"You're a good kind of pussy whipped, Hogan."

"You've got no idea." I winked.

The tones went off for a medical, so I raced to the rig. En route, all the information the dispatcher could give me was that it was for a woman in distress, which meant we could be walking into absolutely anything. *Great.*

When we arrived I knocked on the apartment door and a woman's voice hollered, "It's open." So, I turned the knob and found her splayed out on her living room floor underneath her dog. At first, I'd thought the Rottweiler was attacking her, but then I noticed that the dog's tongue was hanging out, panting, so it couldn't be attacking her.

When I stepped closer, I figured it out. "Shit," I exclaimed as I stumbled back.

Just when I thought I'd seen it all...famous last words.

"You've got to help me please," she begged with wide eyes. "He's stuck."

"What do you mean stuck?" I asked for clarification.

"It won't come out," she replied frantically.

I bit the insides of my cheeks to try and keep from laughing as I turned to the four guys that had come in with me. "Uh, do any of you have a dog?"

"I do," Draper replied.

"You ever, uh?" I gestured to the woman.

He pressed his lips into a line, clearly trying not to laugh either. "No, lieutenant."

I ran my hand over my chin while I debated what to do. "You have your phone with you?"

Draper nodded as he dug it out from under his bunker pants.

"Got the vet's number programed?"

"Yeah." He pulled it up and handed me the phone.

I hit send and waited.

"Animal Hospital," a woman's voice answered.

"Yes, hi. This is Lieutenant Kyle Hogan with the FDNY. I'm currently on scene at a medical incident and I need to speak with a vet immediately."

"Hold on."

I looked at Draper and said sarcastically, "They seem real friendly."

He shrugged.

"This is Dr. Halpern, I understand you have an emergency." She sounded young and I was mortified about what I had to ask her.

"Yes, I'm a lieutenant with the FDNY and I'm on a call where a woman's Rottweiler appears to have been...copulating with her and he's stuck."

Silence.

"Hello?" I asked.

"Um, yes, I'm here. Sorry, but did you say the dog's penis is stuck inside a *woman*?"

"A huh."

"A human woman?"

"That is correct."

"Well, that's a new one."

"For me, too, Doc."

The patient looked like she wanted to crawl into a hole and die. Can't say I blame her.

The vet cleared her throat. "Can you ask her how long they've been stuck like that?"

Kill me, now. "Ma'am how long have you and..." I pointed to the dog.

"Bosco," she offered.

"How long have you and Bosco been stuck?"

"Maybe fifteen minutes. I'm not sure. I tried to get him out for a while before I called you."

"You hear that, Doc?"

"Yes. So when a male dog is mating, there's a gland inside the penis that swells causing it to get stuck inside a female and creating a tie. This tie can last up to thirty minutes. Whatever you do don't try to pull him out because it'll only become more inflamed."

I covered my mouth with my hand. "So you suggest we just hang out here and wait?"

"Correct," she replied with amusement.

"And, um, if the tie doesn't...come apart in thirty minutes, then what?"

"Then call me back and we'll go from there."

"All right. Thanks for your assistance."

"No, thank *you* for calling me."

I handed the phone back to Draper, then bent down beside the woman. "Ma'am, I'm afraid this is normal for a dog when he's..." My face got hot. "When he's mating. The vet said it can take up to half an hour for the swollen gland to shrink back down, so we will need to wait."

Ten minutes later, Bosco was free.

I picked up some of the soup that Allie loved from the deli and drove to her apartment. She'd been sick for a few days and I knew she was upset about it because she had a surprise party planned for my birthday. She's a terrible liar, but I'd pretend to be surprised anyway. And then I would surprise her.

She'd given me a key so I let myself in without buzzing in case she was napping. When I opened the door, I didn't see her so I set the soup down in the kitchen and crept down the hall to her bedroom. It was empty. Seeing the bathroom door closed, I assumed she was in the tub. She enjoyed taking baths.

"Allie?" I asked at the door.

"What are you doing here?" she asked in a panic.

"I, um, I came to check on you. Is everything all right?"

"I want to be left alone," she sniffled.

I jiggled the door knob, but it was locked. "Allie, what's wrong?"

"I said, go away!"

"Not until you tell me why you're crying."

"Dammit, Kyle. Leave," she barked.

Not a chance in hell I'd leave when she's so upset. "Allie, open this door."

Silence.

I jiggled the knob. "You do realize I'm trained to get locked doors open in seconds, right?"

"You wouldn't dare."

"Try me." I pressed my ear to the door and heard her ruffling something. "Come on, love."

"Give me a minute," she snapped. When she opened the door, her eyes were swollen, red, and glossy, and her skin was pale. "Happy now?" she snarled.

I grabbed her arms and bent at the knees so I could look into her eyes. "What's wrong?"

She ran the sleeve of her sweater under her nose. "I don't want to talk about it."

"That's not how this works, Allie."

She shook my hands off and leapt back. "You said you wouldn't leave until I opened the door. Well, I opened it, so please go."

I stepped forward to try and hug her, but she screamed at me in a harsh tone that I'd never heard from her before. "Get out!" Then, she slammed the door in my face.

I pressed my palm against the door and sighed. "I brought you soup. It's in the kitchen."

Her cries were audible through the door and it broke my heart.

"Call me when you're ready and I'll be right over, okay?"

I waited.

"Allie?"

"Ah huh."

"Promise?"

"Ah huh."

I took a deep breath and said, "I love you," then I left and walked over to my brother's.

Both he and Autumn were home and the second I walked in both of their smiles dropped.

"What happened?" Dylan asked as he moved toward me.

I shrugged. "Something is wrong with Allie. She locked herself in the bathroom and she's crying."

"So, did you take the door?" he asked, seriously.

I shook my head. "I told her I would if she didn't open it. She let me look at her for a minute and then she promptly barricaded herself back in."

Autumn came from around the kitchen island where she'd been cooking. Her baby bump was starting to show and it made me smile, but just for a second.

"Maybe I should go check on her. Could be a woman thing." She began untying her apron.

"Would you?" I asked, desperate for any kind of answer.

"Absolutely." She tossed the apron on the counter and gave Dylan a kiss. "Be back in a bit."

"I'll walk with you," he said as she went to grab her coat from the closet.

"Nonsense. I'll be fine, Dyl. Stay with your brother."

Dylan wanted to argue, but she gave him a sharp look that put him in his place.

"Thanks, Autumn," I said as she went out the door.

Dylan went to the fridge and grabbed two beers, then brought one over to me in the living room. I took it as I sat on the couch.

"So what'd you do?" he asked.

"Nothing." I tossed up my hands. "I haven't seen her in two days. I just got off a twenty-four and was bringing her soup."

"Soup?"

"Yeah, she's been sick." I looked at the beer bottle and, deciding against it, I placed it on the coffee table.

"So what do you think happened?"

I shrugged. "I've got no fucking idea." But I had a bad feeling that I wasn't going to like the answer.

44

ALLIE

*O*nce I was certain Kyle had left, I came out of the bathroom. His arrival had taken me completely by surprise. Even though he'd mentioned coming by when he got off work, I'd forgotten about it with everything that had transpired. I couldn't bring myself to see him, let alone talk to him, until I'd processed the situation myself. In the kitchen, I spotted the bag he'd brought over on the counter. The smell of the chicken and celery should've made my mouth water, but the mere thought of food turned my stomach instead. I hadn't eaten much the past few days because I hadn't had an appetite, so I knew I needed to force myself to eat for the baby's sake.

I took the warm container out of the brown paper bag and placed it on the counter then removed the lid. The drawer squeaked when I opened it to retrieve a spoon and my stomach lurched.

"You've got to eat, Allie," I said as I dunked the spoon into the broth and brought it to my lips.

The door buzzed and I padded over to the intercom. At least he buzzed in this time. "Yes?" I asked, annoyed.

"It's Autumn. Can I come up?"

Autumn? "Uh, sure." I wasn't going to leave a pregnant

woman out in the January cold even though I assumed Kyle had something to do with her arriving unannounced.

I unlocked my door and went back to my soup. When I heard a soft knock, I said, "It's open."

"Allie?" her gentle voice called out.

"In the kitchen." I blew on my spoon.

She appeared in the doorway. Her coat was unzipped, showing off her baby bump. My stomach lurched. "Hi," she said.

"Hey," I managed in response before putting the spoon in my mouth.

"Are you all right?" she asked.

I swallowed as the tears threatened to well.

"Oh, sweetie." She wrapped her arms around me and we both cried. When I pulled away, she said, "Let's sit and chat."

I followed her to the living room and sat beside her on the couch. Without prompting, I blurted out, "I'm pregnant."

A smile lit up her face and she hugged me again. "Congratulations! This is so exciting."

"No, it's not."

She stared at me. "I know you're scared, but this is wonderful news. You said you've always wanted to be a mom."

My lip quivered. "I can't..."

She grabbed my hand. "This is a miracle, Allie. It's not like the others."

I so badly wanted to believe that.

"You know how you told me to have faith?"

I gave her a lopsided grin and nodded.

She squeezed my hand. "Have a little faith."

I took a deep breath and covered my belly, already feeling so much love for the child growing there.

45

KYLE

*D*esperation was setting in. The more minutes that ticked by, the more I had to fight the urge to go back over there.

"Give Autumn some time, bro. She'll get through to her."

I fingered the ring box in my pocket. I'd brought it with me because I wouldn't be back at the firehouse again until after my birthday. "Do you think she found out I'm going to propose?"

"Uh, I don't know. How would she have?"

"I don't know, but what if she did and it freaked her out and she wants to run again?" My mind was getting away from me.

He took a pull of his beer. "Do you think she'd freak out?"

"No." I ran my hand over my hair. "Maybe. I don't know."

Dylan sighed. "If you're not sure, then maybe proposing isn't the right idea."

I bounced my knee. "I'm telling you, I'm gonna marry her, Dyl." I had to. The thought of going through any more of my life without her was unfathomable.

"I get that, but does it have to be right now? Look, I love Allie. I'm all for the two of you getting hitched, but if you think she could be that upset because you're going to propose, then maybe it's too soon, is all."

The lock clicked and I hopped to my feet as Autumn walked in.

"Well?" I asked.

As Dylan helped Autumn remove her coat, she said, "She'll be okay."

I let out a breath. "Yeah?"

When she walked over, I could tell she'd been crying. She gripped my forearm and said, "She needs you, Kyle. Go see her."

"But she told me to —"

"Go see her," she affirmed.

I gave Autumn a hug. "Thanks." Then I grabbed my jacket and sprinted down the street.

I didn't use my key this time, so when I hit the buzzer, I crossed my fingers that she'd answer.

"Hello?"

"Can I come up, love?" I asked, a little breathless.

The door buzzed and I raced up the steps, taking two at a time. I knocked on the door.

"It's open."

I twisted the knob and found her sitting on the couch hugging a pillow.

"Hi." I smiled and took a seat beside her, then wrapped my arm around her shoulders, tugging her to me.

We didn't say anything for a while. I simply held her and waited until she was ready. It took longer than I would've liked, albeit a second of not knowing why she was hurting had been too long, but eventually she sighed. Seeing the opening I said, "What's up, Allie?"

She turned her head to look at me and her lips parted but nothing came out, so I waited. Then she got up.

"Where are you going?"

"I'll be right back." She disappeared down the hall and

returned shortly after with the bathroom trash can, which she put on top of the coffee table.

I cocked my head and, unable to think of another reason why she'd bring the can into the living room, asked, "Are you feeling nauseous?"

She remained standing and shook her head. "Look inside."

I picked up the can and found it filled with pregnancy tests. My eyes widened and I gazed up at Allie with my jaw slack. "Are you...?"

She nodded and her eyes filled with tears. I dropped the can and jumped up to pull her into my arms. I held her tight as she cried into my chest and I let the magnitude of what she was telling me sink in. She was pregnant. *Holy shit.* My heart swelled and the tears fell from my eyes. "I love you so much," I cried into her hair. "It's going to be okay."

She stepped back. "You don't know that. It's *never* been okay."

"That doesn't mean it won't be this time."

She bit her lip. "I can't go through that again, Kyle." She sniffled. "It'll kill me."

I put my arm around her and led her to sit on the couch beside me while I held her hand. I'd do anything to protect her from having to feel that pain again. "Have you called your doctor yet?"

"I went to urgent care. That's how I found out."

"And what did they say?"

"Nothing I didn't already know." She stared at her lap. "Every miscarriage I've had has increased the chances of me having another one. After three, the odds of it happening again is forty-three-percent."

I squeezed my eyes closed and swallowed. "That's a fifty-seven-percent chance of success."

She sighed. "Sure, if that's how you want to look at it."

"Think positive, love."

"I've done that before. It's not that simple."

"I know." I brought her hand up and kissed the back. "But this time you have me to help you through it." I grasped her chin. "Look at me."

The fear in her eyes was heartbreaking. "No matter what happens, we'll make it through this. Together."

She bit her lip.

"We need to call up that faith again, like we used to do when things got scary, remember?"

She nodded.

"Besides, this is different. This is *our* baby. Yours and mine." I mustered up a smile.

Allie placed her hands over her stomach. "I want this child more than anything."

I tucked a strand of hair behind her ear. "So do I, love."

Her lip quivered.

"I'll call the doctor tomorrow and get us the next available appointment. We won't leave that office until every question is answered. *Whatever* we need to do we'll do it. If the doctor says you need a six-week vacation in Bali, I'll have it booked before we leave the exam room."

That earned me a smile, but then she sighed. "You may not be too far off. What if I have to be on bed rest?"

"Then you'll stay in bed and I'll take care of you. When I'm working, my mom, Autumn, Lana, Zoe, Dylan, Jesse, Ryan— someone will take care of you."

"But my job—"

"You can take a sabbatical."

Her brows furrowed. "I can't afford to do that. My divorce depleted my savings."

I squeezed her hand. "Allie, I have more than enough to take care of us both. I make good money and I've lived a modest life, so I have a substantial savings and my house is paid off. If you want to be a stay-at-home mom, we can easily make that work."

She shook her head. "I won't leach off you."

"You wouldn't be. This is my baby, too. I want to take care of our family and I have the means to be able to do it." I put my hand out to touch her belly, but paused before making contact. "Can I?" I asked.

She nodded. "Of course."

When my palm touched her warm skin, I got goosebumps simply from the knowledge that our baby was growing beneath my hand. "Hey little one. Your Mommy and are excited to meet you, but you stay in there until you're good and ready. No rush. We can wait."

Allie sniffled and I kissed the tip of her nose. "Have a little faith," I whispered.

"I...I don't know if I can."

I kissed her forehead. "Tell you what: I'll have faith for you and you have faith for me."

She gave me a sad smile.

I allowed my lips to brush lightly against hers. "This is something to celebrate. We're going to be parents, Allie. You and me." It was a dream I'd long ago given up on because there was only one person in the world I'd wanted that with.

And now I had her.

Well, almost.

I grinned broadly as I slapped my thigh. "I had this whole plan, but screw it. This is already the best day of my life; what do you say we make it even better?"

She tilted her head. "What do you mean?"

I got down on my knee and fished the ring box out of my pocket.

Her jaw unhinged and her eyes lit up. "Kyle, what are you doing?"

I grabbed her left hand. "Allie, my love for you spans decades. My heart has belonged to you since we were four. I love you with everything that I was, everything that I am, and everything that I will be. You are my past, my present, and my future. Be my wife. Let me love you the way you deserve to be loved."

Tears pricked her eyes again, but this time they were accompanied by a smile.

I opened the box and she gasped. The way her face lit up was even better than I'd imagined.

"Allie, *my* Allie...will you marry me?"

She nodded with vigor. "Of course I'll marry you."

I swear my heart smiled. My fingers shook as I removed the ring from the box and slid it onto her hand, then I cupped her cheeks and kissed her until we were both breathless.

She gazed down at the ring, a plain platinum band braided with a pave cut diamond band. In the center, were two brilliant cut stones stacked diagonally. "It's us," she uttered in awe.

I nodded. "The bands represent how our souls are inter-twined and the center stones represent us—together, always."

"It's perfect."

"There's an inscription, too."

She slid it off her finger and read the engraving. "It's always been you." She blinked away tears.

I stared straight into those familiar bronze eyes and proclaimed, "And it always will be." I placed my hand on her belly. "You, me, and baby."

EPILOGUE – DECLAN

amn, did I look good in a tux, I thought as I checked myself out in the mirror. My emerald eyes—the same as my sister's—stared back at me. My cropped strawberry blonde hair and that scar in my eyebrow I'd had for years, normally fit my image, but with my tattoos hidden beneath the tux, I looked a lot less rough around the edges. It was an image I could get used to, as long as it wasn't all the time. Too bad the thing was uncomfortable as hell. I was already tugging at my tie and I'd only had it on for five minutes.

We were in the room that had been set up for the guys in the wedding party to use before the ceremony and it reeked of some kind of puffy white flowers. My boy, and almost brother-in-law, Jesse Hogan would be marrying my sister, Lana, within the hour and I truthfully couldn't be happier about it. Being at the wedding though, well…that presented a whole other challenge in the form of a classy-as-fuck blonde in a pink tweed suit.

Kyle put his hand on my shoulder. "You're wearing the tie."

"Yeah, yeah."

"You can take it off once the reception starts," he conceded.

"Already planning on it."

His phone buzzed and he answered it with urgency. "Hey, love. You all right?"

Kyle's wife, Allie, was pregnant and she was high-risk, so Kyle the control-freak was insanely overprotective. They'd gotten married in an intimate ceremony in Ann Hogan's back-yard a few weeks back. She was due at the end of August and they'd wanted to get married before she got too far into her pregnancy just in case she had to go on bed rest or something.

"Okay, see you soon. Love you." He hung up.

"All good?" I asked him.

He nodded. "She was letting me know she was in her seat."

"Guess Allie could've been in the wedding party after all," I commented.

Lana had asked her to be a bridesmaid after she and Kyle had gotten engaged, but with the baby, Allie had been concerned that if she had to go on bed rest, she'd miss the wedding, and she didn't wanna have to bail.

He shrugged. "Probably for the best this way. Less stress. I'm just glad she and the baby are doing well enough for her to be here at all. It would've really upset her to miss this."

Dylan came over and joined us. "You hear from Allie?" he asked Kyle.

"Yeah. You hear from Autumn?"

Dylan's petite wife was very, very pregnant and he was a nervous, overprotective husband. "She said she's holding up all right," he replied, sounding doubtful.

Having had my fill of pregnant wife talk, I excused myself and went to have some whiskey with Jesse, Ryan, and Jesse's friend, Chris, who was in town from Hawaii. I was the only single dude in the room. That had happened way too fast. When Lana and Jesse had started dating, Dylan was the only other one in a relationship. Normally I'd be hyped to have my pickings of the single women at a wedding, but I only had eyes for one particular woman who was buzzing around wearing a headset and clutching an iPad: Gwendolyn Roth.

As if on cue, there was a knock on the door, then Gwen appeared. The skirt and jacket she wore fit her prim and proper professional demeanor, but she wasn't fooling me. I knew exactly what was under those tightly-fastened buttons. I gave her a sly smile, which she promptly looked away from. I'd get her to cave later, though. Always did.

"Are you all ready?" she asked.

"Hell, yes," Jesse replied, making everyone laugh. A lot of guys are nervous as hell before their weddings, but not Jesse. He was chomping at the bit to marry my sister.

"Wonderful," Gwen replied. "Let's go then."

Everyone filed out, but I hung back to get a moment alone with Gwen. As though she recognized my intent, she tapped her foot and warned, "Come on, Declan."

I smirked. *Oh, I'd 'come on,' all right.* When I'd boned the wedding planner after Dylan and Autumn's wedding, I hadn't expected her to keep popping up in my life. Then, my sister had gone and hired the woman to do her wedding as well. I was shit for her good girl image, but damn did I like being bad with Gwen. She'd told me we needed to stop whatever it was we were doing, but I was too consumed by the way she felt, smelled, tasted, fucked. And as much as she pretended to hate me, she couldn't stay away either.

As I passed her in the doorway, I brought a battered and calloused hand up to her cheek. "I've got plans for you later, baby, and they involve a much better use for this tie I'm wearing."

Her skin flushed and I winked before following the group down the hall, all the while having the satisfaction of knowing my words had caused her to warm between the legs.

I'm a crass, Scotch-Irishman with tattoos who fights fires for a living and beats the crap outta guys in a cage for the hell of it. She's the daughter of a billionaire real-estate tycoon. The

Roths own a serious chunk of Manhattan. If they knew their daughter had so much as looked at me with less-than-innocent intentions, they'd disown her. For her own good, I should keep my distance, but I was an addict, and she was my drug of choice.

BONUSES

Want a Bonus Epilogue from Kyle and Allie?
Get it now for free by going to www.kayekennedy.com/allie

Get the Extended Happily Ever After in
Burning for You: The Wedding

Help others fall in love with Kyle and Allie by leaving a review
on Amazon and GoodReads.

Your reviews are critical for keeping my books visible, so the
more reviews I get, the less time I need to spend on marketing,
and the more time I have to write and bring you the content
you want!

Kaye Kennedy

BURNING FOR LOVE

Can the good girl and the bad boy really be destined for love?

Declan

Everything about Declan Murphy screamed bad boy. He didn't just look the part, he owned it with his tattoos, cut up knuckles, and that scar in his eyebrow he refuses to talk about.

After spending a night with the ultimate 'good girl,' he can't seem to forget about her. Six months later, the woman he'd dubbed princess re-appears and while he's no good for her, he can't stay away.

This New York City fireman works out his frustrations by fighting in the MMA cage, but when he finds himself in the fire after a fight goes wrong, his princess gets caught in the crosshairs and he'll do anything to protect her.

Gwen

Gwendolyn Roth has always been a good girl. As the heiress to her family's billion-dollar real estate fortune, she'd never questioned the expectations she must uphold...until she'd found herself in bed with Declan Murphy for her one and only one night stand.

They have no business being together, but the heart wants what the heart wants...though, that doesn't mean they can have it.

Declan and Gwen will steam up the pages while also proving that love can be found with the most unlikely

person...even if there are forces determined to keep them apart.

Pre-Order Now: www.kayekennedy.com/books

Release Date: April 14, 2021

Sign up to be updated on the release and get the first 5,000 words for free
http://www.kayekennedy.com/declan

———————

You can interact with Kaye, chat all things romance, and get access to freebies in her exclusive **Facebook Group**: **Romance Reads that Kiss & Tell**
www.facebook.com/groups/kayekennedy

Join Kaye's Romance Readers Club and be the first to find out about new releases and giveaways! You'll also get free bonus scenes and fun extras.
Sign up at www.kayekennedy.com

ACKNOWLEDGMENTS

Without the following individuals, this story may never have been told:

- My husband, who has cheered me on from the beginning of this journey. His input on the high school experience was crucial since I was a total goody two shoes growing up.
- My grandmother for fostering my love of reading from a young age and for always being my number one fan — no matter what I do.
- August Head of Walter's Writing Emporium for guiding me to make this the best it could be and for loving this story as much as I do.
- Jaycee DeLorenzo for bringing my vision for the cover to life.
- Dr. Carina Alyce for her valuable medical expertise and input
- My friends, Joe and Mindy Miller, for being so understanding as to why I had to basically ignore them for an entire week while I finished this book

when they were staying with me at my house. Love you guys!

- My street team and early readers for being awesome and for loving Kyle and Allie as much as I do
- YOU for taking a chance on love with my characters
- Lastly, I'd like to acknowledge those who are battling with infertility. Unfortunately, I've had several friends struggle with conceiving and carrying to term. I wrote this book for them and for all women who have the same struggle. You are not alone.

ALSO BY KAYE KENNEDY

Burning for the Bravest Series

If you like alpha males with soft centers who love hard and make love harder, then this series featuring New York City firefighters is for you!

Burning for More – Dylan & Autumn

Burning for This – Jesse & Lana

Burning for Her – Ryan & Zoe

Burning for Fate – Jace & Britt

Burning for You – Kyle & Allie

Burning for You: The Wedding – Kyle & Allie

Burning for Love – Declan & Gwen

Burning for Trouble - Coming Spring 2021

Burning for Christmas - Keith & Brielle

Standalone set in the same world

ABOUT THE AUTHOR

Kaye Kennedy is a CEO by day and a romance novelist by night! She earned her degree in English Literature and taught college composition & literature classes before switching gears entirely and becoming an entrepreneur, starting three businesses. She writes steamy contemporary romances because who doesn't love love?

Kaye is originally from New York, but now lives on the Florida coast with her husband, who often inspires her characters (she's a sucker for an alpha with a soft side). When she isn't busy writing or running one of her companies, Kaye spends as much time as she can cuddling with her rescue mutt, Zeus, paddling on the water, or relaxing on the beach with a good book.

You can interact with Kaye and get access to freebies in her exclusive Facebook Group: Romance Reads that Kiss & Tell

facebook.com/writtenbykaye

twitter.com/writtenbykaye

instagram.com/writtenbykaye